For Victoria Policeamore —
Thanks for helping make
Mulligans! a comedy classic!
Niles Hood Swartout

Easterns and Westerns

Also by Glendon Swarthout

NOVELS

Willow Run (1943)

They Came to Cordura (1958)

Where the Boys Are (1960)

Welcome to Thebes (1962)

The Cadillac Cowboys (1964)

The Eagle and the Iron Cross (1966)

Loveland (1968)

Bless the Beasts and Children (1970)

The Tin Lizzie Troop (1972)

Luck and Pluck (1973)

The Shootist (1975)

A Christmas Gift (previously published as *The Melodeon*) (1977)

Skeletons (1979)

The Old Colts (1985)

The Homesman (1988)

Pinch Me, I Must Be Dreaming (1994)

JUVENILE FICTION

(co-authored with Kathryn Swarthout)

The Ghost and the Magic Saber (1963)

Whichaway (1966)

The Button Boat (1969)

TV Thompson (1972)

Whales to See the (1975)

Cadbury's Coffin (1982)

PLAY

(co-authored with John Savacool)

O'Daniel (1947)

Easterns and Westerns

SHORT STORIES BY

Glendon Swarthout

EDITED BY

Miles Hood Swarthout

Michigan State University Press
East Lansing

∞ The paper used in this publication meets the minimum requirements of ANSI/NISO Z39.48–1992 (R 1997) (Permanence of Paper).

Michigan State University Press
East Lansing, Michigan 48823–5202

Printed and bound in the United States of America.

10 09 08 07 06 05 04 03 02 01   1 2 3 4 5 6 7 8 9 10

LIBRARY OF CONGRESS CATALOGING-IN-PUBLICATION DATA
Swarthout, Glendon Fred.
Easterns and westerns: short stories / by Glendon Swarthout.
p. cm.
ISBN 0-87013-572-4 (alk. paper)
1. United States—Social life and customs—20th century—Fiction. I. Title.
PS3537.W3743 E27 2001
813'.52—dc21
2001000310

Cover design by Ariana Grabec-Dingman
Book design by Sharp Des!gns, Lansing, Michigan

Further information about all of Glendon Swarthout's novels and their availability, as well as family biographies and still photos from the films, can be found on his official literary website on the Internet, *www.glendonswarthout.com*. Video copies of the comic short film "Mulligans!" made from the short story in this collection, can be ordered directly from *Amazonassociates.com*.

Visit Michigan State University Press on the World Wide Web at:
www.msupress.msu.edu

Contents

Autobiography (1992)

I was born April 8, 1918, on a farm near Pinckney, Michigan, which is a very small town some twenty miles northwest of the university city of Ann Arbor. My father's family origins were Dutch. I once visited Groningen, in the Netherlands, and thought I'd ring up a relative and perhaps we could fire back a Heineken together. The local phone book had a full page and a half of variations of the name "Swarthout." My mother's maiden name was Chubb, and her forebears were English farmers out of Yorkshire, dependable as puddings. By coincidence, both the Swarthouts and Chubbs headed west in covered wagons from upper New York State in 1836, and homesteaded sections of land only five miles from each other in southern Michigan a year before it became a state. It was probably proximity, not fate, which effected a meeting between young Fred Swarthout, who played shortstop on the Pinckney ball club, and young Lila Chubb, who ruled a one-room schoolhouse. They wed. I resulted.

It was a dark and stormy night, according to my mother, and a difficult birth. Shortly thereafter, my father, on the theory it was less effort to push a pen than a plow, quit farming and accepted the position of cashier and CEO of the Pinckney State Bank. The other employee was a teller who also swept out. For the rest of his working life my father toiled in various one-horse banks in Michigan, though finally, at retirement, he was shuffling mortgages for the Detroit Bank.

My childhood was unremarkable. I tipped over a highchair and broke my nose. I required the average number of diapers. World War I ended. At age four I suggested to a friend that we steal a loaf of warm bread from the bakery wagon that peddled our street, and eat the entire loaf. This we did. We had bellyaches of epic proportions, we learned a lesson, and I lost a friend because his parents told him that if he ever played with me again I would kill him, and if I didn't, they would. As I traipsed through the elementary grades I collected bottle caps and cigar bands and measles and scarlet fever; while other boys were playing ball on vacant lots, I was devouring books, entire books, warm with adventure, without ever an ache. In the ring and on the radio, Gene Tunney defeated Jack Dempsey. My favorite Christmas presents were a bicycle and a Daisy air rifle and a Boston bull pup named Beans who died of distemper before I could love him enough. My three heroes were Lucky Lindy, Sir Lancelot, and Fred Thompson.

By now I was deep into my first vice: the movies. Almost every Saturday afternoon I blew a dime at the local celluloid palace and watched a hell-for-leather Western, which was usually preceded by a chapter of a serial, which frequently starred Fred Thompson and his "great horse" Silver King.

About that time, my parents treated me to a live show, a program of dances staged by a traveling troupe of real Indians from the real West. I was thrilled by the drums and chants and pounding feet. I lay awake half the night.

Other nights I lay awake listening to my mother and father talking in the bedroom next to mine. They had just lost almost everything in the great stock market crash. They couldn't sleep. They lay awake wondering what they would do, comforting each other.

When I was thirteen, we visited an uncle who had a cottage on a lake. There I met the girl next door, a twelve-year-old, whose name was Kathryn Vaughn. She expressed a serious interest in learning how to kiss by playing Post Office. I was pleased to take her through a beginner's course, and assured her that in another year, when she was thirteen, I would offer advanced osculation.

Fourteen was a fateful year for me. Doors opened. I got my driver's license. My farmer-grandfather suddenly brought out of safekeeping an old Colt revolver and a cavalry saber. His father, my great-grandfather Ephraim Chubb, had carried them with the 10th Michigan Cavalry in the Civil War.

Since I was the eldest grandson, when I reached twenty-one I could choose, taking possession of the gun or the saber. I'd have seven years to decide. Finally, I entered Lowell High School. Lowell was a picturesque burg of two thousand souls and thirty Rotarians seventeen miles east of Grand Rapids.

I had a fine, frenetic time in high school. I pulled A's in English from Mrs. Roth and D's in geometry from Miss Hawes, who confused me with the most geometrical pair of jugs in town. Outside of school I took dramatic art lessons, and could soon orate "Spartacus to the Gladiators" with classical gestures. I took lessons on the piano accordion, and could soon play "Boulevard of Broken Dreams" in the key of C minor. I weighed ninety-nine pounds and went out for football and lasted less than a week as a blocking back. I wrote some poetry and short stories, which I judged excellent. I read Joseph Conrad and Somerset Maugham and daydreamed about beaching around on tropical islands and writing novels. I dated farmers' daughters and town girls. The farmers' daughters smelled of buttermilk and moonbeams, the town girls of Saturday Nite #5. You could put a gallon of gas in your dad's car for eighteen cents, take a girl to the movies for thirty-five cents each, buy her a cherry coke for a nickel each, and still have two cents worth of your dollar. For a few bucks more you could drive her to a big shindig in Grand Rapids and do "The Dip" to the swing music of Duke Ellington or maybe Benny Goodman.

The summer before my senior year I spent with relatives in Charlevoix, on Lake Michigan, playing accordion with Jerry Schroeder and his Michigan State College Orchestra for ten dollars a week. This summer of 1934 was when our skinny, four-eyed squeezebox player began to grow up. There was a larger world than Lowell, I realized at last, and a more glittering one than Grand Rapids; for some people there was no Depression, and never would be. In Charlevoix chauffered limousines lined some streets, and the harbor groaned with yachts. Mrs. Horace Dodge's "*Delphine*" carried a crew of forty. I had my first gurgle of champagne, and decided I could develop a taste for it. I decided, too, that senior year, what I would do with my life.

I loved the English language. I loved books. I lusted for travel, adventure, fame, and fortune. Above all, I wanted freedom and independence, and I believed the surest way to have these things was to be a professional writer of fiction. An author. I didn't dare tell a soul.

Three dramatic events occurred while I was in high school. First, the town cop was blown off his motorcycle with a submachine gun by bank robbers. Second, a local girl, age fourteen, took to walking the streets by night and accepting rides with some of our most prominent businessmen. Third, the banks were closed, first in Michigan, then nationwide. My father ran the bank. The first rumor was that he had flown the coop with the cash.

I graduated from Lowell High in 1935, after which I was off to Ann Arbor and the University of Michigan. With help from my parents I could afford it now. For three college summers I had a gig at the the Pantlind Hotel in Grand Rapids, the largest hotel in Michigan outside Detroit, playing five nights weekly on the terrace. We were four pieces—accordion, bass, guitar, and a double on tenor sax and clarinet—and the other guys were all pros who'd been on the road with name bands. I averaged $60 a week, a sweet emolument for those days, lived in my own room at the Pantlind, and became sophisticated as hell. With increasing frequency I drove to a certain lake to weekend with the family of the aforementioned Kathryn Vaughn, who had graduated from Albion High School and was now attending a girls' school, Ward-Belmont, in Nashville. Now and then we enjoyed night fishing, in a red canoe, across the lake, under the stars, in the reeds.

I majored in English, was initiated into the Chi Phi fraternity, and was honored by the company, my senior year, of Miss Vaughn, who joined me at the University for the festivities. Count Basie played my J-hop, Glenn Miller my Senior Prom. I kept my literary ambitions a secret. Writing would be unlikely to support one, much less two. On April 8 I turned twenty-one and had to choose between the Civil War revolver and the saber. I chose the revolver, and it has hung, mounted, on the wall over my desk ever since. Six weeks before graduation I began work at the General Motors Customer Research Center in the General Motors headquarters in Detroit. My salary was $100 a month, and my future bright, for I was assured that one of the fastest tracks to becoming a GM executive was a lap around the Research Center.

So, in June of 1939, I went forth into the world of trade and commerce. I was twenty-one and two months old. That September I was fired. My work, I was informed, was "unsatisfactory." I later learned, from a friend there, that he had watched this happen three years in a row. Summer was the heavy workload for Customer Research; each spring they hired a couple of U. of M. grads, and each fall they gave them the boot.

After two months pounding the pavement and starting a consummately bad novel, I found gainful employment at MacManus, John and Adams, a big advertising agency, writing copy for Cadillac cars and Dow chemicals. In a perverted sense, I had finally begun to write for a living. The following spring Kathryn Vaughn, by now a real buddy of mine, graduated from Ann Arbor. To celebrate, I bought my first automobile, a new Pontiac, a club coupe, loaded, radio and heater, through my agency for $612.72. That was the only General Motors car I've ever owned, and I bought it only because of the special deal.

On December 28, 1940, I wed Kate Vaughn, the girl next door who, only nine brief years before, I had tutored in the rudiments of the kiss. Oh, she'd be glad she married me, I promised her, because very soon I'd be pulling down fifty thou a year in the ad biz and we'd live in Bloomfield Hills with a three-car garage.

Six months later I came home from work, burst into our apartment, and announced to my bride that I must confess at last—I'd always secretly yearned to be a writer of fiction, forget fifty thou, forget Bloomfield Hills, I was quitting my job and we were going to South America. To my dismay, the dear girl burst into tears, ran from the room, and sought refuge for the night in her bed and a box of Kleenex.

Yet that's exactly what we did. I quit my job, I drove madly around Michigan all summer, selling small-paper editors on a column a week from me from South America, and by summer's end I had signed contracts with twenty-two newspapers, adding up to a sensational $212.50 per month. We sold our only asset, our Pontiac, for $500 to jump-start us, packed pencils, paper, and an antique typewriter, and drove a haulaway car to Miami for free. We had never seen an ocean. We sailed to Havana, Puerto Rico, Curacao, Trinidad, and Barbados. Now, for a second time I was making a living at writing, but that was advertising and this was journalism—would it never be fiction? On December 7, 1941, while sucking up a rum punch on Barbados, we heard over the BBC that Japan had attacked Pearl Harbor. With bombers that were handsome, well-engineered, and maintenance-free. End of adventure. I was hot to go home at once, for I knew America needed me. But it required five months to reach the Statue of Liberty, sailing on an old, coal-burning tub a roundabout route to Dutch and British Guiana, Trinidad again, Curacao again, Haiti, and up the East Coast through the German U-boats. Our sister ship was torpedoed, and we picked up the crew in their lifeboats. In any event, our first sight of Manhattan was from the sea.

Just as my bully-kick-sand body kept me from being a star football player, now it denied me the chance to become a war hero. I applied for OCS, the infantry officer school at Fort Benning, stuffed myself with water and bananas, weighed in at 117 pounds for the physical, and was out the door. Then I had a lightbulb idea. A new bomber plant had just opened at Willow Run. I'd go to work there and write the first American novel set in a war plant, which was sure to be published. Kate and I settled in Ann Arbor, I got a job, trained as a riveter of B-24's, worked nine hours a day, six days a week at the plant, and, writing at night, finished my novel in six months and sent it to New York. It was bought at once by the Thomas Y. Crowell Company. I was ecstatic. I was paid an advance of $500, and the only rewriting I had to do was to rewrite the entire book. *Willow Run* was published in the spring of 1943, the reviews were kind, and it sold enough to earn the advance and another $125. At long, long last I held in my hands my own novel—and read it—and it was a piece of shit. It was, I knew in my heart, a really lousy book, not nearly up to my standards or talents. I was ashamed of it.

What did I do? I came home one night from work, burst into our apartment and announced to Kate that even though, as a married man, I had so far been spared by the draft, I was volunteering for induction into the Army. Tomorrow. To my dismay, the dear girl burst into tears, ran from the room, and took refuge in her bed and a box of Kleenex.

I had made up my mind: I would not send a second book to New York until I had learned how to write. Yet I wasn't running away to atone for my literary sins. I was intensely patriotic. My great-grandfather's cavalry Colt hung over my desk. I desired to beat the hell out of Hitler. Besides, this war, I believed, might be the most important experience of my generation, and if I were still resolved to be a writer, I had better participate in it.

I took the oath in Detroit, was shaped up at Camp Custer, and shipped out to Fort McClellan, Alabama, a large infantry training post. What the Army needed by 1943 was warm bodies, rifle replacements, and after four months of basic training, it had another one in Private Swarthout, 36874394. I was well versed in the art of the M1 rifle, BAR, light and heavy .30 cal machine gun, mortar, grenade, bazooka, and bayonet. I recall being only a fair shot with the rifle, but quite accurate with the light machine gun when firing in bursts. After leave I was ordered to Fort Meade, Maryland, which was the East Coast POE (point of embarkation) for Europe. There followed three weeks in convoy aboard a Liberty ship from Norfolk, Virginia, to Naples. For entertainment we had a U-boat attack by night on the convoy in the Mediterranean, which was very exciting. I debarked in Naples on April 8, 1944, my twenty-sixth birthday, was turned over to a "repple depple," a replacement depot, and was soon assigned to Co. A, 15th Regt., 3rd Infantry Divison, and issued a rifle, bayonet, and combat boots. The 3rd Div was up at Anzio, preparing to bust out. Everyone passed around a grim statistic: that the life expectancy of a rifleman in the lines was 17 days.

On Anzio, mine was 17 hours. I was transferred to G1, Personnel, Div HQ, to assemble info and write awards for the Medal of Honor, DSC, Silver Star, and so on. My ID card, following me around the Army, had labeled me a "writer," and G1 had been looking for one. Except for meeting a red-headed, twelve-year-old girl desirous of learning to kiss, it was probably the largest piece of luck in my life. And frustrating—for the third time I was writing for a living, but not fiction.

The 3rd Division exploded out of Anzio and took Rome. I shared a bottle of brandy with some buddies in the Colosseum by moonlight. We dropped down to Naples to prepare for the invasion of southern France. When the fleet was assembled, Winston Churchill himself, in an admiral's launch, saluted every ship with a V for Victory. On August 15, 1944, I hit the beach near St. Tropez in an LST (landing ship transport) with the second wave. This was the greatest spectacle I had ever seen, and still is. We moved north into France rapidly, and here I saw my only combat: six days with the Div Battle Patrol, getting eyewitness statements from some GIs for a couple of posthumous Medals of Honor. The Battle Patrol numbered about sixty men, used jeeps and six-wheeled scout cars, and was always out in front of the Div, eyes and ears, probing. In my six days we moved north over a hundred miles, had two firefights, found among abandoned Kraut gear several thousand dollars worth of new French francs, and had some spectacular poker games.

By late September we were about to invade Germany when, unloading our truck, I ruptured a disc in my spine. Five days later I was on the slow mend in a hospital in Italy, trying to walk. Two weeks later I was in mid-Atlantic on a hospital ship. I finally wound up in Wakeman General Hospital, Camp Atterbury, near Indianapolis. Here the decision was made to discharge me rather than do the surgery, and so, on January 8, 1945, eighteen months after I entered the service, I was a civilian again. Kate had waited for me, toiling as a timekeeper at the bomber plant. Now, at our first embrace, I burst into tears and she gave me a box of Kleenex.

Let me digress for a paragraph. In my duty writing awards, I was uniquely exposed to the phenomenon of courage. I met and came to know heroes. I wrote about incredible deeds on the battlefield. I came to believe profoundly that heroism lies latent in all of us, and that all we need to evoke it is the right circumstances. I believe this still. It has been the central theme of my best books. We are all, every one of us, capable of great deeds.

My postwar years were typical. I returned to the University of Michigan for a master's degree on the GI Bill. Kate and I had one of the earliest yuppies: Miles Hood Swarthout was born on May 1, 1946. The English Department offered me some classes of their brightest freshmen, and I tried teaching. I liked it, but they were so damn smart that I ended many a class wet with sweat. I won a Hopwood Award of $800 for a novel, bought a new suit, and moved us to the Washington, D.C. suburbs, where I taught for two years at the University of Maryland. Then the fiction fever hit me again, I am ashamed to say. I took my gallant wife and small son to Mexico. Under the palms I wrote for six months, read the novel over, knew in my soul it wasn't good enough, uttered a foul oath, burned the manuscript for hot water for a shower, took that shower, packed us up, and it was Gringoland again.

That autumn, 1951, I began teaching English at Michigan State University. There, in East Lansing, all the pieces of our chaotic lives fell finally into place. Over the next eight years, the following occurred. Kate got a master's degree, and a teaching certificate, better-looking than ever, and commenced teaching in the elementary school system; Miles got a Cub Scout uniform and the chicken pox; I got a Ph.D. in Victorian literature. I wrote and began to sell short stories to magazines like *Cosmopolitan*, *Saturday Evening Post*, and eventually *Esquire*. One of these stories, titled "A Horse for Mrs. Custer," was sold to Columbia Pictures by my agent and was made into a film called *Seventh Cavalry*, starring Randolph Scott and Barbara Hale. I was paid $2,000 for it, a princely sum to a college instructor on a salary of $6,500 a year. The day after my last exam for the doctorate I started a novel called *They Came to Cordura*. Its subject was the phenomenon of human courage. Its characters were troopers of the U.S. Cavalry in 1916. Its setting was Mexico, its ambiance that of a Western. And there were Indians, who danced. Random House bought it immediately, and New American Library, a paperback house. In early November of 1957, two months before publication, our phone rang. It was my agent.

He had with him my editor at Random House and a vice president of Columbia Pictures. That studio had just bought *Cordura*. For a quarter of a million dollars. Would I prefer payment in a lump sum or spread over, say, ten years? Ten years, I said. Presently I hung up the phone. Kate and I looked at each other.

We had done it. I was an author. The freedom and independence we had so long struggled for had just been handed us on a silver platter. I was thirty-nine years old.

Meanwhile, back at the typewriter, I had almost completed another novel. MGM bought it on first sight. It was a comedy, set in Fort Lauderdale, about college kids on spring break. It was called *Where the Boys Are*.

I worked on the script of *Cordura* for ten weeks at the Columbia studio in Los Angeles. We moved to Arizona in 1959, to what is now Paradise Valley, and discovered how easily a standard of living rises to meet an income. Creatively, I was full of fiction, and the books came every two years till there were sixteen in all, and also six childrens' books we wrote together, Kate and I, at irregular intervals. For material I used much of my own experience. In the novel called *Welcome to Thebes*, for example, a young girl walks the streets of a small town by night, and a police officer is shot off his motorcycle. Another, called *Loveland*, is set in summertime Charlevoix in the 1930s, and there's a chapter about the closing of the banks, and the hero is sixteen. Plays the accordion. In a band. I wrote with complete freedom—what I wanted, when I wanted, publishers and market be damned. I was fortunate. I changed agents, moving to William Morris on both coasts. They produced more film sales for me and built a network of publishers for me overseas. It has been a happy literary marriage.

The last thirty years of my life have been comparatively uneventful. I have traveled considerably, always with a bright and shining girl at my side. Last year Kate and I celebrated our fifty-first wedding anniversary. We have lost our parents. We have put on pounds and take pills. Miles, our old kid now, graduated from Claremont Men's College and USC, and has long resided in Malibu, California, where he bodysurfs, dates wannabe scriptwriters, and pursues a screenwriting career. Kate has written columns for *Woman's Day* magazine for fifteen years. I wrote the last page of my last book, *The Homesman*, on September 17, 1986, put down my Scripto, stubbed out the last cigarette, and retired.

◆◆◆

Remarks

on Receiving the Owen Wister Award for Lifetime Achievement from the Western Writers of America

I AM SUPPOSED TO MAKE SOME REMARKS. I CERTAINLY SHOULD. THIS IS CERTAINLY remarkable. I'm thrilled to have it.

I'm going to tell you why I often wrote about the West. I've set novels in Michigan, my birthplace, and in Fort Lauderdale and Los Angeles, and I had some fun with Bat Masterson and Wyatt Earp in New York City, but I always came back to the West. Why? I've asked myself lately, and I think there are three reasons.

I was twelve years old, living in Lansing, Michigan. My parents took me to a program of Indian dances in an auditorium. I was spellbound. The costumes, the chants, the drums. I lay awake half the night. My mind made pictures.

Then, real pictures, moving pictures. Throughout boyhood I went almost every Saturday afternoon to a movie matinee, a Western, which was preceded by a chapter of a serial, also a Western. Oh, this was crackerjack entertainment. Stagecoach over a cliff. Justice at the end of a rope. Gunplay and galloping, galloping. What a feast! For a dime, ten measly cents. I stuffed myself. My imagination put on pounds. My spirit soared six inches. My heroes were Fred Thompson and his great horse, "Silver King."

Delivered June 27, 1991, in Oklahoma City at the annual convention of the Western Writers of America.

Then, when I was fourteen, something *real* happened. Something I could touch. My parents and I were visiting my maternal grandparents on their farm. Suddenly my grandfather Will brought something out, something wrapped in an old union suit. He unwrapped it. First a cavalry saber, gleaming, the upper blade intricately patterned and bearing the words "York, PA," where it was made. Next, a big Colt revolver, stamped "1863." Saber and gun, my grandfather said, had been left to him by his father, Ephraim, my great-grandfather, who had served with the 10th Michigan Cavalry, Company K, from 1863 to the end of the war. He'd been puzzling about what to do with these relics, Will said, and finally decided. Since I was the eldest grandson, when I reached twenty-one years of age, I could take my pick. Gun or saber. The next grandson in line would have the other. So it would be up to me. I had seven years to make my choice. Seven years to think about it.

Well, that enlisted me in the 10th Michigan Cavalry. For a seven-year hitch. I rode every road in the South, galloping, galloping. I yelled and waved that saber and skewered the foe by regiment. I hauled out that Colt and mowed 'em down, and U. S. Grant himself patted me on the back.

Once, during those seven years, Will got out the Colt and fired it. The report was very loud, and the recoil flung up his hand.

Another time he unwrapped the saber and took it and me to the barn. The beams in that barn were 16" by 16". We went up into the hay mow and he jabbed the saber point into a beam. He bent the saber almost halfway around the beam. I shut my eyes, sure the blade would snap. It didn't. He said he wanted me to see what fine steel could do.

I don't know what he intended with these two demonstrations, but the horns of my dilemma were sharper than ever.

Finally, finally, I was twenty-one. You can easily guess my choice. I assume you can. That I don't even need to tell you. Right? Wrong?

The saber was romantic.

The Colt was real. And how perfectly it tied together all the rest—the drums, the chants, the cowboys and gunmen, galloping, galloping. The West. The Great American West. I had been born and brought up to possess that gun.

A few years later, in the archives at the state capitol in Lansing, I found a complete history of the 10th Michigan Cavalry. There, in the roster, I found his name: "Corp. Ephraim B. Chubb." I read every word. The Colt has hung over my desk for fifty years now, mounted on oak, with a copper plate listing the battles. They resonate in my soul. "MacMillan's Ford . . . Bull's Gap . . . Henry Court House . . . Stoneman's Raid."

Well, then. These are my reasons why. Dances, movies, and an old, historic Colt. These things have inhabited me most of my life. The last word of my last novel was "dancing."

What were your reasons? I'm sure they were just as personal and imperative as mine. At some point, some day or night, some taking in of breath, you said to yourself, our West is an unprecedented place. The settling of it is a proud and epic story. I have found the scene and subject for my fiction. Thank God. And Western Writers of America, I thank you.

◆ ◆ ◆

Easterns

A Glass of Blessings

Cece was so hung, her tongue clave to the roof of her mouth. She groaned. This roused Sandy and Paula, who were nearly as hung. She had never been so bombed as last night, the Costume Ball in Cabin Class. Wearing the bikini she had bought in Cannes, holding high the clothesline to which were pinned damp nylon pants and a bra, she had pelvised down the stairway to flashbulbs and cheers as "Miss Drip Dry of 1958" and won first prize, a bottle of champagne she had promised The Group to uncork today.

Sandy swung out of the lower berth opposite and said they had missed lunch, which was unsensational since they always did, and of course the breakfast bit had anyway gone out with the Renaissance. Cece mumbled for an herb and Sandy stuck one between her lips and lit it for her. The three of them had thought her winning so keeno that they had let themselves be talked into drinking Layaways and much later being herded down to the boys' cabin. She remembered necking up a storm with Jenk, but after that she drew a complete blank. Great with her because it must have been ultra-sordid.

Like vast snakes in their lairs, the propeller shafts writhed and coiled, and the cabin smelled like a wrestling team after some hot hammerlocks. Cece absolutely abhorred squalor. Sandy was deterging a slip in the washbasin. That was the thing about Tourist Class—the squalor, the scaly people, professors and low-budget honeymooners and schoolteachers and war wives going home to show off their S. Klein wardrobes, oh, and also being stuck down with the ship's viscera. She would never forgive her folks for sending her steerage.

Sitting in the upper berth, Paula hit her head on the pipe again, asked Sandy to hand her the electric razor, and said there was something under the door. Cece had not been so bombed since Rome, which had been mad, mad. They had run into Carl and Jenk at the American Express and drunk lunch at Doney's and dinner at Passetto and wound up around 3:00 A.M. with a horse-cab at the Fontana di Trevi. What was under the door was their customs declarations and a notice that they were to be filled out and turned in to the Purser by 8:00 that evening, as they would dock in New York at approximately 7:30 in the morning. Paula said she didn't know how, she was anyway too flaked out, and began to shave her legs. The floodlights on the fountain were out and she and Sandy went in wading while the boys, really bombed, tried to drive the cab into the fountain, actually getting the forelegs of the horse in the water and the animal whinnying and the cabman yelling and eventually some *carabinieri* or *cherubini* or whatever they were hauling them off to the tank. So she had never seen Keats's house or the Sistine Chapel, but when she came to in the hotel that afternoon she found a dime between her toes.

Her legs dangling, accompanying herself with the razor, Paula was singing *Arrivederci, Roma* off-key. Cece forced herself to sit up and agony out of her berth. *Arrivederci*, youth. Twenty, and what had she to look forward to? An Organization Man, three kids, and varicose veins. Possibly not even that, because the summer after your junior year at Loftus was the either-or point. Either you were engaged and getting married at graduation so you pooped around home all summer building a tan or you had no prospects so you sweat the folks into giving you the Grand Tour of Europe. Half-dressed, smoke from the cigarette watering her eyes, she leaned against a wall and took a fix on the bottle of champagne. Sandy said to bring the declarations and their purchase receipts, the boys could help them. Scrummaging in her luggage, Paula said she had no receipts. Cece got her hair in a tail and fumbled a rubber band around it. Our trouble, she gloomed, is that we are the all-time uncoordinated. Maybe because we average about one meal a day and lack calories. We shave legs and do washings on empty stomachs and we have no receipts. Thought for the day: when it's over, do they give you a receipt for life? It was also like college. Concentrate as she might, she could recall nothing from any of her courses except the motley types who taught them and the beginning of some poem by some metaphysical poet which had really clicked with her: "When God at first made man, having a glass of blessings standing by, 'Let us,' said He, 'pour on him all we can.'"

They lipsticked and found their handbags and, with Cece lugging the champagne, went out and down the passageway. She felt so grisly she was afraid any minute she would barf.

They opened the door into Cabin Class with the key Carl and Jenk had made for them by twisting a piece of coat hanger, and, walking up a deck to the lobby, found the ship's photographer had already covered a bulletin board with developed shots taken at the Costume Ball.

"Cece, look!" Paula shrilled.

"Oh, no." Where had she raised the nerve to wear that bikini? She had a sensation alien to her. She wondered if it could be anything as childish as shame.

"Miss Fleshpot of 1958," Sandy said. "You going to buy one for the folks?"

"I am not. Let's tool before I'm recognized."

"With your clothes on?"

They decided, before going to the bar, to window-shop the ship's store, Galeries Mirabeau. The door between Cabin and First was open and they walked across the Grand Salon to the store, its windows crawling with gloves, scarves, perfume, and men's ties and socks. Cece saw a man's red waistcoat with gold buttons in which her father would be really slick. She went in to price it and emerged grimacing.

"*¿Quanto costa?*" Sandy asked.

"Thirteen thousand francs. Around thirty dollars. I know I don't have it."

"I wish I could buy more perfume," Paula sighed.

Cece pressed her nose to the Galeries window. The vest was very sharp. She could see how great her father would look wearing it, under a brown tweed jacket, say, how its red and gold and daring would contrast with the silver at his temples and, wanting it so much, swept a second time by the alien, childlike sensation, felt a sudden, oysterous lump rise to her throat, angering her.

"I really need another bottle of Canasta," Paula said.

"Get off my toe," Cece snapped.

Passing back into Cabin Class, they went directly to the bar. Carl and Jenk were already there, beers before them, slouched at the corner table The Group had taken over on the first day out. Sandy and Paula went on while Cece paused to give the bottle of champagne to Emil, the bartender, to chill.

Going on, she was stopped by the sight of the sea, which she had not taken time to look at in Southhampton, blue and glittering and really oceanic, so perfect in its undulance that it seemed to have been sprayed with a wave-set product from some cosmic container, so illimitable in its beauty that she was absolutely clutched.

After Emil brought the girls beers, they began to play bridge, as they always did after missing lunch, until second dinner sitting at eight, drinking and dealing and often, when they progressed from beer to liquor around five, singing school songs at the tops of their voices. One day, when an elderly couple had inadvertently usurped the corner table, The Group sat nearby making rude remarks until the couple left. From that point the other passengers avoided them as though they were leprous. Today the game soon disintegrated. The boys were hungover and needy. Jenk, who had another year at Dartmouth, threw in his cards every hand unless a slam were bid, and Carl, who had flunked out of Harvard in the spring, told Cece he had bought a print of her bikini shot and would arrange for old buddies of his to run it in the *Lampoon.*

"Help us with our declarations," Sandy said.

"List your loot, that's all," Carl said.

The girls spread out their declarations.

"I tell you about ol' Carl an' I in the canal in Amsterdam?" Jenk demanded. "It was one of those night tours with the canals all lit up. We're on this boat, see, an' this guide boring the hell out of everybody in three languages."

"How do they expect you to remember everything?" Paula complained.

"What is it, you're allowed five hundred worth of stuff duty-free?" Sandy asked.

The beer made cigarettes taste better to Cece, but it was no help psychologically.

"We're already drinking our tip money," Carl said.

"You're not," Sandy said.

"I forgot about tipping!" Paula wailed, opening her handbag and counting her money.

"You get off the boat, these jokers never see you again," Jenk said. "The hell with the French. They struck oil in Algeria."

Large Animal joined them. The Group had forgotten his name. He was big and smily and went to some Oriental place like Michigan State, where he was going to graduate a veterinarian and specialize in large animals, such as cows and horses, as opposed to small, such as dogs and cats.

"Anyway, we're on this boat in Amsterdam, ol' Carl an' I, an' we're bombed of course or we'd never go on a damn tour. The boat comes up this water gate an' the guide hollers out to open up an' the gate guy is out to lunch. So there we sit, about eighty passengers, an' dark as hell."

"Emil, *garçon*, beers, hey!" Carl called.

Large Animal was showing the girls his completed declaration. He was good for laughs and he made a date with Paula so they tolerated him. But he was a real cube.

"What's a Bavarian bird?" Sandy asked.

He tried to explain. He had done Europe on a shoestring, and the bird, a gift for his mother that he had bought in Lucerne, not Bavaria, was his only declarable purchase.

"Animal, I didn't know you had a human mother," Carl said. "I thought you were anyway dropped in some field."

"Funny," Cece said.

"Go bring it," Paula ordered him. The beer was getting to her. " I wanna see a Bavarian bird."

"Well, ol' Carl an' I climb out on the poop deck an' shinny up the canal wall to find the gate guy. But there's nobody in the gatehouse an' we don't have the faintest how to work the machinery."

Cece was listing gifts. English doeskin gloves for her sister, five dollars. Small bottle of *Numéro Cinq* for her mother, six. Her purchases for herself came to two hundred four. Her father had given her, besides the boat ticket, a thousand to spend for the six weeks. Eleven dollars for gifts out of a thousand.

Emil brought the beers.

"I'll never know," Sandy said, "going into my last year of school, why I bought six cashmeres."

Cece wanted the red waistcoat bitterly.

Large Animal returned with his mother's gift. It was a small metal canary perched in a large, hand-painted cage. Under the tail a tiny key, when fully wound, caused the bird to sing for half an hour. A button at the base of the cage started and stilled it. He wound the key, pressed the button.

The bird tweeted.

Large Animal listened with rapture. The Group sat stunned. It was so hicky, in such bad taste, that they were speechless. Large Animal turned it off.

"Emil, *garçon,* Screwdrivers, hey!" Carl called.

"An' peanuts!" Paula called.

"So we see a light across the street an' it's a bar or something so we can go in an' try to clue these jokers there's a boat can't get through the damn gate. 'Der boot iss schtuck!' we say but we can't get our message through to these jokers. Everybody's drinkin' this Dutch gin called Bols or something so what the hell, we have one."

"Are we playing bridge, hey?" Carl demanded.

Cece drank half her Screwdriver and had some peanuts. Jenk was anyway the bore of the world. Twenty years old and a beer belly and beer jowls and partly bald. To imagine kissing him was to barf. And what a beast.

"So we go on drinkin' Bols an' sayin' 'Der boot iss schtuck!' an' after a while we're so plowed we take off for the hotel. Could be that damn boat's still stuck in that damn canal!"

Large Animal had wandered off to the deck to look at the sea, leaving the Bavarian bird on the table.

"We heard that story the first day out," Cece said.

Paula pressed the button.

"And the second day out."

The bird tweeted.

"What's her problem?" Jenk asked injuredly.

"Paula, shut off that bird," Cece said.

"Oh, she's gone ape over a red vest in the store. For her father," Sandy explained.

“But I love it!” Paula wailed.

“Her father?” Carl tossed peanuts into his mouth. “What complex is that, hey? Oedipus or something?”

“Shut it off!” Cece commanded.

“The opposite,” Sandy said, trying to remember her Psych. “Daughter for father. Electra, I think.”

Cece was recounting her money. “Five to the cabin steward and ten in the dining room and maybe five for Emil.”

“Who tips?” Jenk belched.

“How much is the jiving vest?” Carl asked.

Cece closed her eyes and chug-a-lugged her Screwdriver. She got spastic inside. “Sandy, my four cashmeres. I’ll sell you the lot for twelve dollars.”

“Cece, you know I don’t have it.”

“Paula, you can wear my size,” Cece begged. “How about them for three apiece—they cost eighteen!”

“When you absolutely ruin the last afternoon of my summer?” Paula sniffed.

“*Voilà!*”

It was Emil bearing the champagne in a silver bucket. The Group cheered. He placed the bucket and glasses on the table beside the Bavarian bird.

“No,” Cece said, swaying up. “Emil, wait. How much would that bottle be if I ordered it from you?”

“Twelf dollare. *Pourquoi?*”

“Would you buy it back from me for ten?”

“Bud no,” Emi said. “*Maintenant* we nod need.”

“You won’t give me anything?”

“Bedder you drink.”

“Then don’t open it,” Cece said, tossing her head. “We’re not going to have it.”

Emil shrugged, slipped the bottle into the ice.

The Group stared at her as though she had announced she were entering a convent or suggested they panel the world situation. She sank into her chair and put her head down on the table.

“How chintzy can you get?” Paula demanded.

"Why not have an auction in the cabin, Cece?" Sandy offered.

"We'll put up signs and sell all your stuff. That should swing the vest."

"I didn't even get to see the Sistine Chapel!" Cece sobbed.

"Don't be so damned Michigan State," Carl said.

"I wanted to see where Keats died!"

Paula tweeted the bird.

"Thirty bucks, what the hell," Jenk said. "You anyway got tonight. Put on your bikini an' sell yourself. I'll pimp for you."

Cece reared, her cheeks flaming, struck the table a blow with her fist.

"Shut up all of you! That champagne is going home to my father because I've cheaped out on him! None of us saw Europe—we went on a bombing raid! We're selfish and uncoordinated and I hate us, hate us, hate us!"

Her eyes awash, she flung her head down on her arms again. She could hear them sweeping up cards and money and declarations.

Carl punctuated the bit: "Miss Drip of 1938."

Suddenly Cece understood they would leave her. She panicked completely. She would be the all-time isolate. Word of how gung-ho and preachy and childish she had been would circulate and there would be no Group for her anywhere. She stood. She made them wait until she unfoiled and uncorked the champagne. Against tears of terror she played out the scene by serving them herself. She cried that when this bottle was killed she would buy more. She laughed that her father was anyway past the red vest phase. So terrific was she, so her real self again, that she won: they stayed, and by second sitting they were singing and absolutely stoned.

◆◆◆

Four Older Men

THEY WERE IN A BOOTH IN THE BAR OF A HOTEL ON CONNECTICUT AVENUE IN Washington, and by this time she had had a Daiquiri and a Pink Lady and a Roman Candle and a Singapore Sling. She was wearing a big black picture hat and a dress like a sheath and mink around her shoulders. She was the finest thing on Connecticut Avenue that night, including the embassies. Her divorce had become final that day. She had gotten the little boy and girl, the house in Chevy Chase, the big car, half the investments, and a large sum yearly. She had come up from a small town in North Carolina to start nurse's training at eighteen, and a doctor twice her age had married her out of it her first year. They had the children quickly and after that there was no chance for her and her husband. Now she was only twenty-six and beautiful and she was going for life as though it was something new and exotic in a glass she had never tried.

"I guess I know you well enough to tell you," she said.

"About what?"

"About the first date I ever had. On a night like this you remember things like your first date."

"I can understand that."

This was his night as well as hers. Half in love, he had waited a year for this night. He knew how he wanted it to end. He was sure she did too. If it went well he would ask her to marry him in the morning. She knew that too.

So this time in a booth in the bar of a hotel on Connecticut Avenue was very important to them.

"I was just sixteen. The little town I come from is right near Asheville and near an Army camp. On Sundays during the war the people in our town would ask soldiers from the camp to dinner."

"What camp was that?"

"Camp Crawford. This one Sunday my folks invited one and he was twenty-four and drove his own car and was just about the handsomest thing I'd ever seen. He was from the East, I think, and went to college somewhere in Massachusetts. I couldn't eat a mouthful. Afterward he wanted to drive over to Asheville to see Thomas Wolfe's grave, and he asked my folks if I could go with him and show him around and they said yes. It was the first time I'd really been out alone with a boy. I was shaking all over when we got into his car. To go out with someone like that your first date, eight years older and educated and everything, well, you can imagine how I felt."

"I'm ten years older. I went to college."

"But I know you."

"You knew something about Thomas Wolfe?"

"Not the first thing. Oh, I knew there was such a writer who came from Asheville, but that was all. I wouldn't even have known he was dead except that we were going to see his grave."

"That surprises me a little. Wolfe was rather famous then."

"Who cares about dead writers at sixteen? I suppose he's one of your favorites."

"He was when I was twenty-four."

"At that age a girl thinks about boys. At least that's all I thought about."

"I see."

"Don't frown. It's true. Well, we started for Asheville and he told me all about Wolfe and his books and his life and recited pages from what he'd written and I didn't hear a word. I was in love with him already. I didn't want to go to Asheville or see anybody's grave. I just wanted him to park and put his arms around me and kiss me. If he'd wanted to run away and get married that very afternoon I would have. But he was too old and I was too young."

"You don't recall any of the passages he quoted?"

"Yes. One."

"Which one?"

"Don't look at me while I say it."

"All right."

"'For what are we, my brother? We are a twist of passion, a moment's flame of love and ecstasy, a sinew of bright blood and agony, a lost cry—a lost cry—'"

"Oh, I forget," she said. "Let me think." She bowed her head. "Oh, yes—'. . . a music of pain and joy, a haunting of brief, sharp hours, an almost captured beauty. We are the dupes of time.'"

They were silent. He had known the lines once, but had lost them. She had come a long way from a town in North Carolina to Connecticut Avenue and the house in Chevy Chase and the boy and girl and half the investments. Or had she?

"What's another drink I've never had?"

"An Apple Blossom, perhaps."

"Will you order one?"

He ordered one.

"How do you happen to remember word for word?"

"I'm coming to that. We got to Asheville and went out to the cemetery and stood in front of the grave. The stone just said 'Thomas Wolfe, A Beloved American Author, 1900–1938.' I thought we'd never go. I had Thomas Wolfe running out my ears by then and I didn't care if I ever heard his name again."

She tried the Apple Blossom.

"Mmmm, this is good."

"Is that the end?"

"No. We started home. I sat way over in one corner of the front seat and began noticing how beautiful a day it was. It was April and the air was warm and fresh. The grass and trees were already green and the sun shining made the cuts in the hills redder than ever. The dogwood was all in bloom. I thought I was seeing how beautiful everything was for the first time in my life."

The drinks she had never tried before were beginning to take her now. He had warned himself to watch that, but now he did not care and could not understand why he did not care.

"Then I came to and saw that he was looking at me the way I'd wanted him to at first. He turned off the road into a lane and parked and put his arms around me. But it was too late. Now he was too young and all of a sudden I was too old. I was thinking how beautiful and sad the world and the lines from Thomas Wolfe were, so that instead of kissing him back I asked him to say them again. He didn't want to, but I made him. I thought they were the most beautiful words I'd ever heard, and to think that someone who lived so near and who saw the same world I did had written them. All I could think of now was poor beloved Tom Wolfe, dead but still alive, and that I must go to our library and get all of his books and read them right away. After a few minutes he gave up and took me straight home. We hardly said goodbye."

Her voice was soft as a child's, and he was afraid she might cry, but instead she smiled.

"And that was my first date."

"You never saw the soldier again?"

"Never."

"But did you read all of Wolfe?"

She shook her head.

"I meant to, I honestly did. But I never got around to it because after that my folks let me date all the time."

"I see."

"Don't frown."

"All right."

He did not ask any more questions. She did not try any more drinks. When he took her out to the house in Chevy Chase, which was now hers, he did not go in with her but stood before the door so that she had to come back out to him. She saw what that meant in the same way she had suddenly seen the grass green in the sun and the red cuts in the hills.

"Why?"

"Wolfe, the soldier, the doctor, and I," he said as though to himself.

"Why?" she demanded again.

"We're dupes of time," he said.

Her beautiful face twisted and she pushed a gloved hand against his shoulder in defense.

"I didn't know what that meant then and I don't now and you know I don't."

"You have to read all of us," he said.

She went into the house and closed the door. He drove into Washington. He did not marry her either.

◆ ◆ ◆

Poteet Caught up in Lust and History

POTEET CARRIED, ON NOVEMBER 2, 1950, A DOLLAR'S WORTH OF NICKELS AND THE list into the phone booth. The booth was in a drugstore on the corner of 16th and K Streets in Washington. Across K was a firm of stockbrokers with their names in gold letters on the window: Redpath, Graves, Ponsonby and Marshall. Beside it was a small art theatre showing a French film, *Les Enfants du Paradis.* The Treasury and the White House were within two blocks.

Poteet had come to Washington to get a job with the government. Friends had given him the names of friends and he had stayed in a motel last night, groping through a telephone directory, making a list of the phone numbers of the departments and agencies to which he might be useful. He was a man of lists.

Stacking the nickels, he began phoning. There were long waits as the calls were routed from Information to Personnel and then to a particular person in Personnel. Twice the connection was cut and he had to redial. After an hour he had completed five calls and made three appointments for the following day.

Poteet was hungry. He bought a paper and had breakfast at the counter. Blowing bugles, carrying lances, riding on shaggy little Mongolian ponies, a thousand Mongolian horsemen, said a communiqué from Korea, had attacked an American regimental position, and Poteet, a veteran, tried to imagine what it would be like, standing in your hole, to see over your sights a thousand Mongolian horsemen charging you with lances leveled. What would you think? What would you do? You had been trained to fire at infantry and vehicles and even strafing planes, but that was one thing the Army had never thought of, training you to fire at Mongolian cavalry. He had a second cup of coffee and a cigarette and read the communiqué over again. He tried to imagine what it would be like to see them coming, and he could not.

He went back to the booth. Friends of his friends did not know of anything open in the government right then, but they would be glad to talk it over. A couple of people were out of their offices, probably having coffee, and he said he would call back.

Through half the list, he bought another paper and had another cup of coffee. A full column on the front page was given to a dispatch from Rome. To a throng of sixty thousand people before St. Peter's the pope had proclaimed the dogma that the Virgin Mary had ascended bodily as well as spiritually into heaven. This was a pronouncement the College of Cardinals had been considering for hundreds of years. It was very historic. Poteet thought about it. It was as hard to imagine anyone ascending bodily into heaven as it was to imagine Mongolian horsemen coming at him, but the pope was as much an authority in his line as the Associated Press was in its.

Some of the people of his next calls still out, he gave the number of the phone in the booth and said he would be standing by. Certain people referred him to other departments or agencies, and he listed these. He made more appointments for interviews, and stayed in the booth until noon.

The earliest edition of an afternoon paper was now on the stand. He bought one and read it during lunch. The big deal was that George Bernard Shaw had died at his home at Ayot St. Lawrence outside London during the morning. Poteet sat until one o'clock going through the paper but mostly thinking about Shaw. Vegetarians died every day, but not famous playwrights. It was very hot in the drugstore. The toasted cheese sandwich and the chocolate malted copulated frenziedly in his stomach. He had a kind of gaseous vision of the surprised soul of a lance-killed GI and the wild, foam-flecked spirit of a Mongolian pony and the body of the Virgin Mary and the vegetarian wraith of George Bernard Shaw going up to heaven together.

After one o'clock he waited for calls. When none came he got more nickels and went into the booth again, determined to stay until he was through the list, but after an hour or so of phoning he saw people rushing out of the drugstore into K Street. He rushed out after them. People were running or walking fast down K toward the White House. Everyone seemed to have come down out of the buildings, into the streets. There were the sounds of many sirens. Poteet asked a man what had happened and the man said somebody had tried to kill President Truman.

Unwilling to run the two blocks to the White House, he stood in front of the drugstore. He thought that this was probably a very historic moment. It was very hot for so late in autumn. The limbs of the trees lacing over 16th Street still had most of their leaves, and the sun through the leaves made the street look as though it were covered with skin.

Poteet returned to calling, made more difficult now because the whole government must have been looking out windows and talking about the attempted assassination and paying no attention to phones ringing, but by five o'clock he was finished. He had completed thirty-one calls and spaced twelve appointments over the next three days.

A boy ran through the drugstore with extras. Poteet bought one and sat at the counter, drinking a Coke as he read the lead story. Two Puerto Rican nationalists had tried to force their way into Blair House, where President Truman was living while the White House was remodeled, to assassinate the president. Guards had shot it out with them. One guard had been killed and one of the assassins. The other Puerto Rican, a man named Torresola, had been wounded but would live. When it happened the president had been upstairs in Blair House taking a nap in his underwear while Poteet was sweating in a phone booth just two blocks away, trying to get through to the government, but then, look at George Bernard Shaw, dramatist enough all his life to get play in the papers, and now, the most important act of that life, at least the most final, dying, would be pushed off the front pages by a Puerto Rican nobody named Torresola.

There was certainly a lot going on today, Poteet reflected as he picked up his car and drove out Rhode Island Avenue, a lot going on today all over the world.

He stopped at a Toddle House and had the cube steak plate for dinner. While eating he became interested in a small coin machine that was attached to the counter. It was not a jukebox selector but a machine called "*Fortunato.*" You turned a knob until a question appeared which you wanted answered, then put in a penny and got the answer on a card which popped up beside the question. All the questions were of the type that could be answered by Yes or No. He turned the knob and read them while he ate. "Am I going to inherit money?" was one. "Does my girl really love me?" was another. Others were "Am I going to get the job I want?" and "Am I romantic?" and "Will I take a sea voyage?" Poteet wondered if people would be crazy enough to put pennies into a machine to figure out their lives. "*Fortunato* Knows All the Answers!" it said. He considered the damage that might be done if people took the thing seriously and started everywhere to conduct their affairs according to the answers. He asked the counterman if people really put money into it. The counterman said sure they did. Poteet could not imagine it. But as he sat smoking he thought about the job he had to have. He had enough money to last three weeks in Washington unless he sold his car. Finally he turned the knob to "Am I going to get the job I want?" For a penny he would at least get a Yes or No and on that surety prepare himself. He put in a penny. The machine whirred and the answer popped up: "Don't bet on it." He stared at the card. He became angry. "*Fortunato*" was a gyp. You did not get a Yes or No. You got a damn equivocation. What if you really had to know? What about the people who really depended on the damn machine?

That night Poteet felt not like sitting around his motel room but like going out. He shaved and showered and drove up U.S. 1 to Baltimore to the Club Tigris, about which friends had told him and where the first show started just after he got a table. Blondes, brunettes, redheads, big, small, medium-built, for a full hour one stripper after another came out, four of them, at one point, peeling simultaneously as Poteet watched and drank and became bored by bulk flesh. The last act, though, stopped him. The stripper was a big woman with big everything who stripped from the top down, and when she took off the panels of silk around her hips and the lights came on bright and the band loud, something hung from the G-string down between her legs. Poteet had to lean for support on the table. The back of his neck bristled. It was the head a fox. It was the head of a fox, mummified, with beady eyes, like the heads of foxes on fur pieces. The stripper got a huge hand when she went off. Poteet could not for the life of him figure out why the fox head or the huge hand. After only two drinks he left the Club Tigris and started back to Washington.

Halfway back he started thinking about the fox head and then for some reason about the Mongolian horsemen in Korea and then about George Bernard Shaw and it suddenly struck him what a day this had been. It struck him very hard. When he thought of all the things that had come to his attention this day, there were so many of them it made him tie up intellectually, and it was not the drinks at the Club Tigris. He had to get off the road to think about it. He pulled off U.S. 1 at the next bar, which was called the Prince George's Club, and went in.

. . .

So I am at the end of the bar when about midnight this stupido comes in and I think *hang out the flag.* Monday nights are always slow. Anyway, this one comes in and orders and drinks up and orders again and I might as well be the door to the powder room. It is not very complimentary. I am quite insulted and actually, to be truthful, worried, my birthday being the day before. You know. When a girl makes forty she begins to wonder if she's worth the markup. Joke. Of course, in paint and that blue sheathe I can pass for thirty-five, not a day over. Well, this client has some big problem because after another on the rocks he asks Leonard, the bartender, for paper and pencil and starts writing. When they do this, hello nothing. They may write books and poems in bars in Paris, which I read somewhere they do, but in this country when a man drinks alone on a weeknight and puts things on paper, he has a problem and you can go home and wash out your hose. Anyway, I move down two stools closer to the client. He is very average-looking. He keeps drinking and putting down stuff on paper. I move two more stools. I can't see what it is except it looks like a list, not numbers. I order myself another and light my own cigarette and have some popcorn and by now it is way after one and we close at two. I have been there since nine and I am, I must say, serene. I sort of change my mind about this client. He drinks and works on his list and uses up a lot of paper and really fights that problem. He is no stupido. Maybe he is a thinker after all, really a deep thinker, and is braining up on something big. You know. It makes me very curious. Besides, he is so snockered. Finally, I move next to him, and after a minute give him the teeth and say hi. He looks at me as though trying to decide on my planet. I tell him the bar is closing and he is really too stoned to be driving on U.S. 1, so why not come next door to my place for some ruckabout and he says all right. He is very particular about paying his bill. Then I take his elbow and we go out the back way and he asks where I live and I tell him just a few steps, in this motel here, isn't that convenient. Inside, I turn on the light and hang my dress in the closet and turn around and there he is, sitting on the bed, very ditty-boo.

"What's your name?" he says.

"Just call me Dixie," I say.

"Your real name," he says, very serious.

This ticks me a little. You know. So I say, "I have already had my census took this year, thanks a lot. Whyn't you just transfer a twenty and let us get this action going."

He looks at me like I am conversing in Bulgarian or something.

"I mean," I say, "let the bull out of the chute."

It penetrates, why we are here. "Oh," he says. "That." And takes out his billfold and hands me the twenty. "Now, what's your real name?"

So help me, I tell him. Remember, I have had a lot of sauce myself and am really serene. Besides, you never know what you are going to get in off U.S. 1.

"Charlotte," I say.

"Mine is Radford E. Poteet," he says.

"That's grand," I say. I decide to be very careful. He may be fresh out of the Happy Academy.

"Where you from?" he says next.

"Hinton, West Virginia," I say.

"I'm from Terre Haute, Indiana," he says.

"Listen," I say, "did you go to college?"

"Two years," he says. "To junior college."

I thought so. If they have been to college they always have to be intimate.

I don't know why, unless it's because they have learned nothing is fun unless it's complicated. Anyway, I am very sleepy by now so I yawn and take off my slip, thinking that will satisfy him.

"Okay," I say, "so give me the story of your life."

"There isn't any," he says. "I'm thirty-three and I've had a lot of office jobs and I was married once and in the army and now I'm in Washington looking for a job with the government and that's all."

This caught me short. "Well, that's very interesting," I say, being polite, "but now let's get goaty for about five minutes and then you go back to Washington and get that job, huh?"

"I don't think we ought to do anything like that," he says.

"Why not?" I say.

"Not tonight," he says.

"Why not tonight?" I say.

"Not the night of this day," he says.

"What is it, my God, about this day?" I say.

Try to get the picture. There I stand in all the skin I got at two in the morning, staring at this client, and there he sits on the bed, holding his papers and pencil and looking into my eyes, which makes me know I have to go on a diet, looking into my eyes for about five minutes.

"Charlotte," he says, "today was a very historic day."

A very historic day. I about collapse in the chair. You know. But there are characters so weirdo they will pay a girl to just talk with them. You get one every once in a while. It's sort of scaggy and wonderful both.

"Okay, Radford," I say, scratching a corn and giving him a pal smile, "tell me about it."

Honest, I don't know if I get it even now and I am no stupido myself. Anyway, this list he was making was all the things that had happened to him and to other people and all around the world on this day. He had the date at the top, November 2, 1950, and then all this stuff. Here is some of it. He had Head of Fox and Bugles and Vegetarianism and 1000 Mongolian Horsemen and Am I Romantic? and Torresola and College of Cardinals and *Fortunato* and The Boy of Sparta and Am I Going to Get the Job I Want? and George Bernard Shaw and Toddle House and Ascension of Virgin Mary and Will I

Take a Sea Voyage? and Ayot St. Lawrence and Don't Bet on It and St. Peter's and President Taking Nap in Underwear and *Les Enfants du Paradis* and Street of Skin and Does My Girl Really Love Me? and Tigris and Euphrates and a bunch more stuff I can't remember plus the names of all the government places he'd called looking for a job like AEC and Agriculture and VA and State and Civil Defense and FBI, oh, yes, and of course at the end Charlotte and Hinton, West Virginia, which made me sort of proud. And this was his problem. All these things had happened in one day, a day people hundreds of years from now might put down in books. The cosmos, he says, has been just about exploding with events and significances. He says there was something metaphysical about it, whatever that is and I don't think he knew either. And his problem was, what was the connection between all these events? He was sure there was one, and he was sure if he could figure it out he would have something for the whole human race.

Don't laugh, remember, he's been to college. Absolutely forgetting about being bare as a tuba I sit there looking over his list while he gives me part of the message. For example, there was some juvenile in Sparta, a real dead town, who carried a pet fox around under his pants because he wasn't supposed to have a pet and it chewed his guts out and he never said word one and tonight he'd been to the Club Tigris in Baltimore and seen a strip-teaser wearing a fox head and way back when, about the same time of Sparta, the two most important rivers in the world were the Tigris and Euphrates. So there was a couple of connections. And St. Peter's and Ayot St. Lawrence was another. And his looking for a job and finding the machine *Fortunato* was another, so don't laugh.

I wasn't. The more he tells me the more interested and frantico I get and pretty soon I get a pint out of the closet and we belt a couple and go on talking and the more we talk the more I'm sure he does have something. All these things had happened today and it really ticked him to be trapped inside a telephone booth on a day that might never come again, the rest of his life or the century. He says he is not going to be trapped again, either with his underwear on like the president or in bed with some babe. Now I understand about his not wanting to bunny up and I tell him it's okay.

"Charlotte," he says suddenly, "neither one of us is going to be trapped in case anything else happens before morning. Put on your clothes and come on. I am going to take us where if anything does happen we will be right in the middle of it!"

I stand up too and get hold of the chair. There is something real kicks and historic about it.

"I will, Radford!" I say.

I get on my clothes and turn off the lights and we go out to his car and he starts driving down U.S. 1. He may be vined but he is steady as the Rock of Ages, driving. We come in on Rhode Island Avenue and turn on First and park on the mall and start up the steps. It takes us about ten minutes to get all the way up, helping each other, we are so gassed but finally we do and have to sit down and rest. Then we stand up. We are in the middle of everything, for sure. On the top steps of the U.S. Capitol. I have never been here before and I never expected to be here at four o'clock in the morning with a client. It is like the whole country is asleep and you are the only ones on the whole national ball. What you see is but glorio. You can see the 14th Street Bridge over the Potomac and the red ball on top of the Washington Monument with a plane coming in over it with lights winking on its wings and way past that the Lincoln Memorial. And over you the great big dome of the Capitol all lit, sticking way up into the glorio sky. I was supposed to come here with my senior class from Hinton High but I got married after the eleventh grade and didn't graduate. I thought they were all just juveniles and it was better anyway to be married but when they took the trip to Washington and I had to stay home I cried all the time they were gone. I was only seventeen. You know. So I had never stood on the steps of the Capitol before and here I am. I feel like I have on a too-tight girdle, not a fatso but busting. With beauty. Radford Poteet stands beside me with his head up high, waiting. And I start to bounce tears big as tennis balls. I knew we would wait here in the middle of everything and then I would ask him to take me to that Toddle House for something to eat and where I could ask that machine some questions myself and that he would take me because he was a very nice, interesting client.

"Radford," I say, really boo-hoo now, "I thank you."

"Charlotte," he says, "you're welcome."

◆ ◆ ◆

What Every Man Knows

For months after my mother died, my father and I were very united. We lived in the same big house and kept it exactly as it had been. To fight loneliness we did the housework together, went fishing often and to many movies, and he told me stories about his boyhood I had never heard before. We isolated ourselves. This was probably natural.

Then the year I was fifteen a lot of things happened. I shot up three inches and went out for the basketball team and started messing around with a razor. My father began dating. I found out who, too, even though he didn't tell me. Widowers are more interesting to small towns than world events. To think that he could commit such a sacrilege hurt and enraged me, and to maintain self-respect I started to smoke a pipe on the sly, but limited myself in order not to stunt my spectacular growth. I hid the pipe and tobacco can on a beam in the basement, and whenever my father went out in the evening I would sit on the steps in front of the furnace and smoke up a mutinous cloud.

But most of the really symbolic things happened all in one day. It was not only the coldest but the most symbolic day of the year.

We were just closing the front door of the house in the morning. He always walked as far as school with me. We heard the telephone ring and went

Originally published in *Collier's*, February 17, 1956.

back inside. He answered, standing up. It was long-distance for him from the state capital.

"You don't mean it," he said. He sat down. It was the first time I had ever seen the face of a grown man go completely white. "Bill," he said, "we're all right here. We *can't* close. We're all right, I tell you."

Whatever it was, he could not comprehend it. He sat at the telephone, wearing the beautiful brown Cheviot overcoat that I liked best of anything he wore. He had paid eighty dollars for it, and though it was four years old it looked as fine as it had when new. It was big-city, that overcoat, not small-town, and so was my father when he wore it.

"We're all right, we're sound," he kept saying and shaking his head. But it was no use. Finally he put down the telephone, and after a while he said, "That was Bill Devore at the State Banking Department. I am not to open the bank this morning."

"How come?" I said.

"None of the banks in the state will open this morning," he said.

What we did not know was that in a few weeks none of the banks in the whole country would open.

He rose and reached for my arm. "You're not to tell anyone," he said. "Anyone. You don't know what this means."

"I won't," I said.

As we walked to school I realized he didn't want me to ask questions. It was January and below zero, and the cold silences you anyway. Our shoes squeaked in unison on the hard snow, and that was the only sound we made.

The news reached school in the middle of the morning. The kids always found things out before the teachers. The girls looked at me in the halls, not saying anything, just looking at me and whispering together, but the boys kept hissing things like "How much did your dad get?" and "Your father going south of the border?" and "Tell your old man to leave a little for mine!" They kept it up. I had a fight with Orton Hill, going home at noon, and cleaned his clock at the cost of a nosebleed.

I ate lunch alone. I was beginning to learn what it meant.

The first class in the afternoon was Latin. Mrs. Ames was the teacher. She was really Miss Ames, but we all knew how many years she must have wanted to get married, so we called her Mrs., though not to her face. She was nearly as old as my father, small and comparatively dumpy with bobbed blonde hair. She did everything possible to interest us in Latin, keeping on her desk a bust of Cicero—on which someone was always penciling a mustache—talking constantly about how she had once seen the Coliseum by moonlight, and discussing culture and antiquity and stuff; but the tenth grade in a small-town high school is not apt to be very classical, and she, as far as we were concerned, was pretty antique herself.

About all we had learned the first semester was *Gallia est omnis divisa in partes tres* and how to conjugate the verb "to love": "*Amo, amas, amat.*" The only time Miss Ames had ever made a hit was the day we were to play Carthage High in football, and she wrote on the board *Delenda est Carthago!* That means "Carthage must be destroyed!" Personally, I despised her. She had given me a D at the end of the first semester. And I had other reasons.

Today Miss Ames seemed very tense. I felt her looking at me often. She talked a lot about the ancient Stoic philosophers and how they endured disaster stoically. So the teachers must have heard. I'd sometimes seen them come into the bank to cash their checks at noon the same day they got them. Miss Ames must have been wondering how she would cash her next check. She might have been wondering if there would *be* a next.

After class she asked me to stay a minute. When the kids had gone I stayed in my seat and she stayed behind her desk. "If I were you—" she began.

"Which you aren't," I butted in. That was one thing I could be thankful for.

"If I were you I would leave school and go to the bank."

This was phenomenal, a teacher telling a student to skip school. "I've got chem lab and basketball practice," I said.

"They aren't important today," she said. "Only your father is. It would be a source of strength to him if you were there."

Her voice was very tight. It suddenly struck me that she was suffering—not about her check or the bank, but about *him*—and trying to be stoic about it. It burned me that she should suffer when only he and I had a right to. I took my books and started for the door.

"You don't know what this means," she said.

I stopped. Being told like an adolescent that I didn't know what it meant was becoming insulting. I couldn't advise her to paddle her own canoe because I had to get through Latin, but I could at least be dignified and adult and aloof. "Don't tie me up, Miss Ames," I said aloofly. "Stay loose. You'll get paid."

Then I left. I put my books in my locker, sneaked out the gym door, and went downtown. It wasn't what she had said—I just had a feeling that with my father was where I ought to be.

The bank was a yellow brick building on a corner in the middle of the main street. It gave me an odd sensation to see the door shades drawn early in the afternoon when they should have been up, with people going in and out the doors. I knocked shave-and-a-haircut-two-bits on the glass, which was the signal for Dan Wingeier, the assistant cashier, to let me in.

It was very peculiar. On the tops of the two tables in the middle of the floor, the deposit and withdrawal pads had not been moved or the blotters blotted, and the pens were all in their inkwells. Yesterday's date showed on the calendar pages. My father sat at his desk in the front, talking on the telephone. He didn't say anything about my being there instead of in school. As I pushed his half door open and went past his desk I saw his *Chicago Journal of Commerce* still folded; he usually had it read by the time the bank opened.

I went around the glass partition into the cage and sat on top of the hot-air register to warm myself. It was the best place in the bank to sit, and when I had been small, Dan Wingeier would lift me up and I would sit there for hours watching him and the lady teller work, watching the faces of the farmers and storekeepers and teachers as they came to the windows and telling myself stories from their faces.

From the register I could see the two floor buttons of the burglar alarm and the two drawers, one by each window, in which the guns were kept. Once it had been exciting to be lifted up and have the drawers opened so that I could see the oily, death-still .38 automatics, and to imagine the alarm clanging and my father and Dan Wingeier shooting it out with bank robbers and killing them. One of my earliest resolutions in life was to stay at my post on the hot-air register, no matter how close the bullets came, and see it all.

There would be no bullets this afternoon. Dan Wingeier figured in a ledger and had no jokes about locking me in the vault. The lady teller and the girl who did the typing whispered together at the back. My father talked quietly on the telephone most of the time. Every few minutes someone would pound on the front door, pound and pound because he had not heard the news, pound until his blows sounded through the whole bank. Finally whoever it was would give up and go away.

Just after three someone else knocked shave-and-a-haircut-two-bits. Dan Wingeier went to the door. In came Miss Ames. She had come as soon as school was out. Since she knew the signal too, I knew she had been here before, after hours. In a small town that was pretty scandalous.

She sat with my father for an hour, not saying much, until Dan Wingeier and the women were gone. They did not pay the least attention to me. I was overheated from the register but I would not leave them alone. When Miss Ames rose at last she stood behind my father's chair and put her hands on his shoulders. It was as though she had put them on mine. I closed my eyes and recoiled from her touch. I let my imagination go and thought of taking one of the .38 automatics and assassinating both of them for treachery. When I opened my eyes she had gone.

I went to my father's desk and faced him. "You can't be serious about her," I said.

He leaned back. He looked tired and drawn, even though he had done little all day. "I was considering getting married," he said.

"Again?" I cried.

"It would only be for the second time."

"She's just an old maid!" I said violently.

His face softened. "Your mother would have been an old maid if she hadn't married. Did you ever think of that?"

At the mention of my mother my eyes began to burn, but I had to be too old for tears. A guard in basketball cannot be emotional.

"She thinks as much of you as she does of me," he went on.

"Horsepucky!" I said.

"It's true, son. It surprised me too. She came in to talk about you, not me."

"Why?" I demanded.

"She's afraid this is going to affect you most."

That made me maddest of all. As if I cared a whoop about losing the seventy-four dollars in my savings account. "I hate her," I said steadily.

We looked at each other, each of us locked in his own vault. My father picked up the *Journal of Commerce.* "The directors are meeting at six, as soon as the stores close," he said. "You'll have to get your own supper."

I went home and sat on the basement steps in silence and betrayal and smoked one pipeload after another.

That night I had a date with Dorothy Phoebus. Her farm was north and east of town, up over the hills and into the flat country near Bowne Grange. It was good to be by myself out in the open, driving. Our car then was a 1928 sedan with just over forty thousand miles on it. The temperature must have been ten below zero. The snow was banked car-high on each side of the road, but they had plowed it down to the gravel and I could open up the car. The sedan would do a little over seventy but it was a very special seventy, for at that speed a stream of sparks always shot out from the exhaust and made you feel you were doing a hundred. It was fun to watch in the rearview mirror and see the sparks burning red and snapping into the snow.

At one corner I stopped and got out and stood for a minute beside the car. The night was very dark and the stars were so high and small I could hardly see them. A winter's night in Michigan is much lovelier than the Coliseum by moonlight. I cleared my lungs with ice-cold air and shot a basket at the stars and told myself that nothing had changed, really. The kids in my grade would soon forget about the bank closing. The teachers would be paid. My father would go on drawing his salary and eventually get over his passion and perceive his irreverence to the memory of my mother.

The main thing was, I was all right. Inside I had not been touched or hurt in any basic way, and my life would be the same. I got back in the car feeling a lot better.

Dorothy Phoebus was the first girl I had formally dated, and my dates with her were always the same. I would go in the side door of the farmhouse and into the big kitchen and sit and talk for an hour with Dorothy and her folks around the table. Her mother would often give me a slice of cake she had baked that day, and sometimes I had a glass of elderberry wine with her father. Mrs. Phoebus was round and sturdy and cheerful, and Dorothy would be like her someday. Mr. Phoebus was giant and spare, with big hands and a lantern jaw. I could tell they liked me and were glad to have me going with Dorothy.

Then after a while they would say goodnight and go to bed in the bedroom off the kitchen. Dorothy and I would wait a few minutes and then tiptoe into the dim parlor and sit on the sofa and kiss. We would sit there close together for two or three hours, not saying much but kissing all the time, long damp kisses, so long that we had to stop to breathe. She was fifteen, too, and kissing was very vital to us and to our friends at that age. We were always playing post office and spin the bottle at parties. There was no arrangement between Dorothy and me about ever being engaged or getting married or even going steady, just the kissing. We both enjoyed it and found it more interesting than anything else.

But tonight Dorothy was alone in the kitchen. When I asked her about her folks she said they had gone to bed. I felt the same peculiar way I had felt when Dan Wingeier had let me into the bank that afternoon. Dorothy was very quiet. I stood around a few minutes and then took her hand and led her into the parlor. But when we were on the sofa she sat beside me stiffly, and when I tried to kiss her she wouldn't let me. The skin of her arms was cold and goose-pimply. I couldn't help noticing how plump and cold she was. I asked her what was wrong.

She started to cry with little sniffling noises and said the bank closing would ruin her father and mother because they had a mortgage and would probably lose the farm. I tried to tell her it wasn't my fault or my father's fault or anybody's, and that the bank would open again soon. But she just sat there, plump and cold, in one corner of the sofa, making sniffling noises. It was certainly not very conducive.

From the bedroom off the kitchen I could hear her folks talking together in bed—not understand what they said, but hear their voices—probably talking about me or my father or their farm. The below-zero cold outside made the joists of the old farmhouse creak loudly. Besides the sound of her crying and her folks' talking together in bed and the creaking of the joists I could still hear the pounding on the glass doors of the bank. I had never felt more detached. I didn't know anyone in the world could be as lonely and detached as I was.

Now I knew that I had been wrong in what I'd thought when I stood by the car under the stars, and that an old-maid teacher had been right. The closing of the bank was going to be very important to me after all. My life would not be the same. For one thing, I would probably never have another date with Dorothy Phoebus. And worse, I might never again date or kiss any other girl in the tenth grade. Suddenly a whole series of kissless years stretched before me—all the way through high school and maybe even through college, if someone from my town went to the same college and word about the bank got around. It was a dread prospect.

"Dorothy," I said, "you've *got* to kiss me."

"I won't," she whimpered.

It was too serious a thing to be stoic about. With long strides I marched from the parlor and into the kitchen and stood before the closed door of her folks' bedroom. "Mr. and Mrs. Phoebus," I said, "there's something I have to tell you."

My voice was high-pitched and scary, but I had to go on, now that I'd started. I was as determined about this as I had been once about staying on the hot-air register right through the shooting.

"Dorothy won't kiss me because she thinks it's my fault or my father's fault that the bank closed today," I said. "I've tried to tell her it isn't but she won't believe me. And I don't think it's fair of her. I don't know how you feel about it but I just want you to know this—my father said the bank was sound. And besides, he would never let you lose this farm no matter what happened. Not after your being so nice to me, giving me cake and elderberry wine and letting me go with Dorothy and everything . . ."

Then I heard someone sitting up in bed. It must have been Mrs. Phoebus. "Dorothy," Mrs. Phoebus said.

"Wha—what?" quavered Dorothy.

"You ought to kiss him, dear," her mother said gently.

"Noooo . . ." Dorothy sniffed. She was a very stubborn girl.

Then I heard someone sitting up in bed with a giant grinding of the springs and I knew who it was. "Kiss 'im!" thundered Mr. Phoebus.

"All right," Dorothy said meekly.

"Thank you, Mr. and Mrs. Phoebus," I said.

I marched back into the parlor. Dorothy came to meet me. She had stopped crying. It seemed to me, in fact, that she was glad to obey her parents. She kissed me.

It unlocked the vault. I stood there realizing so many things at once that I felt almost imperial. It was *Veni, vidi, vici,* but in different order. I had come, I had conquered, and now I saw.

I saw that my father had already spent a couple of kissless years. He and Miss Ames probably didn't kiss on their dates. People that age do not play around with the physical.

I saw that if Miss Ames was not as beautiful as my mother it was not her fault.

I saw that my father did not belong to me entirely, any more than the bank belonged to him, or Dorothy belonged to Mr. and Mrs. Phoebus. All Gaul was divided into three parts, and that was the way it had to be with people. They had to be shared.

I saw that I deserved the D in Latin.

And I saw that I had to leave.

Dorothy had already taken her place on the sofa, but I found my coat and told her I had to go. I promised to come out the next night and kiss her amply. Then I took off. I really red-sparked the car back to town.

When I turned our corner I saw someone on the front porch. I drove into the garage and went to investigate. It was my father, standing there alone, looking up at the faraway stars, just as I had done out in the country. I would never have thought people his age did that, either. I stood beside him and noticed for the first time that I was as tall as he was.

"How was the date?" he asked.

"Okay," I said.

I was so busting with what I wanted to convey to him it was hard to be adult and aloof. "When are you getting married?" I asked.

I heard him draw a deep breath, filling his lungs with ice-cold air. "Oh, in a few weeks," he said.

It must have been twenty below zero by then, but we were very warm. "We'd better bank the furnace," he said.

That was something we always did together. We went into the house and down the basement steps, and while he banked the big furnace with ashes for the night I sat on the steps. It was a pleasant, private moment. On the fruit-cellar door was painted the head of a fox and the words *Fox Patrol.* We had held patrol meetings there a long time ago, when I was fourteen. Some of my mother's canned pears and raspberries were probably still on the shelves, for we hadn't been able to bring ourselves to eat many of them, even though she would have wanted us to.

When I looked at my father again he had my pipe and tobacco can. I had left them in plain, defiant sight that afternoon. My heart began to pound but he just handed them to me stoically. To be doing something, I packed the pipe and lit up.

"I keep it under control," I said. "I have to stay in condition for basketball."

He lit a cigar and sat down beside me. The furnace rumbled and radiated even more warmth.

"I was thinking," I said. "I think you ought to get married right away. It would be good for the town. It would show people that you're not worried about the bank closing and that in your opinion everything is going to be basically all right. It would be symbolic."

"It might at that," he said.

After a while he said, "It would be good for your Latin, too."

We sat together, smoking. Both of us had several emotional things to think about.

◆ ◆ ◆

Gersham and the Saber

WHAT MY FATHER TOLD ME WAS THAT EVERY BOY SHOULD HAVE A SUMMER ON A farm and therefore he was sending me way out west to Michigan to stay with my grandparents south of Constantinople. Such a summer would exalt my spirit. A phrase like this my father savored the way he did a Sheepnose apple.

What he told my mother, as I lay that night in bed listening, was the real reason. He believed between music and movies I was becoming too citified. This was because she made me take flute lessons and because I had seen *Hell's Angels* three times and fallen quickly for Jean Harlow and considered myself an ace for shooting down, from the cockpit of my Spad, Baron von Richthofen. He told her a summer on a farm would make a man of me.

I resigned myself. Being made a man of is a thing a boy of thirteen-threatened-with-fourteen cannot fight.

My grandfather met the train in Constantinople. L. D. Pierce was a small man and spry, with sparky black eyes and little tufts of white hair screwing out of his ears. He hustled me to a Model A and there was a girl. Her name was Cassy Rubbins. She was my age but taller and thin with long braids. L. D. lifted them up to show me and called her a "pippin" and said she was the step-daughter of a nephew of his, which made us kissing cousins, which did not mean we were to go lovering around all summer, for he calculated to get a lot of work out of us. The farm was six miles south and L. D. talked a streak all the way. His first car had been a two-cylinder Pope-Tribune, red. He had a dandy Model T, too, full of get-up. We came to the top of a high hill.

"See this hill? Well, I was coming down 'er in that T one day when out runs Montaig's sow! Hit 'er square in the bacon and you know where I was?"

"Can you milk a cow?" Cassy asked me.

"By Jehu, the ex of that T set right on top of that sow!"

"No," I said.

"High and dry on that critter, I was!"

"I can," Cassy said. "Have you ever seen a lamb born?"

"No," I said.

"Well, I honked the horn and fetched Old Man Montaig a-running cross-lots."

"I have," she said.

"So what," I said.

She was spoiling L. D.'s story. One of the troubles with girls is that they have no sense of the dramatic.

"And when we hoisted the T off, that sow took out like blue blazes. But you know what?" L. D. looked straight at us. "Next month she littered and not a one could grunt. Montaig's Honking Pigs, they was known as!"

I stared.

He winked at Cassy.

"You're really citified," she said.

I felt awful and isolated. When we turned onto the county road I did not notice how beautiful the farm was. There were fields of June wheat and alfalfa and rolling pastures with sheep in the shadows of the clouds and all of it fell far away into hollows for three joined lakes. I did not notice the foxsquirrel woods or the orchard or the huckleberry marsh or the line of pines which led up to the white house. An ace deserved at least a Jean Harlow. I had drawn Cassy Rubbins.

My grandmother Nola Pierce was very glad to see me. She was cutting out fillers from the weekly paper, the Putnam *Argus-Vigilant*, which everyone shortened to "The Piecrust." This was her hobby. She memorized them because they were useful in conversation and a body never knew when the information might come in handy.

L. D. kept a close watch on me during dinner. He seemed to be searching for something in me. To defend myself I ate more than usual.

"No wonder you're fat," said Cassy.

"May have to run him over with the Model A," L. D. said.

Cassy giggled.

"The floor of the Atlantic along the Brazilian coast," my grandmother began reciting a filler, "is made up of red, blue, and green muds, which get their color from volcanic rock and coral."

It was nice of her but not very handy.

After dinner she took me into the parlor and suggested this would be the best time to practice. I certainly did not want to. It takes a long while for people to accept the fact of a flute. But I jointed up and started a finger exercise. In a minute Cassy appeared at the window, gaped, then fell back in the snowball bushes, dying laughing. I turned my chair. In another minute my grandfather stood in the parlor door.

"Lordamighty," he said. Then he walked away. Whatever it was he was searching for in me, it was not music.

Right after supper I went to bed. When it was nearly dark my grandmother came in and sat down beside me. "Did you know," she asked, "that the Baltimore and Ohio Railroad was completed by engineers of the United States Army in 1828?"

I didn't.

She took one of my hands and held it. I was surprised hands so old could be so soft. Then she said goodnight and left me. My spirit was not exalted so far. I cried.

In the morning L. D. and Cassy and I sat on the side porch steps in the sun. Hollyhocks grew there and everything was warm and Junish. L. D. had a chew of Red Man plug. My grandmother would not allow him to chew in the house.

"Think you'll ever make a farmer, boy?"

"We don't farm much in Philadelphia," I said superiorly.

He studied me. "Your dad ever tell you about his Grandad Gersham Pierce and the Great War?"

I shook my head.

He rose, chewing hard. "You wait."

He went into the house. When he was out of sight I fired a stone at a hen and sent her squawking.

"Don't scare the hens," Cassy warned.

"Go lay an egg," I said.

L. D. came down the steps. He had a bundle of long winter underwear and he was unwrapping as fast as he could, the underwear arms and legs flying. Suddenly something long and bright flashed in the sun. He swung it round his head in wild and silver circles.

"Yaaaaarrrr!" he roared, advancing on me.

I retreated. "What is it?" I cried.

"Why, Gersham's saber!" he said, puffing. "Didn't you know he was in the cavalry?" My eyes stretched.

"Well, by Jehu, he was. Tenth Michigan Cavalry, Comp'ny K!"

Now I held the saber. It was a thing of magic. The blade was cool, as long as I was, and slightly curved. There was a design below the black hilt and the words *York, Pennsylvania,* and the date, 1862. It trembled in my hands.

"What happened to him?" Cassy asked.

"He was kilt," my grandfather said. "Down in Tennysee and they shipped him home to be buried. Why, he lays just down the road here in the township ground."

He sat down and had another chew of Red Man and began to tell about the battles, at places with names like Bull's Gap and Henry Court House, and I felt undutiful because I had never heard of them. On Stoneman's Raid, in 1864, Gersham Pierce was killed. My grandfather must have talked an hour. Part of it I listened to and part I didn't. I was far away, down South in the long ago, charging down red clay roads with a bugle belling in my ears. And all at once my heart went high. I knew why L. D. had brought the saber out for me to see. He meant it to be mine. I was the only grandson. I might not make much of a farmer but I was a Pierce.

"Can I have it to keep?" Cassy asked.

The ground under me tilted. I could not comprehend how any girl could dare ask such a thing.

"She can't!" I burst out. "She's a girl!"

"So was your great-grandma," L. D. said.

“She isn’t even a Pierce!” I cried.

“Being a Pierce ain’t who you are but what you are,” L. D. said.

I was beside myself. My voice split.

“You have to give it to me!”

My grandfather snatched the saber. The tufts of white hair in his ears fairly bristled. “Have to, do I, you young Reb!” He began to wrap the saber all whichway in the underwear. “I’ll teach you! When the summer’s over it goes to the one who’s made the best farmer!” He stomped up the steps. “The best farmer!”

From that morning the summer became a second Civil War between Cassy Rubbins and me. We helped L. D. with the chores. I was very unsuccessful at milking, and once, down in the shed where the barn swallows’ wings pulsed the evening air as they dipped through the door, she squirted milk right in my face. She was much faster at hitching up the team and bringing up the cows. Cassy was the worst kind of boy a girl can be—a tomboy. Several times I tried to beat her up but could not catch her. Once, though, we were looking for nests in the haymow and I cornered her. She fought like a cat but I knew if I could get her down I’d win and finally I did and sat on her and bent over to tie her braids in a knot first. Then a strange thing happened. She was breathing hard, looking up at me, and her eyes were not angry but wide and deep blue like the lakes. A bar of sun made her hair shine like the hay.

“If you’d kiss me,” she whispered, “you could have the saber.”

I was so surprised and disgusted that I jumped up. And before I knew it she was past me and down the ladder, her nose high. At the bottom she crossed her eyes and stuck out her tongue.

Through July and August I labored. I tanned and toughened and leaned until my grandmother said my folks wouldn’t know me. But as I lost weight I lost hope. What Cassy could not win by force she took by guile. By late August the cause was lost and I saw Appomattox coming.

It came one afternoon when I shut myself in the parlor to practice. I jointed up, positioned my arms, and blew the first note of a scale. There was no sound. I blew again. Then I unjointed the flute. It was plugged with beeswax. I looked up. Cassy and my grandfather were outside the window, clutching each other.

I sat there a long time, long after they had gone, Cassy to play and L. D. to his nap. One of the most despicable things anybody can do in this world is to plug up a flute. Finally I realized what I had to do.

Putting the instrument away, I tiptoed into the kitchen. Opening the bedroom door, I saw my grandfather asleep. Inching across the room I opened the lower drawer of his bureau, found the underwear. I sneaked out of the room, over the porch and down the steps. As soon as I touched ground I began to run and cry both.

When I could run no more I found myself supported by a low iron fence rusted with age. I had come all the way to the township ground. It was not a scary place. The sun was obliging, the grass green and deep. Crickets sang. On the gravestones were names like Montaig and Weatherly and Rouncifer, and three or four markers had little iron standards with the letters G A R and a small faded flag. The ground rose to a level canopied by several great oaks. I opened the gate and made my way upward among the graves. The hallowed prize glittered on my shoulder. Crows flew, cawing loudly, from the tops of the oaks and left silence.

It was at the foot of one of the great oaks. The headstone said simply Gersham Ralph Pierce, April 4, 1825—August 16, 1864. There was an iron G A R standard and a faded flag.

I tried to decide what to do. At first I thought of sticking the saber in the ground, hilt down, and impaling myself on the point the way Mark Antony had, way back when. They would be sorry, all right, when they found me. Then I thought of throwing it in the lakes, as King Arthur had ordered Sir Bedivere to throw his magic sword Excelsior—it was ex-something-or-other—in the mere when he was about to die. Finally I decided the most revengeful thing would be to break the saber. And I must do it quickly, before I changed my mind.

I jabbed the point in the ground as far as possible and then bent. But the resilient blade loosened and sprang free each time. At last I had an idea. Leveling the saber, I charged full tilt at the towering oak and thrust it home into the black trunk. I began to bend, further and further, straining against the hilt until the fine steel curved the blade almost double, and just at the last instant I almost stopped, afraid to be the one to destroy so much splendor and history. Then something snapped, threw me headfirst against the trunk, then flat on my back. A high ringing sound lifted through the leaves of the oak right up to the blue sky. It was done.

Immediately, from down the road, I heard the roll of hoofbeats. In a moment horse and rider came into sight. The rider wore blue. The horse's hoofs at a gallop raised puffs of dust.

I was not surprised or shivery or anything but I had the sensation that time stopped. I waited.

Roan horse and rider slowed, passed through the open gate, and picked their way among the headstones. The rider pushed back his box cap, looked at the saber half in the oak, the hilt half in my hand, then down at me from the lathered horse. His eyes were cutting black and quite young but there was gray in his beard.

"Thought I wouldn't hear it, hey, sonny?" he demanded.

He slid from the saddle, took the hilt half from me, and went to the tree.

"A fine piece of work you done," he said, shaking his head. "I ought to lick you proper." He came back and sat down on his headstone. His horse cropped the long grass on a nearby grave. "L. D. tell you about me in the War?"

"Some things." I decided to change the subject. "Did you have music?" I asked.

"Why would we?"

"I just wondered," I said.

He shot a glance at me. "Oh, well, we had a bugler boy and a fifer," he corrected himself. "Fife's near kin to a flute."

Everything in the township ground seemed held in suspension. The crickets were stilled, the leaves of the oaks did not stir.

"Reckoned I wouldn't hear," he said, half to himself. "Why, fine steel cries when it's broke the same way boys do." He plucked a blade of grass from his plot and chewed it. "And all the ruckus over a saber. Fightin' with that girl and mad at your Granddad and do you know something?" He held up the hilt half. "I never told and don't you. But I never used it much."

"You didn't?"

"Thunder, no!" he said. "Not worth a pinch of dried owl dung at close quarters! You can shoot 'em easier'n you can shave 'em!"

I stood foolishly, my mouth plugged up as though with beeswax.

"No matter, the harm's done," he said. "It's broke and got to be mended."

"It can't be," I said.

"Oh, it can't hey?" he snapped. "Kids today know it all, don't they?" He strode to the tree and with one tug pulled the point half from the trunk, then joined the two. Then he saw me gaping. "Getting your eyes full? Now if you be so all-fired smart you can just guess how it's done!"

And with this he stepped behind the tree. I heard him mumble "hokus-pocus" or something, which was probably for my benefit. I didn't dare peek. I noticed the air around the tree looked blue and smoky and his horse's head was reared. Still, I was skeptical. In less than a minute, though, he appeared again looking mighty proud of himself. The saber lay in his hands, the blade whole.

"Now take it home to your Granddad," he said.

It trembled in my hands, restored as though by Merlin, beautiful as before. I could see Cassy with it. My eyes filled.

"I won't," I said.

"Won't! Why, you young Reb!" He looked angry enough to snatch me up by my overall straps. "You'll mind your elders!"

I could picture L. D. waiting for me back at the house. I would catch it if I went or if I stayed. It is tragic to have three generations against you.

"I won't!" I cried.

"You will so, by the Great Gin'ral George Thomas!" he cried. Then he stopped. "Now you march," he said gently. "You march and I'll tell you how to get that sticker just the same."

"How?" I said.

"Why, here you was," he said, "in the haymow with that girl!" He fetched me an enormous wink, took the reins of his horse, hopped up, and swung the animal around above me. "You put this in your pipe, sonny," he said. "There's times when a smack's a damnsight mightier'n a sword!"

He bumped his boots and hollered "Yaaaaarrrr!" and the roan gave one leap into full gallop over the graves, right over the iron fence and off down the road. The last I saw of the cavalryman, he was leaning low and swinging his cap and charging east. He was showing off, of course, but he made a splendid sight.

. . . .

Time moved again. The crickets struck up. But the high ringing sound was in my head now. Rubbing my forehead I found a lump nearly as big as a cannonball. That must have been where I hit the trunk when the saber snapped. I opened my eyes and sat up. The saber lay at the foot of the oak. It was unbroken. I pulled myself up to my feet, whirled suddenly. Cassy stood watching.

"You'll catch it when you get home," she said.

I was dizzy. She must have seen me running away with the saber and tattled.

"I didn't think he could mend it," I mumbled.

"Who?"

I was more confused. She must have seen him.

"Why, Gersham!" I blurted.

"What are you talking about?"

I dared not answer. Perhaps the saber, of truer steel than I, had not broken. Perhaps it was only the lump on my head. Perhaps he had not been there after all. It was up to me to decide. I made up my mind. I would test the cavalryman not wishfully but adultly, by his advice.

"Cassy," I said, "I'm going to kiss you."

She gasped, blushed, and turned to run. But she did not know what a summer on a farm had done for me. I caught her and held her down on the Weatherly plot and despite all she could do gave her a good smack. I hit her somewhere between the eyebrow and ear. It was pretty rustic.

When it was over she sprang up, blushing worse than ever.

"That kind of kiss doesn't count!" she wailed.

I just threw her a wicked wink, picked up the saber, and went calmly down to the gate. On the road again I did not even look to see if there really were hoofprints in the dust. I marched.

Back at the house my grandfather waited. Some old omniscience must have signaled him I was coming. My grandmother Nola waited on the porch, wringing her apron. I trudged up the hill, Cassy following silently. I simply handed the saber over and L. D. gave it to Cassy and said it was hers, for by stealing it I had lost claim. Then he took me down the hill by the ear. While Cassy watched he licked me in the wellhouse. He was a little uncertain about it because it had been years and years since he had licked a boy but I had toughened up all over and I did not yip once, though it is a shock to be spanked by your grandfather. It hurts in a historical way.

When he was through I stood up. To my surprise, Cassy's eyes were teary. All at once, not like Jean Harlow but like Guinevere, she held out the saber. Knighted, I took it.

"Thank you," I said.

"Lordamighty!" my grandfather said.

That evening we played out till dark, refighting the Stoneman's Raid. Swinging the saber, I led Cassy in savage charges up and down the hill. She was obedient to every command and I felt not only a new sense of power but of pity for her. She was only thirteen and she was having an awkward time growing up. Besides, she was right about the cemetery smack. So after a while I led her into the pines and backed her into the branches and gave her a long, citified kiss.

"Ohhhhhh," she whispered. And then, "How did you ever learn to do that?"

"The flute," I said.

She begged me to come back next summer and said she would, too, and I said I might.

In a few minutes I let her take a turn with the saber and went up to the porch. L. D. sat on the steps having a last chew, my grandmother beside him. I still had the lump on my forehead but it had been a small price to pay for such good advice. I looked away, first at the huckleberry marsh and the three lakes lost in the dusk, then beyond, to the township ground where great oaks rose in peace. The cavalryman had tested out. There was a high ringing sound in my heart. I was exalted. I looked down the hill where Cassy stood faithfully by the pines, desiring, I supposed, to be taken into them again. I turned to my grandfather.

"Can you use another man next summer?" I asked.

He chewed reflectively. What he had been searching for in me these months he had suddenly found. He grinned.

"If he earns his keep, by Jehu," he said, "and won't go lovering around all the time."

"Now L. D.," my grandmother said.

◆ ◆ ◆

O Captain, My Captain

One afternoon in February, Mason H. McCord, 0–13170, Captain, Infantry, was relieved of his duties in Decorations and Awards, the Pentagon, and ordered to report to Walter Reed Hospital. He went without protest. The next day he was subjected to an examination by a medical officer who inquired not about his physical condition but about things that seemed irrelevant to him. At four o'clock the next morning, alert to his situation for the first time, he somehow obtained his clothing and made his way out of the hospital undetected, to disappear into one of those Confederate fogs that still sweep up out of Virginia and haunt the city. An hour later he moved slowly along a street in southeast Washington, checking numbers under the streetlights until he stopped before the darkened window of an appliance store, through which the screens of dollar-down television sets stared at him like blinded eyes. Stepping to a doorway, he climbed a narrow flight of stairs to the floor above, searched the doors for a name, then knocked on Jess Kinyon's door.

The door was opened a few inches, then shut sharply.

"Jess."

It had taken several seconds for Jess's eyes to adjust to the light, for he had been asleep less than an hour, but the instant the face came clear he shut the door and stood stock-still.

"Jess."

At the repetition of his name, in a low tone that was almost a command, he began to tremble over his entire length. He had sworn to his wife, drunk and sober, that if he ever met the man face to face again he would beat him to a pulp.

"Jess."

But they had met, the year before, and Jess had fled, not fought. He had not told his wife. And now he had seen in seconds by what had happened to the face that there was no need to fight, that the man was utterly at his mercy, at anyone's.

"Jess . . . Jess."

The voice got into him and he leaned, helpless, against the door a moment.

"Jess . . . Jess . . . Jess."

He opened the door.

Captain McCord sat down heavily, or rather collapsed in a sitting position on the davenport, and without removing his cap or loosening the belt of his rumpled service raincoat, asked for liquor. Clad only in shorts but covering himself with a blanket, Jess shut the bedroom door tight, turned on the floorlamp, and brought half a glass of rye from the kitchen. Holding the glass in one hand, and holding the wrist of that hand with the other, McCord got it down and in a minute was steadied enough to light a cigarette after two tries at the end with a lighter. He was seated directly under the lamp, with a leather briefcase across his lap, and Jess sat sullen across from him, shivering, listening to the sound of the man's lungs using the smoke he fed them, and waiting.

The change in him was so shocking that Jess closed his eyes in order to remember him as he had been so that he might hate him as much. This had been Lieutenant McCord overseas: thirty-eight or nine, of average height and build, swarthy of complexion, brown-haired, with sideburns worn at an antiquated length, with a small moustache waxed to spikes that could have bloodied a woman's flesh. One resented the white sword of his unnatural smile as much as he seemed to resent smiling. Set in shadows beneath the high forehead and lowering brows, his black eyes kept enlisted men at attention and the rest of the world at a distance. The face had his commission writ on it in deep lines, which, strangely enough, preserved its youth. No matter how much he had drunk, his walk had been direct and purposeful, as though he had strung wires from tent pole to tent pole, tree to tree, officers' mess to officers' latrine, and guided himself by them. In fourteen months, through Italy and France and Germany, Jess had never heard him laugh out loud. Jess knew he had no heart, no soul, only a broken bottle in his belly. Yet, with the arrogant moustache, the gaudy silk handkerchief he flaunted at his throat, the haughty sheen of his combat boots, the way he plumed his smoke, there was something dashing and theatric about him, as he intended. Had he been issued gold epaulets and cavalry boots, he might have resembled the daguerreotype of a young Rebel officer Jess recalled in his history book from the year he had left high school.

Jess opened his eyes. The man, four years older, was a shambles. His face had gotten fat and his black eyes were veined with red and couched in deep fat caves. Smoke dribbled out of flaring nostrils and over red lips. Silver flared at his temples. The lines that had once made him younger were melted away, and he was middle-aged. There was no banner at his throat now, there were no combat boots agleam; the knot of his regulation tie was grimy; and his regulation oxfords were ordinary. The mystery of the man, the drama in him Jess had had to admit overseas, was gone. Time had worn down the wires.

At that moment Jess Kinyon believed himself the master of their situation, believed their positions to be exactly reversed, and the sweetness of it swelled in him; but that triumphant notion lived only until Captain McCord raised his head and stared about the room, picking out with his eyes the pertinent data. They selected three things—a worn pillow on the davenport stenciled with the words "God Bless America" above an unfurled flag, the pink-crusted lampshade on which two green lovebirds were branched and from which frayed tassels hung, and the right front ceiling of the room where the wallpaper was cracked open like a wound—and with these three things he seemed to pass silent, merciless judgment. Then Jess could hate again, as easily as before, and make his cold hands into fists beneath the blanket, for it was then the old trapped feeling came upon him. He had known it all his life, really, but a town in Sicily, named Agrigento, had first forced him to understand what it was, an officer in uniform named McCord had built it up inside him until he was still choked with it, and neither beer nor sleep nor labor could free him of it.

The Captain smiled at him, comprehending, and gestured with his glass, and automatically he obeyed him, all his lean body mutinous under the blanket. The Captain smiled again to see him obey, and when he returned the red-black eyes pushed him down into his chair and the voice began to question.

"You're married, aren't you?"

No reply.

"Have you children?"

No reply.

"How long have you lived in this—here?"

No reply.

"I know how you make your living, Jess. You drive a cab. Does it satisfy you?"

Jess would answer none of them, but only sat there, his twenty-six-year-old face stone.

"Are you happy, Jess?"

No reply.

"How do you like the way the world is going?"

No reply.

Finally the interrogation became a rambling, reasonless monologue.

"I'm sorry to trouble you at this hour, Jess, but it is not my fault. Do you sleep well? I haven't for a long while, I don't know anyone who can. Wouldn't it seem good to go to sleep to the sound of the guns again, just once? Or see another decoration ceremony—ah, that would be the finest of all!" The puffy face reddened with rye and excitement at the thought. "There were only primary colors then, Jess. Now everything is gray or—" a murderous look at the lampshade— "or pink. In my opinion what is needed is a month of war every year. Set aside a month for it and give ourselves to it, there's no equivalent. It brings out the best."

In Jess's imagination the high forehead seemed to bulge outward and he remembered reading somewhere that alcohol, in sufficient quantity over sufficient period of time, would eat, actually eat, away the cells of the brain, and there must come a point, of course, when one additional cell would make the difference.

"I have only a little time, Jess, only enough to do one last thing with you.

To tell the truth, I've gone AWOL just the way you did once, remember? I've been at the Pentagon more than a year now, and day before yesterday they sent me to Walter Reed. An observation ward. By today they would have had me in a detention ward, with bars on the windows." His head jerked from this side to that as though he, too, were afraid of being trapped. "Out of sight, out of mind, they thought. Or perhaps out of mind, out of sight. Yet they do not understand me as well as I understand them. It was not me they would hide away, but a part of themselves. As though questions about dreams and bars on windows would help either of us. I've gone AWOL so we could do one more thing together, something which needs doing and is very vital to the world, take the train to New York. One last trip together, Jess, the last case to complete. You must shave and dress as quickly as possible."

"I wouldn't go across the street with you."

The distended eyeballs glistened irritation. "I'm sorry, Jess. You must."

"No."

"That's an order."

"An order?" Jess came out of the chair, clawing at the blanket as though he were suffocating, his sallow face twisted. "The war's over, you sonofabitch!"

His cry brought McCord to his feet and they faced each other and everything between them exploded.

"An order, Kinyon!"

"Go to hell, McCord!"

"*Captain* McCord!"

With a snarl Jess put both hands against McCord's raincoat and shoved him sprawling onto the davenport. He might have tried to rise except that Jess let the blanket drop from him, and at the sight of his body the man cringed as though at a whip-fall. The machine gun bullets that day in Agrigento had stitched Jess expertly across the front and back. The scars were white pieces of patchwork skin sewn round his lean middle with far less craftsmanship, and thus revealed in the light they flashed and seemed inset with diamonds. McCord had never seen them and he stared with mouth agape, his breath whistling, fumbling for something in his raincoat pocket while Jess loomed over him.

"Get out of here before I beat the life out of you, Lieutenant, get out of here and leave me alone. My wife's in that room, and my kid—" Jess was unaware that he was begging, not threatening, and that his fingers writhed like snakes over the terrible scars, touching them. "I can't go to New York or anywhere with you. Just go away and leave me alone. You're drunk and sick and God knows what all. I just want to forget you and forget the war—"

His lips continued to move, but no sound came. He was looking down the muzzle of a small pistol McCord had pulled from his pocket and now held no more than two feet from his face. He recognized the weapon at once as the Beretta Billy Dow had given the Captain in France, and the threat of the thing straightened him up. He began to shiver again, his thin ribs rising and falling.

"Don't make me use it, Jess. Even I wouldn't miss at this distance." His eyes hid in their caves from the scars. "But I will unless you follow orders. I have no alternative. You're my only eyewitness, Jess, and we both know there must be eyewitnesses. So go shave and dress, on the double. We must take the seven o'clock train. I'll pay your ticket. Just dress—and put on your best." He smiled and the Beretta did not waver. "We are going to see some important people—as the world gauges importance. We are going to do our last case together, our greatest. William Harold Dow." He spaced the names softly. "William Harold Dow. Now go."

Jess obeyed, dragging the blanket behind him into the bedroom as though he were sleepwalking. Once in the darkness he began trembling again and his mind worked with such violence that it was almost audible to him over the soft breathing of his wife and of his child in the crib. If we woke her she could call the police later and have them picked up at Union Station. He had only to put his hand over her mouth and whisper in her ear. Yet he did not. At that moment it was impossible to conceive of her as his wife, or of the child as his. To himself he seemed an intruder: the man outside had made the past the present. He had made Jess Kinyon a stranger in his own bedroom.

When Jess reappeared he had shaved his hard, almost ugly face and put on what was obviously his best—a light blue suit which hung awkwardly across his shoulders, a white shirt, a red tie, black shoes—and he had combed his sparse, sandy hair, plastering it tight against his skull with water. He took his topcoat from the back of a door.

"What are we going to do in New York?"

The fog seemed to have gotten into the room, and Captain McCord was only a figure in it. He stood near the front door, his briefcase under one arm, one hand in his pocket, over the gun. From the other pocket protruded the neck of the rye bottle he had taken from the kitchen.

"You called me 'Lieutenant,' Jess. It's like old times. Only it's 'Captain' now."

"What are you going to do?"

McCord mused a moment. "After you make a hero, Jess, can you unmake him?"

He put his cap on thoughtfully, and Jess heard the meaningless words repeat themselves in his brain. He knew the one cell that made the difference had in fact been eaten away. He wished he had never opened the door. He wished desperately he had awakened his wife. Now it was too late. He thought then that the only way out of his trap was to kill, and that if he were careful it could be done. He had killed before. McCord never had. His eyes narrowed, he opened the door for the officer and stood back.

Captain McCord's teeth gleamed and he moved his hand in his pocket. "Thank you, Sergeant. After you."

. . .

They were seated stiffly opposite each other, nearing Baltimore, and outside there was rain. Five other passengers were dispersed along the length of the car. Captain McCord had emplaced himself beside the window and removed his raincoat, spreading it on the seat beside him so that the pocket opening was never more than inches from his right hand. He had directed Jess Kinyon to sit across from him, at the aisle end of his seat, and indicated there was an unseen line between them which it would not be advisable to cross. And so they sat, watching each other, each calculating his chances.

"Will you fight me all the way, Jess?"

"You know what I'll do."

"But this wouldn't be an appropriate setting, now would it? In an alley somewhere, perhaps, but surely not the Pennsy." He smiled and caressed the neck of the bottle. "Put your head back, Jess. Rest."

Jess put his head back and the past leaped nightmarish into his mind. He had joined the division just prior to the Sicilian invasion in June 1943. Four weeks later, entering Agrigento in the lead jeep of a Reconnaissance Troop platoon, he had gotten his from a Kraut gunner, and the next five months he had spent in a general hospital, returning to the division on the Anzio Beachhead in April 1944. It was not the Recon Troop to which he went, though; it was Division Headquarters Company, and more specifically Lieutenant Mason McCord. It was the worst thing that had ever happened to him. And how had it happened? Smiling, the officer explained that he had long needed a driver, and since he himself was a Virginian and sentimental, he had asked G-1 to watch the incoming cards and give him the first replacement from Virginia. Shortly thereafter, Jess's card had listed his home address as Alexandria.

Within two weeks Jess had a gutful. There was comparatively little danger, but there was all the old rear-echelon stuff—shave every day, sir every shoe clerk with gold or silver on his collar. He made no buddies, for the other enlisted men were not his kind, and the lieutenant would never have permitted him time for them. He had none himself. He lived for his work. He made Jess live for it.

The lieutenant was the division's sole writer of awards for valor. On Distinguished Service Crosses and Congressional Medals of Honor he lavished a scrupulous and almost manic devotion. He would go into the lines night or day to take statements direct from the mouths of eyewitnesses to heroic deeds. The more gory a case, the more care and dedication he would give it. Jess was sure that he preferred posthumous awards, that he resented the occasional soldier who was presumptuous enough to live to receive the award in person and be sent home a hero. Yet at the slightest rumor of a deed above and beyond the call of duty he would have the man out of the lines and peril at once to the safety of headquarters, there to remain in comfort until Washington had approved the award. One could not deny him this. Through his efforts the men of his division had, by that time, been awarded by the Congress of the United States twenty-six Medals of Honor—twenty-two of them posthumous—more than twice the number secured by any other division in all the armed forces. He had been promoted. He had been assigned his own field telephone, his own jeep, and, finally, Pvt. Jess Kinyon.

He gave Jess a bad time. Not only did he demand that the jeep be serviced and ready at all hours, but he ordered his driver to get behind a typewriter and learn to use it so that he might devote all his time to "creation." He kept Jess totally occupied and totally wretched eleven hours a day, seven days a week. What he did not see, or would not, was that he was forcing a sincere, simple, yet ordinary and quite unlettered enlisted man into an environment and an activity that was altogether alien to him. He was attempting, without reason, to make of Jess Kinyon something he could not be, and in the process he was not only demeaning a combat soldier but twisting and torturing a personality. There was something paradoxical about it: he would save Jess Kinyon's life, literally, by keeping him out of the lines, yet he would render Jess Kinyon's life not worth the living.

For the duration of the war and two months of occupation and fifteen more Medals of Honor Jess remained Lt. McCord's typist, driver, assistant, and mortal enemy. He never saw another day's combat. He never again fired a weapon. He never had a day's respite. And although the war for them ended twelve months later, the war for him was not over until the day in August 1945 that he took the train for Le Havre. An enslaved Europe had been liberated, and so, at last, had Jess Kinyon.

He had heard Wilmington called long before, had not moved during the stop, but now he let his eyelids part a fraction, and when he did the war was not over at all. For the officer still sat opposite him; they were together just as they had been for those fourteen months; circumstances had simply shifted them from a pyramidal tent to a train in Delaware. Then he saw that the other's eyes were fixed on the countryside, and in an instant he hurled himself forward, his arms outstretched for the raincoat, his shoulders rammed across the other's chest. But even more suddenly the Captain's right arm leaped outward so that Jess's fingers, clawing for the pocket, fastened instead about his wrist, and for the first time he touched the flesh and bone of the man. He gasped. Something in the shock of the touch, something in the man himself seemed to flow into Jess's fingers, loosening his grip. It was as though his fingers made contact with something so immeasurable that it weakened him, made him powerless before it, and as their eyes met, recognizing it, Jess's fingers unclenched one by one and with a groan he fell back on his seat.

"You couldn't, Jess. You couldn't even touch me, you see. I saved your life—"

"It wasn't worth it."

Jess wanted to cry. All the fight was out of him. A curious expression came over McCord's face, and he took another pull at the bottle, a long one, then lit a cigarette.

"You're not happy, are you, Jess?"

"None of your business."

"It is. You will never know how much my business you are." He blew smoke. "Or perhaps you will today."

There was still rain outside. The windows were awash.

"Why did you drive away from me that night?"

He meant the night Jess had fled from him. It had been a year before. Around two in the morning Jess had been driving his cab beside Union Station Plaza. He had just passed the station, heading toward the Capitol, and had paused for a stoplight when he heard a voice shouting "Kinyon!" His head had jerked round and in one look he had seen the man coming toward him across the street. He had gunned the cab and run the red light and gone four blocks before the pounding of his heart slowed and the voice faded from his ears.

It was as though you were running away from me. I only wanted to talk with you, to find out how the world was treating you. I had been in Washington just a month. It was the first time I'd seen you in three years." He leaned forward dramatically. "Do you know how I recognized you, Jess? A miraculous thing—your cab was lit by a kind of white light—and suddenly I knew you would be in it."

"You were drunk." Jess remembered that he had been headed south, and anyone approaching the cab from the northwest would have seen it silhouetted against the floodlit Capitol dome.

"Yes. I was drunk." He sat back. "After that I got your address from the cab company and wrote you two letters."

"I flushed them."

"You shouldn't have. I merely wanted to know why you were driving a cab when what you wanted to be was a projectionist. I remember that. Which should prove how interested in you I was—and still am."

"Interested—"

"You were already apprenticed, and all you needed was a thousand dollars to join the projectionist's union. That's why I made Headquarters give you the stripes, made you save the money before you left me." He bent forward again. "What happened to the money, Jess?"

"I spent it."

"What for?"

Again Jess feared he would cry. He knew now with a deadening certainty that he could no more refuse to answer than he could have refused to open his door three hours before.

"Clothes—a car—I got married—furniture—a kid! I don't know how it all happened, but it did, just the way everything does," he choked. "My card came up—just the way it did to you with Alexandria on it. Somewhere they've got all the cards in a big file and every so often yours comes up and there's nothing you can do about it! Now are you satisfied?" He turned his face to the window.

"And you think yours has been coming up all your life?"

Jess nodded miserably.

"Having to leave school early. The Army. Then me."

"You most of all." He pressed his lips together. He had never told anyone about the trapped feeling. For a time there was nothing but the rumble of the wheels below and the click of the bottle against a button. When he looked again at the officer, McCord was staring down at the wrist Jess had grabbed and there was something in his eyes, when his head raised, Jess had never seen before. It might have been malevolence; it might have been tenderness.

"At ease, Jess. We will not need to watch each other any more."

When they were stopped momentarily in Newark, Captain McCord took his briefcase across his knees and patted it with one hand. "Do you know what I have in here, Jess? All my heroes, all the living Medals of Honor—Murray, Searles, LoPresti, Weitzel, Oliverio, Longshore, Roberts, Pogoncheff, Scarbrough—their citations, I mean. I've written to all of them, to see how they were. Adjutant-General has their addresses."

He went on to describe the circumstances of each, where they were now, what they were doing. His speech became swifter and there was a new animation, almost an exhilaration in his tone. The names seemed to intoxicate him where liquor evidently could not. It was as though he considered these men his personal concern, almost his property, that when he praised them, he praised himself.

It was the attitude that had added fuel to Jess's hatred overseas. A fierce, insufferable pride had burned in the man. He considered himself absolutely infallible in his field—and he was. Week after week, month after month he went on writing statements and citations that would make a man stand at attention, his eyes wet when he read them. In this peculiar labor he made new and epic prose out of the heroism of other men; in it, the genius of Mason McCord came to full flower. And he did it all, Jess realized with slow sickening, for himself. Jess saw in time that to the man the heroes he made were no longer human beings, but characters he had created, whose life and fortunes he might manipulate as he chose. The power of life and death lay in his pen, for a Medal of Honor meant coming out of the lines, going home, living—a DSC (distinguished silver cross), remaining. His was the decision, the power, and he enjoyed his omnipotence. He could not alter facts, to be sure, but he could so dramatize them, so contrive and stage-set and ennoble them in prose, that they became not facts but something else. When Jess saw this, he had nothing left—no faith in honor, in the war, in anything. His trap was evil. And there were times then, as afterward, when Jess wished he had not gotten out of Agrigento alive.

McCord was looking at some snapshots some of the men had sent him. "We had pictures in our quarters, too—my father was Regular Army, you know."

Jess did not. He knew nothing of the man's history other than that he had enjoyed several desultory years of study at a southern university.

"Old Blackjack Pershing hanging over the fireplace," the officer mused. "And in my mother's room a lithograph of Edgar Allen Poe. We never owned furniture. When orders came we took down the pictures, that was all. One post after another. Wherever we went, all I had to do was look on the walls and there they were. Pershing and Poe. I knew I was home." He smiled, and said sincerely, "You know, I'd give a great deal to think you had one of me up somewhere at home."

"For what I think of you, you don't want to be remembered."

"I'll send you one, Jess."

"I don't need any brownie photograph. I see you automatically here—" he indicated his head—"every day and night. I wash you out with beer and work and sleep, but you won't disappear."

The Captain frowned and returned to the subject of his men. Jess shut his eyes. He waited for Billy Dow's name, but the officer did not mention it. The omission was odd, for Billy had been his favorite. Moreover, he had been Lt. McCord's masterpiece. Jess remembered him well, for he had lived in a tent beside McCord's for five weeks, high up in the snow and sleet of the Vosges. Billy had been only nineteen then, only a boy, a short, slight, thin-faced boy with wide blue eyes. Dirty and mud-caked though he was when brought out of the lines, his brown hair still curled, and one unruly lock lopped forward as soon as he doffed his helmet. His pink ears grew close to his head, his nose was pug, his hands small, with stubby fingers. He made older men think of the time they had first shaved, or of their first pair of long trousers. Only in the nervelessness of his hands, in the inscrutable clarity of his blue eyes was there any sign that he could have been credited with killing more than one hundred of the enemy—which he was. And when someone pointed him out and told you that this boy, now recommended for the Medal of Honor, already wore the DSC and the Silver Star, you swore under your breath and wondered about things like mankind and the world and Almighty God's intent.

Jess talked to him often during those five weeks—whenever McCord would let Billy out of his sight long enough to go to chow or the latrine. They might have been friends had Billy stayed longer. Billy was his kind. He hailed from Deep Cut, Pennsylvania, a mining town in the Alleghenies, where his father and elder brothers worked in the anthracite. He had two sisters, who wrote him regularly. He liked baseball. He played shortstop. He graduated from high school directly into the army. He had the same seventeen-week basic training as Jess. He did not mind it. He had been only average on the rifle range. He liked assembling and disassembling the various weapons, though, BAR (Browning automatic rifle), machine gun, mortar. He did not want to mine. He thought he would like to be an auto mechanic after the war. He liked cars. That was all.

That was all. But he joined a rifle company of the division on Anzio and went directly into the lines. In March 1944 he was decorated with the Silver Star for gallantry on a night patrol. In August 1944 he was decorated with the DSC for extraordinary heroism on the road to Rome. In November 1944 in the Vosges of France he performed an act of "conspicuous gallantry and intrepidity at risk of life, above and beyond the call of duty, in action involving actual conflict." Word came to Lt. McCord. "It can't be the same Dow," he protested. It was. In six hours Billy Dow was out of the lines and into Division Headquarters. In thirty-eight consecutive hours of interviewing eyewitnesses and writing and typing, a completed case for the Medal of Honor was on its way to Washington.

Billy Dow baffled Lt. McCord completely. "Billy boy—my Billy boy," he would muse to Jess. "Did you ever see such a face, Kinyon? The face of a child. How could he do it? It's difficult to believe myself, yet I've double-checked everything. More difficult to believe than all the others. And do you know, Jess, I've looked into the records—only one other man in the war has the Medal, DSC, and Silver Star—a Marine, posthumous." He was even more solicitous of Billy than the others. Jess could not fathom it—they had nothing whatever in common—and he went so far as to fish for information.

"What is there about Billy?" the Lieutenant said in reply. "I wish I could put it in words—not that it's any of your business." He tapped a pencil on his field phone. "Billy is not only great, he's—good. Healthy. Pure. Unspoiled. Untouched." His eyes grew faraway, the way they did when he was writing a citation. "In the temple of war, Billy is a choirboy."

He seemed unable to do enough for the boy and, at first, Billy had seemed to reciprocate, had, in fact, given McCord the Beretta he prized, as he might have an older brother.

One incident Jess would never forget. One night late he passed Lt. McCord's tent and heard him questioning Billy. He was very drunk, and over and over again he would ask the same question: "Why did you do it, Billy? When the moment came, why did you do it? Billy, why did you do it?" His voice was agonized, rising almost to a shout, and Jess, standing outside in the sleet, had heard no answer. Perhaps there was none. But for that moment, that night at least, Jess Kinyon believed he saw into Mason McCord's soul. He did not know what he saw, but he was profoundly moved.

For the next week the lieutenant was never sober. The interrogation had seemed to change Billy, to make him sullen and rebellious, and his impatience to go home, once his Medal of Honor had come through, was somehow akin to ingratitude.

The snap of a cork, the clink of a ring against the bottle. Since early morning the man had drunk more than half the fifth of rye. Jess had not heard of Billy again until he read a feature story about him in the paper—it had been much later, in 1946, he guessed. Ex-Pvt. Billy Dow of Deep Cut, Penna., had been just awarded the last, the most minor of the four medals for valor that an American might receive from his government, the Bronze Star. He had thus become the first man to receive all four. It was a rather long article, and he recalled the phrase "America's Greatest War Hero." He also remembered thinking it peculiar the Bronze Star should come a year after the war was over. A month or so after that he had seen a little piece which told how Billy had been called to Hollywood to be trained for stardom. And another time, just this last autumn, he had seen Billy's picture in a magazine ad, dressed in his uniform with all his ribbons, standing very erect and saying he liked Pep-Cola better than any other cola drink. It also seemed to him he had read somewhere that Billy was engaged to some Hollywood starlet. Jess had been glad Billy was quite famous and was getting something out of his medals. It was certainly queer Captain McCord had not mentioned—

William Harold Dow! Jess's eyes flew open. The full name! He felt the sweat break out on his body beneath his shirt. The train was still stopped. Not for three or four minutes, not until it moved again and he heard the officer speak, could he get control of himself.

"That was Newark, Jess. About fifteen minutes more."

He had put the citations and letters and snapshots away in the briefcase and lit a cigarette.

"Did you—did you write to Billy Dow?" Jess asked thickly.

"Of course. Oh, he didn't answer. The only one. But someone sent this." The captain brought forth a large photograph from his case.

Jess took it. There was Billy, his hair waved appealingly, looking boylike as ever, and his shoulders were posed so that the rows of ribbons on his battle jacket were prominent, every one distinct. It was not a real photograph, but the glossy, impersonal, somehow insulting print of one—the kind people in

Hollywood always sent out—and there was the usual inscription. "Best wishes to an old buddy—Billy Dow."

"Billy's famous now, you know. 'America's Greatest War Hero,' they call him." While the officer's voice was easy, his eyes were withdrawn and cruel. "I don't know about that, but he's certainly the most decorated. All four. The first time in history."

The fog had lifted and once more rain fell, the large drops rippling the scum pools along the tracks. The train snaked sinuously across the Jersey flats.

"I was sorry Billy didn't write himself. But he's very busy, I presume. He's being married in New York tomorrow, I understand, to a starlet named Gloria Kean—a perfect match, the papers say. And he has a book coming out Monday. I bought an advance copy. Here—"

Jess looked at it only long enough to see the cover. The title was *Out of the Grave.* Below it, on a gold background, were spaced four ribbons.

"I hadn't imagined Billy was in the least literary. You must read it sometime, Jess. All his war experiences. Very vivid. I thought it might mention us, but it doesn't. It scarcely refers at all to his awards. 'Winning modesty,' I'm sure the critics will call it."

Ahead of them, around a curve, was the black hole of the tunnel into which they would soon disappear, and Jess recalled that there was no exit, no escape, but only darkness and wet cement walls until the train stopped in Penn Station, still below the earth. His hands clenched. He thought he could not stand to be trapped below the earth with the man opposite him.

"As I say, I was disappointed Billy didn't write. But naturally, when one is busy and famous he can't be expected to carry on a correspondence with the man who—" Captain McCord returned the book to the case abruptly, dropped his cigarette, heeled it, and began to draw his raincoat about him. The other passengers moved restlessly to the far end of the coach.

"You—you got him the Bronze Star—" Jess managed.

The officer pulled his belt tight. "I did."

"You knew—what it would mean—"

"I did."

Suddenly they were in the tunnel. The wheels shook and pounded. The dark walls pressed in on Jess and red eyes winked in the blackness.

"What are you—what are you going to do—"

McCord's face was livid in the artificial light. He did not answer.

Jess pulled himself upward, crouching. "You're going to do something awful, but I'll stop you," he said hoarsely. "I won't let you do anything to anybody. You've done enough to me, the world shouldn't have people in it like you—"

"Here we are, Jess."

Five hours they hunted Billy Dow. He was everywhere, but they could not find him.

The papers, especially the tabs, fairly slavered over the wedding the next afternoon, Sunday. There was shot after shot of the pair's young, ecstatic faces: Gloria Kean seemed small, blonde, pretty, and in every picture her doll's face wore an expression of adoration for him. As a *Post* columnist put it, "She worships the ground Billy walks on—and shouldn't she?" She was, it seemed, twenty-two, and a starlet with a bright future in her own right. One shot of a chaste kiss bore the caption, "The Dream Couple." There was a picture showing Billy Dow having the Medal of Honor clasped about his neck in the White House, and an old publicity shot of the bride-to-be in a two-piece bathing suit standing bust-thrust on a diving board which a *Mirror* editor had located, with unfortunate taste, in his files and run with the carnal, one-word caption, "Billy's." There were timetables for the wedding day, descriptions and sketches of the bridal gown, lists of Billy's decorations and of the personages flying in from the Coast for the nuptials, and half-page ads for Billy's book, which would be officially "out" on Monday. New York, according to one writer, had "taken the young couple to its heart." The windows of the bookstores around Times Square displayed massive, military arrangements of *Out of the Grave* and blown-up photostatic copies of Billy's citations, and before them the captain would pause, unmindful of the rain and slush.

Yet nowhere was there information concerning the couple's whereabouts. The captain called the newspapers, to no avail, and Jess followed him about the city, from hotel to hotel, in a kind of coma, overcome by the strain of the hours since morning. He seemed to be involved in something so evil, so unreal, and so vast that he could neither guess its dimensions nor foresee its consequences. Not until four that afternoon did the officer think to call the Jonathan

Farmes Company, Billy's publisher, and then it was only by rasping that he was Captain McCord of Decorations and Awards, the Pentagon, and that he must locate Billy Dow, that he got what he wanted. The famous pair, it was divulged, were secluded in the midtown apartment maintained by the man who was perhaps Hollywood's best-known independent producer, Sidney Lewin.

In a matter of minutes Captain McCord and Jess Kinyon stood uncertainly in the foyer of the apartment, having been admitted by a manservant who took the officer's card into the next room and returned with the request that they wait. Mr. Lewin would be finished telephoning presently. The captain paced the area around the door, hesitated, extended a hand toward the knob, then looked at the younger man.

"He said to wait," Jess murmured.

"My ears were open. When you commit yourself, you don't wait."

"But he said—"

"When I am in command we do what I say. That includes you, the admiral in the servant's suit, and the other people who frequent this place. God, what a mausoleum!"

McCord had just noticed the series of tremendous portraits hung along the wall. Except for their gilt frames they looked like Coca-Cola advertisements or Hollywood posters done in oil, and the subjects who had been thus immortalized were recognizable at once. A director, a male star, a scientist, a priest, and a producer among others, all of whom had been zealously publicized.

"By their heroes shall ye know them!" McCord snorted. "And Billy's next in line for consecration!" He took a savage draught from the bottle. "It sickens me. It sickens you. Mr. Sidney Lewin may foist his phony gods on us—but I'll be damned if I'm going to let him make something phony out of the real thing!" He laid a hand on the doorknob.

"You don't just bust into a place like this," Jess protested.

"You may not. I do. We're going in!"

"No!" The officer's eyes pulled at him. "If I thought—by going with you—I'd get rid of you—I could—"

"The door, Jess!" McCord's head reared high in triumph. "And remember, Sergeant, we're a team!"

"Yes, sir."

Jess followed him through the door.

The room was beyond belief. It was huge. Four high windows, undraped, let in only a little light from the gray day which was rapidly darkening. The walls were bare and done in a cold white. The floor was bare. In the center, four chrome and canvas lawn chairs were grouped around a reclining chair and a low table, upon which were two telephones.

"But that's what I'm trying to tell you," Sidney Lewin was saying into one of them. "Twelve-forty-five in the church. You'll never make it. Acapulco. A-C-A-P-U-L-C-O. In Mexico. You could send them air express. Not that she'll need them."

A young and pudgy forty-five, Sidney Lewin shot a quick look at the intruders. Though neat and trimly dressed in an expensive sharkskin suit, there was somehow something sticky about him. The tailor had not been able to hide his wide hips and narrow shoulders. The manicurist had been able to taper his nails, but not his fleshy fingers.

"Sure. Sure. Sure, if you like. But no endorsement," he concluded. "Just the publicity. These kids are different—if you follow me. Adios." He dropped the receiver onto its cradle. "You were Billy's officer during the war, Captain?"

"Mr. Kinyon and I were in the same division."

"Everybody was. And you would like to present your compliments in person, I suppose." The second phone rang and he answered. "Say, what's the name of that lingerie outfit? Yes. Well, they're giving her four negligees especially designed for the honeymoon. One for each of his medals—with silver stars embroidered on just the right places. Cute, eh? Sure, feed it to the papers. But check with public relations. We don't want anything smutty. Right."

He rose and gestured expansively. "The whole country's going to bed with those kids tomorrow night."

"And you?" McCord asked.

The producer stiffened. "What's your pitch, Captain?"

"Are you the man who brought Billy to Hollywood?"

"I am."

"Then you have a considerable stake in what happens to him."

"Look, Captain. Billy's not here—"

"I have a stake, too, Lewin. And my claim precedes yours. I wrote all of Billy Dow's awards for valor. Mr. Kinyon typed them."

Sidney Lewin stared, then rose and came forward, hand outstretched. "Captain, my Captain! Let me shake your hand—the hand that held the pen!" And while he pumped the other's hand he said of course they must stay, Billy was only out shopping, surely they could appreciate how it was, everybody in the war was his buddy now, the world was full of crackpots running around loose. Just sit down, he would hustle them a drink, he kept the liquor in the bedroom. Still talking, he went nervously through a door into the room adjoining.

As soon as he was gone, Captain McCord had a pull at his bottle, then put the raincoat over the back of one of the chairs and sat down. "Take off your coat and stay at ease, Jess," he directed, propping the briefcase against a chair and lighting a cigarette. "This may take quite a while."

Jess remained standing. "I want to know what you're going to do."

"What we always did first. Get the facts."

"And then?"

"Measure the case on its merits. There are unwritten laws that govern such decisions."

"I'll stop you," Jess threatened mechanically. "I'll tell them you're crazy and AWOL from a hospital and they'll call the police and—"

Sidney Lewin rolled a small bar table into the room. He had put on a silken dressing gown of pure, monkish white. The room had become very dark and before making drinks he flicked a wall switch. Suddenly the two men were each struck by a single shaft of light which plunged from the ceiling and cut the dimness like a dagger. They looked up, startled.

"It scares the pants off everybody, first time," said the producer, pointing to the modernistic cone-shaped fixtures that hung from the ceiling like spotlights. "The whole room does. The other rooms are Hollywood, but this is my retreat. Bare walls, no frills. A cell for a twentieth-century monk. So what do I care if they call me an intellectual, just so I'm authentic!"

He began to make drinks. "After I was *converted* I could take the Coast and twenty rooms with a pool just so long. So I cleared this place out and got a decorator to do some interior *un*decorating. It was gross before, gross. Now it's clean and hard. When I have friends in we can sit in light, nothing but light. We come alive to each other." His voice lowered respectfully. "Sometimes Jim Farmes comes over. He's publishing Billy's book, you know. And he talks to me and I just listen. He's authentic. If he had a beard—he'd look like God. This room is for him, too." He brought their drinks. "Billy told me about you, Captain. How many Medals of Honor did you write?"

"Forty-two. Most of them posthumous."

"What a twist. A ghostwriter for ghosts."

"I prefer the classical allusion," the officer said sharply. "I believed myself to be writing a new *Iliad*."

Lewin looked doubtful. "Yeah. You must have had a lot of material for stories—stuff that would sell."

"I kept a file. I never had an award disapproved."

"Spectacular," the producer marveled. "A hit every time you raised the curtain. Genius. But how do you decide who gets what?"

"An implacable justice. An inflexible formula. Tell him, Jess," McCord ordered.

"Kill two Krauts—the Bronze Star," Jess repeated dully from memory. "Wipe out a machine gun nest—the Silver Star. Call down artillery on your own position and kill five or six—the DSC. Butcher at least ten and get yourself at least partially mutilated—the Congressional Medal of Honor."

There was a pause. Then Lewin spoke. "Just like a teacher giving A's and B's in school. Jim Farmes says you've always got to give people what they deserve." He drank hastily. "And that's the way I felt about Billy, Captain. When he got the Medal of Honor and Silver Star, so what? So did a lot of red-blooded American kids. Then the DSC—he made the papers, that was all. But when that Bronze Star came through for him a year *after* the war—" he stopped. "Say, you must have written that one, too—"

"I did."

"Did you know what it would mean?"

"I did."

"It made him the only kid in the war to get all four!" the producer proclaimed. "Unique! When I read that I knew what I had to do. You guys are not the only ones with a formula. I reached into the mountains of Pennsylvania and I pulled him out!" Becoming excited, he lit the reclining chair with another spotlight and seated himself, Buddha-like. For half an hour he discoursed to his visitors, bending forward at the waist. Before the war, he explained, he was gross, gross. Pure brain, no soul. Then, during the war, something happened. Did they remember *The Story of the Combat Soldier?* He had made it himself, independently, without changing a word of the original script. "The finest picture of the war, gentlemen—a million dollars profit after taxes! I was converted. I'd never do another picture that didn't mean something!" But on his next two pictures he lost four, five hundred thousand, and his second wife divorced him. No brain, no soul, she was pure body.

"And now you have pure Billy," the captain observed.

"If you knew me better, Captain," said Sidney Lewin, hurt, "you'd know I'm the sincere type. Billy Dow is a great man," he insisted passionately. "He's a symbol—know what a symbol is? A symbol's something that stands for something else. Billy's a symbol of the world's heroism—and Sidney Lewin will see the world recognizes him!"

Jess scarcely breathed. It was what Mason McCord might have said, and indeed, Jess had seen on his face the same look that now transformed the producer's. He watched the officer's expressionless face.

In Billy Dow, Lewin went on, every Gold Star mother would see the son she lost, every girl the sweetheart for whom she had waited in vain, and they might say that their sons and lovers had done as much, had fought as gloriously, and Billy Dow was only accepting the honors on behalf of the dead. "Say," he repeated, "that's a good title—*In Behalf of the Dead.*" All this was why he had watched over Billy with such sleeplessness and devotion. He had not let Billy appear on the screen as yet, because he had only recently finished drama school. He had permitted him to make only such advertising endorsements as would be appropriate to his status—no liquor or cigarettes—just such things as watches, a cola drink, a low-priced automobile, the Red Cross. Billy was not to be used by anyone. "You see," he finished fervidly, "if I can keep Billy the way he was during the war—well, I'm doing something that means something!"

"The Socrates of Santa Anita—"

Their heads swung. A tall, majestic man with high forehead and thinning gray hair had come in unannounced and entered the light, a faint smile playing over his patrician features.

"Will you not introduce me to your disciples, Sidney?"

The producer's face reddened, and getting up hastily he identified the captain, faltering at Jess's name. "James M. Farmes, gentlemen. An authentic intellectual. Never made a mistake on a book. A businessman with a soul. Everything I am I owe to him. There I was, slinking round the Coast. One day the phone rings. It's Jim Farmes. From right here in New York he reaches across the continent and picks me—Sidney Lewin. He's got *The Story of the Combat Soldier* on his desk. "Sidney," he says, "you can have it for a quarter of a million. But take my advice and don't change a line." And I didn't, either. He's the one said Billy should write a book, the country was ready for a book by Billy Dow—"

"I'd take a drink if one were offered," the publisher said easily.

"Oh. Excuse me, Jim." Sidney Lewin went quickly to the bar table while James Farmes took a chair at some distance from the visitors'. "Billy and Gloria'll be right back. He saw an ad in the paper, something he wanted to buy—you know, kid stuff."

The publisher smiled patronizingly. "Just so long as he autographs the books tonight, while his glands are in good order."

"He will, he will, Jim." The producer brought the drink and, flicking another wall switch, spotlighted the chair in which Farmes sat, his topcoat still on.

"Sidney has a superb sense of showmanship, Captain," Farmes remarked, on his face the amusement with which one tolerates the antic devotion of an animal. "Note, I did not say drama."

Jess instinctively did not like him. His attitude toward Lewin, he realized, was somehow very similar to that of the captain's toward him—the same awareness of superiority, the same condescension. Jess sat on the edge of his chair, waiting, waiting while the officer judged them as he judged everyone. Looking at him, slumped down, Jess recalled the little signs the Germans would stake up—*Achtung! Minen!*

James Farmes, Lewin was announcing from the reclining chair, had brought forth from his brain the biggest package deal in years. "Tomorrow

Billy is married. Monday morning the book comes out. Monday afternoon the book is sold by the Farmes Company to guess what independent producer? In six months the picture is canned. Then simultaneous premieres in Washington and Deep Cut, Penn., and guess which American hero plays the lead in his own picture made from his own book?"

"Sidney—" the publisher lifted a hand. "Before you confess us further, would you mind telling me who these gentlemen are and what the purpose of their call is?"

"Why, to wish Billy well, what else? The Captain wrote all four of his awards—and after the war the Bronze Star. You know what that did—"

Farmes looked closely at the officer for the first time. "The captain, too, is a creator, I see. Not an artist of your merits, perhaps, Sidney, but still a creator."

"Why, sure he is, maybe he is!" It was a new thought to Sidney Lewin. "And I'm just bringing him up to date on his creation." Vindicated, he turned to his guests. "That's the situation, Captain. I've been mother and father to that kid because I knew what I had on my hands. I took no chances—when he wanted Gloria I made damned sure she was fit for him." His voice became consecrated. "I've been a museum. That's a metaphor. I've been a museum where you keep a work of art and guard it and get it ready to exhibit to the world. If I charge a little admission it's because it's a psychological principle that people don't appreciate anything unless they pay for it." He seemed carried away, his plump face lifted to the light. "I've made Billy what he is today. And I've done it not for him, not for me—but for the country, for the world. For two years I've lived for that kid—and if I had to, I'd die for him."

In the moment of silence that followed, Captain McCord sent a stream of smoke upward. "If I had to," he remarked, "I'd kill him."

This is it, Jess thought. But nothing much happened. James Farmes stirred slightly.

"An interesting statement, Captain—if somewhat obscure. Possibly you could enlighten us—"

"If I thought it were necessary," obliged the other idly, "that there was no alternative, I'd feel quite justified—"

There was a noise and Billy and Gloria came in from the foyer. Everyone rose. Billy remembered the lieutenant, of course—oh, it was Captain now—

and he shook hands readily when the officer stepped to him and offered his, and he did not seem to resent the familiarity of a hand on his shoulder. The captain monopolized him completely, examining him, ignoring the others, and it was some time before Billy was able to introduce his bride-to-be, to remember to shake hands with Jess Kinyon, to speak to his publisher. And then everyone stood about awkwardly for a bit.

Except Gloria. She let Billy kiss her—the badge of possession—and say, "Confidentially, isn't she a package, though, Jess?"

She dimpled. "Honey, maybe the captain would like a seat at the wedding. After all, he did so much for you—"

McCord frowned. "No more than I did for all the others."

Jess thought she was really beautiful, and he knew he would never let anything happen to her or to their happiness. Moved, he did not see that her dress, intended to be chaste and schoolgirlish, had, in the glitter of buttons and the artfulness of lines, the chastity of a century note. Nor that the sadism of Sidney Lewin's lighting system revealed the tinges of dark at the roots of her blonde hair, the overlength of her lashes, the patina of pancake on her doll's face. Billy was showing her off the way a guy does anything he's choice of, Jess thought—a car, a gun, an infielder's glove—and he did not blame him. Billy had been his kind and still was, even though it was difficult to see in him now the boy in khakis and muddy boots. His pin-striped suit was obviously tailor-made; his hair still had its wave, although it was thicker about his ears and the back of his neck and the wave was set in oil. He came to sit beside Jess and to ask about his family, but when he inquired what Jess did for a living, it was McCord who replied.

"Jess drives a taxi."

"A cab. Do you like it?" Billy asked.

"Sometimes."

"How come?"

"You're not tied down," said Jess. "You can cruise."

"What Jess really wants is to be a movie projectionist," interrupted the captain.

Billy grinned. "You want a cut of the business, too? I don't blame you. It's done a lot for me. What's stopping you?"

Jess stared at the officer. "I've never figured it out." He knew his face was as red as his tie. He would have told them all the truth then, and warned them to call the police, except that it seemed now there might be no need for it after all, that the captain might leave peacefully. Sometime soon the liquor, the combination of rye and Scotch, would have to take effect, too, and he might be deactivated, rendered incapable of harm.

"Do you know anything about Deep Cut, Pennsylvania, Miss Kean?" inquired the officer carefully.

"Why, of course. That's where Billy went to high school."

"Have you ever seen a mining town? Where the men are gone all day, digging coal hundreds of feet under the ground?"

"And the wives waiting on top—just waiting, waiting—" She came to herself. "Oh, I've been to the movies. Only I like it better when they're prospecting for gold and silver. That's more like an adventure. Anyway, Billy wasn't a miner. He was a mechanic."

"Almost was, you mean," Billy said. "When Sidney wired from Hollywood, I really took off." To change the subject, he went to the door and returned with a long, cylindrical package, began unwrapping it. "Say, Jess, I want to show you what I bought." He pulled out a gleaming chrome tube. "An extra tailpipe for my car! I saw it advertised in a racing magazine—"

"But I don't see how it can work," puzzled Lewin.

"Oh, it doesn't work—it's a fake. But it makes your car look like it's got a special motor or something. Say, Sidney, I charged it to you. Is that okay?"

"Sure, kid."

"Fake tailpipes, cars," Mason McCord said aloud. "A far cry from France. What this country needs is one month of war out of every twelve. There is no equivalent."

"Or some more good war pictures," Gloria added. "Sidney says the country is ready for another one—providing it's got a twist."

"Wouldn't you like to go to sleep to the sound of the guns again, Billy?" McCord asked. "Just once more?"

"No, Sir. Do you think I'm crazy? Say, you must have liked the army!"

James Farmes moved. "Obviously, since he stayed in uniform."

"I was out for two years."

"Didn't take to civilian life, huh?" said Billy. "What did you do, Captain?"

"I—I was in New Orleans. But before that I spent a year on occupation. And I found another Medal of Honor in the records."

"Is that a fact?" Billy was more interested in the tailpipe. "Say, Jess, I've got a Buick now, but after the picture Sidney says I can have a Lincoln."

"Tailpipes, Lincolns." Mason McCord rubbed a hand over his stubbly chin. "Don't care for Deep Cut any more, eh, Billy?"

Billy's face set at once. "Deep Cut is a grand little town, a good American place to live, and I hope to settle down there someday," he said as though from memory. "But it was my duty to leave. I have a bigger job to do—"

"A bigger job?"

"To keep alive—" Billy hesitated. "To keep alive the memory of those who never came back."

"Do you *like* the life you're leading now?"

Billy shrugged. "What difference does it make? Nobody ever asked me if I liked being a doughboy or a grease monkey. Why should they ask me now?"

Before McCord could pursue the point, the cold voice of James Farmes sliced the room. "You have some autographing to do tonight, Billy."

"Say, that's right, Mr. Farmes." He went obediently to a cardboard box against the wall, took out some books, sat in one of the spotlighted chairs, and began to inscribe flyleaves.

The publisher was a sound tactician. The captain and his companion were now isolated, their position made untenable. It was well after five and it was made plain they had worn out their welcome. The captain sat sullen, his chin on his chest. Jess fidgeted, aware of the glances shot their way, the unspoken invitations to leave. It was time to get the officer out of there, now or never. The man had had only two drinks in more than an hour, and denied liquor for long he became vicious. The air in the room was sticky, the lights hot. He began to sweat profusely. He saw Sidney Lewin go over and say a word or two to the publisher. He saw the latter speak softly to Billy.

"Mighty nice of you to come up, Captain," Billy said presently.

The officer seemed to rouse. He made the rounds of the room with his eyes. "Those your books you're autographing, Billy?"

"That's right."

"I bought an advance copy. Read it last week."

"Like it?"

Jess saw his hand move toward his pocket, grip the neck of the bottle, then fall away. "I was disappointed you made no mention of your awards."

"Sidney thought it would sound too—" Billy stopped.

"Sidney? Did Sidney help you with the book?"

Jess knew it was coming then. Everyone watched the officer.

"A little."

"I see."

Jess saw his hand slip into his right raincoat pocket.

"Remember this, Billy?"

"Why, sure! That's my Beretta!" Billy put down his books. "I've thought about that little sweetheart a hundred times. I'd pay anything to have it back."

"You could now, couldn't you?"

"Can I have it, Captain?"

"In a moment, please." McCord balanced it in his hand. "I'm writing a book now myself, Billy. A case report of all the Medals of Honor in the war. It will never sell, of course, but we'll give copies to all the libraries."

"That so?"

"Yes. I have a little room in the Pentagon. All around the room there are file cabinets, nothing but file cabinets, containing all the records of the awards. Hundreds of thousands of them. When I look out my window, all I can see is the cemetery at Arlington. It's a strange room to work in, these days." All heard the officer's heavy breathing. "A terrible room." He paused. "You've changed a great deal, Billy."

"Have I?"

"You have. Deep Cut is a good American place to live."

Billy got to his feet. "I know."

"You're going back to Deep Cut." Captain McCord leveled the Beretta. "Tonight. That's an order."

No one moved.

Billy Dow swallowed hard, then shoved his hands in his pockets. "Take it easy, Captain. The war's over."

"Mine isn't. The Farmes Company will call in every copy of your book."

The officer's pouched eyes pushed. "The wedding is off. Your contract with Lewin is void. You will pack and start for Deep Cut tonight."

"Just who the hell do you think you are?" Billy demanded.

"I am the man who made you America's Greatest War Hero, Billy. Unless you obey orders I'll make you America's Greatest War Fraud by morning."

James Farmes rose to his full, forbidding height. "I suggest you go and go now, Captain."

"I suggest you listen," McCord snarled, pulling himself up in his chair. "I can do exactly as I say—and I brought Mr. Kinyon with me from Washington as proof."

He went on to tell what he had done. In 1946, recalling Billy with considerable fondness, he had reflected it would be a fitting gesture to add to his record the last possible measure of recognition, the Bronze Star. Every combat man's record had a Bronze Star in it somewhere, so he had searched through the skeleton of the division until he located a man who had been a companymate of Billy's. The man, a corporal, had been able to remember a day in August 1944 upon which he had witnessed Billy Dow crawl out alone near Besancon, in France, and kill two snipers who had been harassing his company. Taking a statement from the corporal, the officer had written up the case. His only difficulty lay in the army regulation that required two eyewitness statements from enlisted men. Assured in his own mind of the corporal's veracity, he had found the name of another buddy of Billy's, killed in action in Germany, and had deliberately forged that name to a second, similar statement and sworn to it. Within a week the award of the Bronze Star had been approved.

His head turned toward Jess Kinyon. "I brought you with me simply to answer one question, Jess. I want the truth. Answer yes or no. I could have done easily what I say, couldn't I?"

Jess felt the eyes. It was worse than Agrigento.

"Yes or no, Jess."

"Yes."

The publisher sat down slowly. Billy, Sidney Lewin, Gloria Kean were statues.

McCord lit another cigarette. "Unless you obey orders, Billy, I'll call the papers at once."

Sidney Lewin was the first to speak. "So what! So the Bronze Star's illegitimate! The kid is still the most decorated—"

"No." The captain threw one leg across the other. "A Marine has the other three—posthumous."

"Then we change it around, give it a twist," Lewin said hoarsely. "America's Greatest *Living* War Hero—"

"Which is not quite the same thing."

Farmes straightened. "You would be out of uniform in twenty-four hours, and in prison. Forgery—"

"I know."

Billy could not comprehend. "But how—why would you—"

"Because I liked you then, Billy." McCord toyed with the Beretta. "At the age of eighteen you were a great man. God knows what you are today."

Billy's fist clenched. "Easy, Captain. I haven't been mad at anybody for a long time." His face became impassive, cold, his eyes hard. "When I get mad—"

"Sit down and shut up," McCord barked. "I don't give a damn whether you're mad or not, just so long as you go home where you belong!" he shouted. "How long did you think you would get away with this? I wrote you a year ago, in Hollywood, and asked you the same question—and this is what I got—" Keeping the gun leveled, he unzipped the briefcase and pulled out the publicity photograph. "A picture! 'Best Wishes to an old buddy!'"

Billy's face twisted. "I couldn't answer everybody—"

"Of course, not *every*body! The captain sailed the photograph angrily into a corner of the room.

"I know I owe everything to my buddies." Billy clutched at his tie. I only did what they'd have done—"

"Stop it, stop it!" McCord roared. He brandished the gun at Farmes, Lewin, Gloria. "What have you made of him? A ham actor who can't even recite the lines you put in his mouth! You've sold him and sold him in bits and pieces until there's nothing left but the name! The real Billy Dow is already dead—already posthumous! Look at him, damn you!"

They looked. What they saw was a Billy Dow whose hands moved constantly as he attempted to control himself.

"Symbol!" the officer groaned. "There's your symbol, Lewin—of the world's sickness!"

Billy spread his legs, delivered an ultimatum. "Have you finished blowing your top, Captain?"

"No! What I made I can destroy!" McCord rose to face him, waving the gun recklessly. "You be what I made you and go home where you belong, or I'll kill what's left of you!"

Something made him swing round sharply. Jess Kinyon had gotten up. "Listen, you people! Don't pay any attention. Don't let him hurt you—"

"Shut—your—mouth," the officer growled.

"He's crazy!" Jess cried. "He's drunk, he's sick, he's AWOL from Walter Reed Hospital!"

"I warn you, Jess!" The officer stood erect, his back ramrod.

"Maybe he did what he said about that Bronze Star—but he didn't do it for Billy!" Jess continued, spilling out his hate. "Every medal he got, he got for himself. The star writer of citations—and the only thing left for him was to make somebody the most decorated soldier of the war—his masterpiece. And he picked Billy!" His lips curled. "All that stuff about Homer!"

"What about Homer?" the publisher asked sharply.

"He used to say Homer was a piker compared to him—that he was the high priest of heroism or something like that." Every word broke a chain for Jess. "Crazy for glory—as long as somebody else got shot for it!"

"Kinyon has a grudge against the world because he can't join the projectionist's union," said McCord, sneering.

"It's not that—it's not the world—it's you, damn you!" Jess turned to the others. "Fourteen months I sat across from that face. I used to call him Lieutenant God—sitting behind his desk deciding who gets what, who goes home, who lives and who dies. Now it's Captain God—and he tries to give grades to us—civilians! He sits in that room with all the files and thinks he can yank out our service records and give us marks!"

"And you don't like the grade you think I've given you, do you, Jess?" shouted the captain. "But you had to come today, you had to find out your mark just the same. That's what hurts, isn't it?"

Jess advanced on him. "That does it, McCord!"

The officer backed away. "I'll shoot if I have to, Jess!"

"I'll wipe you out myself—"

Suddenly the captain halted, lowered the gun. "All right. Lay hands on me if you can. You can't, Jess. Not yet."

Jess stopped, his hands outstretched.

"Neither beer nor sleep nor your hands, Jess," Mason McCord said softly.

Jess's hands fell to his sides.

"Jess. Jess. Jess. Jess," the officer whispered.

"I have to go—get away," Jess mumbled, near tears.

"Without the key—"

"Don't sacrifice yourself, Kinyon." Farmes came forward to take command of the situation. "We have the measure of him now. I underestimated your creative ability, Captain, but not your stature as a man."

Sidney Lewin swabbed his brow with a handkerchief. "Jim, I knew there was something phony about this guy when he walked in the room. Brain maybe, but no soul. The brass of him—taking top billing. I made that kid—not you!" he shrilled at the officer.

"Say, what's he got on you, Jess?" Billy asked. It must be something pretty big—" He put his arm around Gloria. "You all right, honey?"

"Oh, I wasn't worried at all," she assured him. "I've worked in Westerns a lot more noisy than this."

James Farmes moved toward the light switches, flicked on the conventional lights so that the room was illuminated wall to wall. "Are you going, Captain?"

"No."

The publisher's gray brows raised regally. "Then I shall see that you do." He started toward the telephones. "Unless you leave this apartment at once I shall call the military police. I consider you a menace."

McCord got behind the reclining chair and braced the Beretta across its back. "Pick up that phone and I'll shoot—"

Farmes hesitated. "Then I shall call from downstairs. The Secretary of the Army is a personal friend of mine."

"You won't leave this room alive," the Captain warned.

"I think you're bluffing. What are you trying to prove to us?"

"What are you trying to prove to yourself?" McCord asked.

The publisher made his decision. "To put it crudely, I don't think you have the guts to shoot." Slightly pale, he turned his broad back and started toward the door that opened into the foyer. He had not taken two steps before the officer crouched and steadied the gun in both shaking hands. James Farmes was halfway to the door when Gloria screamed. He slowed, then moved on inexorably. As he put his hand on the knob, McCord fired.

The man leaned against the wall as though to keep from crumpling to the floor, but he did not, and Billy ran to him and found the slug in the wall near his shoulder.

"He missed," Billy said in wonder. "At twenty feet!"

Captain McCord was triumphant. "War's not over after all, eh, Jess? Good to hear a gun go off again—I won't miss next time!"

Billy returned to Gloria while Sidney Lewin's head swung from Farmes to McCord in stupefaction. "You'd have killed him—"

"I would, wouldn't I? Have to write myself up for a Bronze Star!"

The act of firing the weapon, even though inaccurately, had seemed to astonish the captain and now he was galvanized, his arrogance restored. And to the others, the report of the gun had made him real. He was not an apparition after all—he could not be drunk away or blustered away or made to disappear by force of will; he was there with them, on a February evening in midtown New York, and there he would remain until he had done with them what he wanted. They watched as James Farmes took a few faltering steps and fell stunned into a chair, as Mason McCord took the bottle from his raincoat and drank, then ordered Lewin to spotlight the chairs again. "Retreat, eh, Lewin? A retreat with two phones—gross, gross!" He walked to the publisher and stood over him. "Snap out of it, Farmes. I missed. Never been shot at before, have you? Lived your whole life out of other people's books! Get a dose of the raw stuff and you collapse! What if the boys at the Harvard Club could see you now?"

Billy also examined the publisher, moving his head up to the light. "I've seen replacements go glassy-eyed like this the first time a shell came in. They'd stay out cold until the Krauts threw in another eighty-eight. Remember, Jess?"

"I sure do." Jess had not taken his eyes from McCord.

"The country's most respected publisher, eh, Lewin?" said McCord. "The hell he is—I know him!"

Farmes tried to reply, but the words came in a kind of hollow mumble. "The man who . . . publishes only to profit—is but a bookseller with his own press—"

"He's quoting himself!" exulted McCord.

"The country—needs an intellectual sedative. I shall—not publish war fiction—"

"Until those writers spawned by the war have developed perspective and the country is ready to hear them," the officer finished. "That's what he wrote to me, word for word! A form letter from the king of books—why, you colossal fake! I molded in a room in New Orleans for two years trying to write novels without perspective. I had the finest material in the world, the real, raw guts of life while it was still bleeding in my mind—and you call me a menace!"

Farmes made another attempt. "The real menace—to the industry is—the publisher who loses contact with his public—"

"But when everybody else started to list war fiction and it sold, that's when you told Lewin to get a quick book out of Billy, wasn't it?" the officer cried, turning to Lewin. "And because the whole deal was his idea, that sanctified it for you. James M. Farmes is just another of your fake works of art—created by you just to fool yourself. 'Put a beard on him and he'd look just like God!'" McCord mocked. "Whose face is God's now, Lewin?"

The producer turned away from the spectacle. The only one in the room who noticed Gloria slip through the door into the bedroom was Jess. McCord bent over Farmes once more.

"A businessman with a soul! That's your soul coming up now—and there's so little of it, all you can manage is the dry heaves!"

He walked to Lewin, who now cringed at the edge of the reclining chair. "Now, Lewin, haven't you a little piece to speak?"

The producer rose. "Say whatever you want, you can't touch me inside. I made Billy what he is for the same reasons as you. What possible good could the kid do the world if I let him stay in the mountains?" he pleaded. "I brought him to the Coast just the way you took him out of the lines."

"I don't like your comparison," the captain snapped.

"You're anti-Hollywood!"

"I'm anti-evil! And when I see you take something clean and simple and mold it into a Hollywood monstrosity just to prove Sidney Lewin's been converted—"

"Billy, Billy—don't listen to him." Lewin begged. "He doesn't understand the business end of art."

McCord motioned to the chair. "Collapse, Lewin. I'm wearing the long, white beard now and I say collapse!"

After a moment the producer sat down and buried his head in his hands. Jess wondered what Billy Dow was thinking. He did not appear to be concerned in the least that the officer now faced him, but merely sat turning the exhaust pipe in his hands.

"Now will you go home?" McCord demanded. "Or must I send you home in a flag for re-burial?"

Suddenly the loud and sickly blare of a crooner singing "Body and Soul" blasted through the door from the bedroom. Jess, McCord, Billy, and Lewin leaped toward it.

"It's Gloria!" Billy cried. "Maybe she called the cops!"

McCord blocked the door, holding them away with the gun. "Come out of there, you!" he ordered. "What in God's name are you doing?"

Gloria appeared in the doorway. "Playing records," she explained innocently.

"Turn it off! Turn it off!" McCord shouted.

Petulantly she obeyed and returned to the room carrying an album. "Aren't you just mad for Mel Torme? The Boy with the Butterscotch Throat?"

McCord mastered himself with an effort. "What's in it for you, Gloria?"

"He just sends me!" she said rapturously.

"Who?"

"Mel Torme."

"I'll see Mel Torme in hell!" roared the officer.

"Listen, Captain, you leave her out of this," Billy ordered.

"Don't mind him, Baby," Gloria smiled. "I don't. If he'd shave he might even be cute."

McCord glared at her. "I can see it all. You looked at Billy and you thought, if I just had his name all the good things of the earth would start rolling in."

"Why, of course. What's the matter with you?"

"How old are you, Gloria?"

She was sugar-sweet. "Twenty-two and twenty-six."

"Twenty-two and twenty-six!"

"Twenty-two in the movie magazines and twenty-six really," she explained. "I just think of myself as *very young.*"

"What's your real name?"

"Gloria Kean."

"You're lying!"

"You're so dramatic, Captain. Of course that's my real name. Mother knew I'd be going into pictures, so she thought, why not give her a good name now? Then she won't have to change it later."

"Your mother!" McCord snarled. "Where do you come from?"

She seemed not to mind the interrogation in the least, but was doing her best to be helpful. "Pasadena. I went to Pasadena High. All the girls in Pasadena High start getting ready for pictures as soon as they can. If you want to be a star you have to start early, get your name in at Central Casting—"

"What's that?" the officer interrupted.

"It's an agency for extras. They type all your experience and measurements and things. Then when a studio needs somebody like you they take your card out of the files and call you up." She seated herself gracefully, crossing her legs. "I understand why you're curious, Captain. How you get to be a star is very interesting."

"Interesting!" McCord flipped his cigarette into a corner. "Is that the word? Leg art! Bit parts in B pictures. Weekends at Lake Arrowhead—"

"But that's what you have to do! You have to be just what people want you to be. Everybody knows that." She smiled at him as one might at a child. "You have to work hard and have a soul and—"

"A soul!"

"Sidney says everybody should have one."

"Oh my God!" The officer was desperate. "Don't you see what's happening? What Lewin and Farmes are doing?"

She frowned. "I don't understand why you're so mean to Sidney and Mr. Farmes. They're just doing things for Billy the way you did—only in a bigger way."

"And you're actually going through with this travesty," he accused. "This vicious, depraved—"

"That's why I'm so happy about tomorrow!" she exclaimed. "It was time I got married and I liked Billy a lot. He was fun. But then, after a while—I fell in love with him!"

Completely baffled, the captain took momentary refuge in his bottle, then strode toward Billy, who had begun autographing books again. "Now. Look at them, Billy. Farmes, Lewin, and the girl you wanted to marry. I've shown them to you for what they are." He took the Beretta from his pocket. "Now will you go home, or must I use this?"

Billy stretched out his legs. "You know I don't scare, Captain. I never did."

"You don't scare! But good heaven, don't you shame?"

"He should be in pictures, shouldn't he, baby?" asked Gloria thoughtfully. "Character parts."

McCord ignored her. "Billy, when I read you'd gone to Hollywood, I refused to believe it of you. Then a few months later I picked up a magazine and there you were—glamorized. America's Greatest War Hero Prefers Pep-Cola! You weren't advertising that stuff—your ribbons were."

"I got five hundred bucks for that ad," Billy said calmly.

"And then this—" McCord got his copy of the book from his briefcase. "Is that what you took a hundred lives for—to get material for a book?"

Billy seemed puzzled. "What have you got against me? What have I ever done that you should try to break me?"

Sidney Lewin lifted his head. "We know the truth about you. This man told us. You were always looking out for yourself. Well, it's Billy's turn. If it was right for you then, why is it wrong for him now?"

"It's more than wrong—it's evil."

"Who are you to judge?" Jess inquired wearily. His head aching, he sat near James Farmes, almost in the same condition.

"I judge what I've created," McCord said loftily.

"What do you want him to do?" Lewin asked.

"Do? This is what I want him to do!" The officer pulled a sheaf of citations from his briefcase. "Here are my boys—all my living Medals of Honor. I know what they're doing and where they are. They're home, living the simple, honorable lives they should. They run gas stations and work on farms and clerk in stores. They've married decent girls and raised families. They're growing in the soil of this country and some day we'll reap the harvest! They've stayed heroes—they're the bread of the earth, the rock of the world!"

"Will you crucify the kid?" Lewin cried. "Should he throw away his future just because those others don't have any?"

"It's simple for you to say 'get the hell back to Deep Cut,' because you don't know," Billy insisted. "You don't know what life in a mining town is like."

"I don't care what it's like, so long as it's real!"

"You don't give a damn about me," Billy said bitterly. "You'd like to see me digging ditches—or driving a cab!"

As soon as the words were out, Billy looked as though he would have given anything to take them back, but he could not. Jess Kinyon did not change his position, but sat with sandy head bowed, staring at his muddied shoes.

"He didn't mean—" began Sidney.

"I'm sorry, Jess," Billy offered.

McCord looked at them. "This was the real reason I asked Jess to accompany me today. Now sit down, all of you."

One by one they did.

The captain took still another sheet of paper from his briefcase. "Jess, stand up."

"What do you want?"

"I want you to stand up."

"You can't hurt me any more."

"Stand, Jess."

Their eyes met and Jess got to his feet, uncomprehending.

The captain spoke slowly. "This is Jess Kinyon. He lives in four rooms over an appliance store. His greatest ambition is to save one thousand dollars—which is the initiation fee into the projectionists' union. In that work he believes he will have security and dignity. It's a humble petition. The gods are accustomed to pleas for much more. If they grant it, Jess will some day put Billy Dow's face on the screen."

Jess's lips moved. "What are you—trying to do to me—"

"When you said you would not drive a cab, Billy, you implied that you would not be a Jess Kinyon. I would to God you were." The captain opened the sheet of paper. "What I have in my hand Jess knows nothing about. It is a citation for a Medal of Honor sent to the War Department in September 1943. Here, Lewin. Read it."

In the silence Sidney Lewin began to read, swiftly at first, then more slowly as the impact of the words struck him. "'Jess Cleo Kinyon, 32014394, Private, Infantry, 301st Reconnaissance Troop, for conspicuous gallantry and intrepidity at risk of life, above and beyond—"

"Skip all that," ordered McCord. "The next paragraph."

Again Lewin read. "On 22 July 1943, at 1400 hours, while driving the lead jeep of his platoon into Agrigento, Sicily, Pvt. Kinyon encountered an enemy street ambush. Although his two companions were killed instantly by the intense machine gun and rifle fire directed at the jeep, Pvt. Kinyon nevertheless elected to draw that fire away from the remainder of his platoon, and to that end drove his jeep head-on one hundred yards into the enemy roadblock—"

Sidney Lewin swallowed and seemed unable to continue. Captain McCord took over, speaking from memory. "'Despite murderous close-range fire which raked the jeep, Pvt. Kinyon rose from his seat and, standing erect, began to operate the fifty-caliber machine gun mounted thereon. Wounded critically by point-blank fire, Pvt. Kinyon managed to fire a full belt of ammunition, killing or wounding at least twenty-one of the enemy, and by the time he fell unconscious, his uniform drenched with blood, the remainder of his platoon, which had withdrawn safely, was able to flank the roadblock and attack its survivors, thus destroying the position.'"

The officer took the citation from Lewin, tried to look at the young man standing, then turned his face so that he could not see.

The sounds Jess Kinyon made were stifled. "But if—why didn't you—"

"Oh my God, Jess!" It was a cry torn from the officer's throat. "There were no eyewitnesses! That roadblock was around a corner! Everybody knew, but nobody saw what happened. I wrote three statements, but it was no good, no good—I wanted to lie but it wasn't in me! I broke my heart over it, Jess, it was the only one I ever lost—but I lost it, I lost it!"

"Then—then that's why—"

"That's why I tracked you down, why I tied you to a typewriter and a jeep for fourteen months. Did you think I would let you go back in the lines, boy—if I saved the others, would I lose you when I knew before God you were as great as they?"

Jess spoke softly. "As great as they—"

The officer's eyes were closed. "If I couldn't bear the sight of you sometimes it was because I couldn't bear the sight of my own crime against you—my own failure!"

But Jess did not hear. "You think you're nobody," he whispered. "You think you're trapped. Right from the time you're born. So you fight—"

"Don't believe him, Jess." It was Billy. "He just wrote it to break me down—"

"Show him, Jess. Show him."

And slowly, proudly, Jess Kinyon took off the cheap topcoat, the blue suitcoat, the red tie, the frayed white shirt, and bared his naked body to the light. He seemed to be alone, whispering to himself.

"The whole world's against you. And it finally gets you alone on a street somewhere. That's the way it happened."

"There," said Mason McCord quietly. "Now you know him. The kind of man Billy would not be. For a few seconds on a street in Sicily he lived beyond the limits of human conduct, lived an idea bigger than life itself."

Jess's eyes were wide. "Then it can't hurt you anymore. It can't touch you. You know who you are."

"No medals. No applause," said the officer. "Just a body scarred to remind him he has felt something more important than his own existence."

Jess stood erect now and they thought they heard him say: "Then—then you can just cruise."

Gloria clasped her hands. "It would make a beautiful movie. How your wife must love you, Jess!"

"Cut the corn," McCord muttered.

"But I fell in love with Billy. What's so corny about falling in love?"

"Nothing, when it's real. In the heart, not on the billboards, selling soft drinks." The officer went to the reclining chair and lowered himself heavily. After a moment he spoke to Billy. "Go back, boy, where you belong. Take a job in the garage, or go down in the mines. Or be like Jess. Drive a cab along the streets of a great city." His voice took on a mystical, faraway quality. "I can see it at night, lit, if the eye could see, by a kind of white light—"

"The Cab of White Light," Gloria breathed.

"I like to dream of my boys pouring their secret into everyday American life," McCord went on. "You are gods—but gods in men! You haven't the right to sell yourselves for trips to Mexico or fake exhaust pipes. You are miracles and you've got to stay real. In Lewin's hands, Billy, you're a monstrosity. Back in your garage you'd be like Jess—a man."

All at once Gloria ran to Billy. "Take me with you, Baby! I want to go to Deep Cut with you!"

Sidney Lewin leaped to his feet. "Oh, no, you don't! Don't listen to her, Kid!"

"Honey, you don't know what you're saying," Billy protested.

"Of course she doesn't." Lewin took her by one arm. "The girl with the butterscotch brain—"

But Gloria gripped both her fiancé's shoulders, her face enraptured. "It would be so beautiful, Billy. All the way from Hollywood to Deep Cut—and maybe you down in the mines—and me on top with the other wives—waiting, just waiting—"

"She's nuts! I just let you have her because you wanted to get married so bad!" Lewin shouted. "She's ten bucks a day on the Coast! She's—"

Billy pushed her aside and stalked the producer, his face suddenly cold again, calculating. Lewin retreated in terror, his arms extended.

"Don't, Kid. I didn't mean it. You wouldn't touch me, Kid—not after what I've done for you—"

Billy pushed him contemptuously into a chair. "I know what you've done. Now shut up."

He turned toward Gloria but she had already run to McCord and knelt by him. "Make him take me along, Captain. You're the only one who understands. I love him and I want to go with him!"

McCord stared at her, a new light in his eyes. "Would you really, girl?"

"Oh, yes!" she cried.

The officer was fascinated. "Why?"

"Because—" she clasped her hands again and rolled her eyes upward—"because—oh, it's so silly—but in Deep Cut I'd be a star!"

"No!" McCord was on his feet, his face working. "No!" He raised the bottle to his lips, hesitated, shuddered, and for the first time in fourteen hours put it down without drinking. Then he stood silent for a time, his gaze resting on each one in turn. On James Farmes, who still sat staring, sightless, his topcoat on, his lips moving soundlessly now and then. On Jess Kinyon, who had put on his clothing and sat near the publisher, isolated by a piece of paper as much as the former had been by a bullet. On Gloria Kean, who watched him with her doll's expression, waiting for him to assert his mastery of the situation. On Sidney Lewin, who sat helplessly on the chair into which Billy had pushed him, his fleshy face drained of color. And on Billy Dow, who, in his bewilderment, tried without success to devote his attention both to the books he must autograph and to the glittering tailpipe he had brought to the apartment in such boyish exuberance three hours before. The officer seemed to be gathering the last of his strength, to be assembling all of his physical and intellectual reserves preparatory to a final assault.

"I have a theory," he began. "If I could pin you down, you would say that self-interest has driven you to do what you've done to Billy—and to yourselves. I can understand that. It's all you have to fall back on. But, more than any other living man, I know men, I know that they are capable of *something else*. And I say it is time the human race became human!"

He bent over Gloria. "Can't you see anything except that ladder to a Hollywood heaven?" When she obviously did not follow him, he put it another way. "Listen. Did you ever sleep with someone you didn't love?"

She nodded.

"With someone who couldn't do you any good?"

Again she nodded. "Yes. Once. When I was with USO. He was a major—and not even good-looking."

"There—why did you do it?"

She dimpled. "I could never figure out."

"Good girl!" He strode to Sidney Lewin. "And you—in that GI epic—

why was it you didn't change a word? Forget Farmes. I want the real reason."

The producer plucked at one ear. "It beats me. It really does."

"See!" McCord exulted. "It's possible even for you!" He came to Jess. "I can ask you now. What made you drive into that roadblock?"

Jess only looked at him.

"You see," he gestured to the others, "the biggest moment of his life and he can't justify risking his neck."

"What are you getting at?" Billy asked.

"You couldn't answer me either," the captain reminded him. "How many times did I ask you overseas?" Noticing Farmes, he dismissed him with a shrug of his shoulders. "And him, he doesn't count. Even without him that's five out of six. Five out of six who have felt in some way—"

"Felt what?" Billy demanded.

"He means why we're nice." Gloria was trying hard. "He thinks it's a miracle if you're nice to somebody who can't get you a part in a picture."

"A tiny one, girl, but a miracle just the same!" McCord cried. He took a stand in the middle of the room, swaying, the liquor and lack of sleep at last taking their toll. "We all think we're smart and that the only law of nature is McCord looking out for McCord. Then along comes a Billy Dow or a Jess Kinyon and with one act they smash the picture. And that's my theory. There's something else, something we're missing, something utterly *unreasonable* that makes a man strong enough to throw his own life into somebody else's game." He had become a kind of evangelist, no longer able to control the fanatic waving of his arms. "Call it anything you like—but in a few seconds it made great men of Billy and Jess. And it's in us, too—in me, in you. It's got to be! And I will keep it alive in you! I will be your circumstance. In my own person I will be war! You will save yourselves by saving Billy Dow—because in keeping Billy human you will be saving the human miracle in which we so desperately need to believe! You will! You will! You will go home, Billy! He pointed a finger at Sidney Lewin. "He will go home!"

The producer stared at him, then at Billy, then rose and went in anguish to James Farmes. "Jim! You have to say something—help me answer. Help me be logical."

Farmes sat unhearing.

"My God, Jim—answer him!"

After a moment, Lewin went to Billy, shaking his head. "What are we going to do, Kid? We could maybe make the picture in Deep Cut—"

Billy pretended to be interested in the tailpipe. "Jess, maybe I'll wait until I get the Lincoln before I put this thing on—"

McCord made a final appeal. "Billy—"

Billy put the tailpipe down impatiently. "You knock yourself out, Captain, but you don't send me. I guess I've grown up too much. I think I know a lot more about the world than you do. In some ways, I think I'm even older than you."

"You're being impudent!" McCord barked.

"I'm being sensible. You can be the best second baseman in the world, hitting four hundred in Deep Cut. But where does it get you? Deep Cut isn't the world. And nothing happens unless someday a scout from the Pirates or the Tigers sees you play and then asks you to sign up for the big time. That is when your life starts to count." Becoming more sure of himself, he stretched out his legs and tightened the knot of his tie. "Look at you. You might have been the best damned award writer since Homer, but you'd never have got to first base if one day somebody in Washington hadn't approved one of your medals and published it in General Orders. That's when you started to click. And the same goes for us guys you picked out for medals. Somebody passed on you. You passed on us. That doesn't change anybody. It's too bad about Jess, but he just wasn't lucky. Don't blame me for that.'

McCord's look was black. "Now you're being childish."

"I'm trying to be grown-up," Billy said easily. "You'd better get out of that room in the Pentagon and see what the world is really like."

"You didn't feel this way once! You couldn't have—"

"I told you. I've grown up." Billy smiled. "Captain, hasn't anybody ever told you this is a rough world? And when somebody rings your phone, answer it! First, of course, you have to get the telephone and your name in the book. That's the trick. There are people who own the phone companies and the car companies and everything. They don't make phones and cars, but before you get any of these things you have to find out who the people are and how to get in to see them. They can't see everybody, of course. So it's a matter of breaks. When they do spot you, you're in. You get the phone, the car, the girl—the works."

"You won't go home!" the officer thundered.

"No. And you can't make me, even with that popgun."

McCord lurched wildly for the reclining chair. "The hell I can't! I know the way!" He scrabbled in the litter of papers on the chair until he found the gun and one of the papers. "All right, boy, we're going to have a rehearsal! Right here in front of everybody you're going to show us what you did in France to get your break—just the way you'll do it in Lewin's picture! I'll do the commentary and you demonstrate the product—show us what you've got to sell!"

"And if I won't play?"

The officer waved the Beretta wildly toward the others. "Move over there all of you. We want an audience." As they were slow about it, he shouted at them until Jess and Gloria and Lewin were together near Farmes. Then he leveled the gun at Billy with both shaking hands. "Won't play? I might miss again—and you wouldn't want a stray slug in any of your friends!"

Billy's face whitened. "Why, you yellow—"

"On your feet and sell yourself, boy! And if you can get through this without vomiting, then you win—you win!"

Billy left his seat slowly, watching McCord out of the edge of his eye. "I'll get you for this—"

"Too late! Lights! Camera! Action! He stepped back and began to read in an ironic, almost biblical tone. "'William Harold Dow, 33684371, Private, Company A, Thirty-First Infantry, for conspicuous gallantry and intrepidity at risk of life, above and beyond the call of duty, in action involving actual conflict—"

Billy had not moved and McCord swept the gun toward three empty chairs. "Get moving, Dow! There's the three positions—two machine guns and the eighty-eight—remember? Now—sell! Sell!

"If you do this to me—"

"'On 18 November 1944, at 1100 hours, near Vesoul, France, Pvt. Dow left the cover of a trench at the height of an artillery concentration in a single-handed attack upon two enemy machine guns and an eighty-eight-millimeter mobile gun—' Leave your cover, boy! Leave it!"

Billy took several faltering steps.

"All right! 'Despite the intense fire from these two weapons which were aimed directly at him, Pvt. Dow ran one hundred yards through the impact area. Although machine gun bullets kicked up dirt at his heels and eighty-eight-millimeter shells exploded in his path, Pvt. Dow nevertheless made his way to the first enemy machine gun and killed both gunners with a grenade—' Run! Crouch and run! Get rid of that grenade! Kill the Krauts!"

Billy went through a few feeble motions while Jess, almost as embarrassed, turned his face away.

"Not very good!" cried McCord. "Have to do better than that for the camera! Now! 'Wheeling on the second machine gun, Pvt. Dow proceeded in a half-run and killed the three members of its crew with a single burst from his B-A-R-! C'mon, damn you, boy! Wheel and run—use that B-A-R! Shoot from the hip! Now the eighty-eight—over there! Give 'em hell!" He hurled the citation away and went on from memory, his voice filling the room. "Hurled to the ground by a shell-blast, Pvt. Dow regained his feet and advanced on the eighty-eight-millimeter gun, firing his BAR from the hip—and with one long burst of fire he killed its five-man crew—and, unable to check his momentum, fell exhausted across the bodies of the dead Germans."

Billy had started a pathetic lunge toward the reclining chair, but when his eyes met Jess's he stopped. The silence was more terrible than the voice.

"What's the matter, boy? Don't you recognize yourself any more?"

Billy waited, then spoke evenly. "All right, McCord. You asked for it. Now you're going to get it." He addressed the others. "In France he was always asking me why, why, why? As if it made him sick not to understand how a man could—could be a man. Then one night he told me about Tunisia."

The officer gasped. "There are laws of decency—"

"You broke them. How do you think he got to write awards in the first place? Because the first day in Tunisia they gave him a rifle platoon and put him in the lines and he cracked up! Got the hell shot out of his platoon and lost half his men—and they couldn't find him! His sergeant found him crying in a hole!" Billy fairly spat out the words. "They don't court-martial an officer for things like that—it's bad for morale. But somebody thought it would be a real laugh to make him sweat out the rest of the war writing awards for other guys! Him—a yellow-bellied coward!"

No one moved.

"So your number is up, McCord! You don't pass!" Billy shouted.

And then the spell was broken. "Kid, you're wonderful, absolutely wonderful!" chortled Sidney Lewin.

Mason McCord began to move away from them. "Why did you do it, boy?" He kept backing, directionless, as Billy walked toward him.

"Put down that gun, McCord—because I'm coming after it."

But Jess came abreast Billy. "Stay away from him, Billy. He's mine now!"

Billy hesitated. "Stay away? Didn't you hear what I said?"

"That doesn't make a damn bit of difference. He still belongs to me."

"The hell he does!"

As Billy advanced once more, McCord flourished the gun wildly. "I'll shoot everybody! I'll save the world from all of you!"

"Give the gun to me, Captain," Jess commanded. "If any part of what you said is true, you don't need that gun."

"Let me handle this," Billy protested. "This is something between me and McCord."

"Oh, no. This is something between you and a lot of people. Do you think you can touch him any more than I could? No, he's not going to hurt you and you're not going to hurt him! But if you don't leave him alone I'll let him have it out with you!"

Billy was completely confused. "What the hell's happened to you? Are you turning McCord on me?" He tensed. "Well, I'll show you both!" He began to retreat toward the bedroom door, trying to goad McCord into following him. "C'mon, Captain—just the two of us alone—aren't scared again, are you?"

McCord could scarcely speak. "You—you—" But he followed and before the others could stop it, the two of them had disappeared through the door.

"Jess!" Gloria screamed. "Don't let him do it!"

Suddenly Lewin threw the room into darkness with the flick of a switch. There were the sounds of movement and then Jess's voice. "Lights, Miss Kean! Turn on the lights!"

The lights flashed on. Jess stood at the foyer door, blocking Sidney Lewin's flight. The producer began to shuffle away, backward, while Jess guarded the door.

Angry voices rose inside the bedroom. They heard McCord yell, "It's a lie! Tell me it's a damned lie!"

And then Billy's. "Oh, no, you don't! You don't pull that!"

A gun was fired.

As they stood, dazed, Mason McCord appeared in the doorway.

Just then James Farmes stirred, came back to life, noticed the officer. "Captain, I believe I've been shot." He shook his head. "No, you missed, didn't you?" He rose. "There are a few things I'd like to clear up."

"Jess, get me out of here!" McCord yelled.

Billy appeared in the doorway behind him, balancing the Beretta in one hand. The officer buried his face in his hands.

"Billy!" Gloria shrieked.

Lewin's mouth opened and closed. "But—how'd you do it—"

Farmes spoke acidly to Billy. "I have no taste for melodrama, young man. Do you mind giving me that gun?"

"I sure do. It's mine, Mr. Farmes. I just risked my neck to get it back."

"Billy—" Gloria clasped her hands. "*Out of the Grave!*"

"But the switch! He had it!" cried Lewin. "How'd you get it from him, Kid?"

Billy grinned. "I been in tighter spots—and I had this guy figured out. Remember that Bronze Star of mine he was blowing about? I told him it really was a fake—that the guy who gave him that story must have wanted a pass to Paris awful bad because our outfit never went near Besancon. So I couldn't have got those snipers." He buttoned his suitcoat. "You should have seen his face. He'd sworn to the thing—and I knew he couldn't take that. You know what he did? He tried to blow his brains out—but I got the gun." He looked at it. "It'll need a cleaning now."

"Were you in Besancon?" the publisher asked gently.

"Sure I was. I got those snipers. It was authentic, Sidney." He flushed and looked belligerently at them. "Say, what's the matter with you people? Whose side are you on, anyway? I thought you'd be glad—"

The tension broke. There was a general movement toward him. Gloria had her arms round his neck crying that she was so scared, Baby, it was so real, while Sidney Lewin was proclaiming emotionally that he'd seen the real thing, the real thing, Billy had saved himself for the world, anything you want, Kid, name it, and it's yours. James Farmes, meanwhile, was inspecting the hulk of a man who stood bent over, his face concealed.

"You understand I'll have your bars for this, Captain. Had I not been momentarily indisposed, I should have thrown you out myself—before your sorry display of marksmanship."

"Jess—" the officer groaned.

"Back to Walter Reed, McCord!" Lewin shouted at him. "Go back and preach your new religion to the other nuts in the theory ward. What a song and dance! The gall of him—trying to give me a guilt complex!"

"I'd still like to go to Deep Cut," Gloria said happily. "Just to see what it's like."

Billy kissed her. "Later, Honey. After the other things."

"I've got him analyzed now. I would have eventually anyway," Lewin assured them. "Why, he's a coward! That explains everything. A coward needs heroes, so he turns them out, one a week. McCord—writer-director-producer!"

"Writer!" said Farmes. "The man is a hack. I remember his stuff now and I wouldn't offer it at half-price in a drug store."

"Couldn't write! Couldn't sell! No soul at all!" taunted the producer. "No place for you anywhere, was there?"

"People like him find a home in the army," Billy laughed.

"Jess! Jess! Get me out of here!"

At last Jess strode across the room, gathered up the officer's papers, stuffed them in the briefcase, then returned to McCord and threw his trenchcoat around his shoulders. The man had gone to pieces completely, and Jess had to lead him to the door.

"Wait a minute!" cried Lewin. "Are we going to let him walk out like this?"

James Farmes moved toward the phone at once. "We are not. I'll call the Pentagon. The man is a menace. Stop him, Billy."

As Billy started to obey, Jess turned to challenge him. "He'll go out of here the way he came in, Billy. He's mine now and I'm taking him home."

Billy hesitated, then turned to the publisher. "The guy is harmless, Mr. Farmes. Jess will take care of him."

"That boy!" Farmes was dialing. "No. This is a matter for someone with authority."

Billy spoke crisply and there was no mistaking his intent. "Mr. Farmes, I want him to go."

Lewin entered the breach hurriedly. "Sure, let him go, Jim. Let the kid take him back to Washington. I think we've taught him a good lesson. And besides, we don't have time to waste on him. Think of what we've got to do before tomorrow! Billy's books to sign, their packing, the rehearsal—good God, they've got to run through their lines!" He put a hand on the publisher's shoulder. "Let him go. The guy's just a crackpot! The country's lousy with 'em. An insignificant crackpot! He comes up here with delusions and we *un*delude him. Well?"

Jess had heard him out. "He may be a crackpot, Mr. Lewin, but I think you ought to know there's an awful lot of people like him who wish they could come up here and say a few of the same things. I've hated him as few guys have ever hated him. But you can't keep hating a man when you see right through him—when you see he's only trying to be better than he was made. Or didn't you understand a thing he's been saying?"

He turned and put an arm around the officer, supporting him. "C'mon, Captain. They've forgotten Pershing and they've never heard of Poe."

"Poe?" exclaimed the publisher. "What's this about Poe?"

But Jess was leading Mason McCord through the door.

As they moved through the foyer Jess stopped momentarily. He was having trouble positioning the officer. And at that moment Billy ran through the door, saw them, and halted.

"Hey, Jess. Hold on a minute." He came nearer. "Do you need any help? You're going to take him back to Walter Reed, aren't you? Need any money?"

Jess shook his head.

"You're not bitter, are you?" Billy talked rapidly. "You know, it's funny. I could touch him but I couldn't see him shoot himself. He'll come out of this. But what about you?"

Jess looked at him steadily. "I can take care of myself."

Billy wet his lips. "Listen. I've been thinking. I can get you in the picture we're going to make. I'll have a buddy in it, see—good contrast. And Sidney'd do it. He'd say you're authentic. How about it?"

When Jess did not reply, he went on hurriedly. "It's going to be no picnic doing it alone. And you saw what a spectacular actor I am—"

"I don't say it's wrong for you. But it isn't right for me."

"Why not?"

"It just isn't right for me."

He stepped toward the officer, who stood with head bowed, but Billy went with him.

"Well, listen. Listen, I've got it. I couldn't go through that scene again after tonight. I couldn't take it. You know how it is. You just don't talk about those things once you've done them. You leave your talking to the others—like letting someone else write your book." Billy touched his arm. "But I could talk about what you did. And I think I could act it. Even Sidney would say it was authentic—"

"No."

"Of course it wouldn't do you any good. But it would sure help me. Jess, let me have your citation. I promise you they won't change anything but the name."

Jess frowned, thinking.

"Give it to me, Jess. That's the only way I can go through with this thing." He took Jess by both shoulders and turned him round. "Look, you can't want me to be pushed back into the big machine. I'd never get out again! Where is it, Jess?"

Billy reached for the briefcase, but Jess refused to let go. Finally he turned questioningly toward the officer.

"Don't let him have it," McCord mumbled.

Jess stood erect. "I know what's on it now."

At that Billy grabbed the briefcase, took out a copy of *Out of the Grave* and a sheaf of papers, and began leafing through them.

"I took it out of the files," said Jess.

"Where is it?"

Jess took a folded sheet out of his pocket. "Here." He held it a moment, then handed it over. "Take it, if it'll do you any good."

Billy tried to shake his hand. "I knew you'd come through for me! You'll see it on the screen, Jess. They'll all see it—all the witnesses in the world this time!"

"I don't need them now. Just be sure—"

Billy clutched the citation. "Nothing changed but the name, I swear." He had another idea. "And listen, do you know what I'm going to do? I'm going to have Sidney write you a check—"

Before Jess could speak, he rushed on. "Don't say anything. Let me finish. A check for one thousand bucks. I want you in that union. Don't you see, that would put us both in the picture business. You on one end and me on the other!"

Jess took back the briefcase, put it under one arm, and supported Mason McCord with the other as they started off. They neared the door when Billy ran to them again.

"Hey! Here's the book." He put it with the briefcase. "Say, if you could only get him off the bottle, what a spectacular book he could write for you!"

◆◆◆

Westerns

Pancho Villa's One-Man War

I was born in Dedham, Massachusetts, in 1923. The same year, near Hidalgo del Parral, in Mexico, they waited for Pancho Villa and they finally got him. Though dead the same year I was born, lying there all sun and blood with the wind of Chihuahua blowing dust through his mustache, he still did a lot for me.

The first movie I really remember was *Viva Villa*, with Wallace Beery as Pancho. There probably wasn't much of the real Villa in it, but it had me on my feet all the way, and my throat dry. I was ten years old and one of those small, quiet kids who live with giants. In bed that night I gave King Arthur and Robin Hood and Boone and Buffalo Bill and Hoot Gibson away and put Pancho in my pocket. I had my hero. I can still see him leading his men hell-for-leather and shooting and taking towns, the bandoliers of ammunition criss-crossed over their shoulders. Before I went to sleep that night I took Dedham, Massachusetts, about ten times.

Then in high school I found a book about my man in the local library. It was written by a retired cavalry colonel. I read right through suppertime, for now I was getting fact that my imagination could build on. I'd never known he crossed the border in 1916 and raided the town of Columbus, New Mexico.

Originally published in *Cosmopolitan*, February 1953.

I'd never known he had the whole United States so heated up about it that President Wilson sent General John J. "Blackjack" Pershing with four regiments of cavalry, a couple of infantry, some artillery, and one of the first air squadrons down into Mexico to bring him back dead or alive. But they never caught Villa. Later it was learned that he lay wounded in a cave in the mountains near Guerrero and watched a column of troopers ride past, hunting him. I could picture him grinning and the big mustache spreading as he watched them ride by. That was the only book I ever stole from a library. It was more lying than stealing. I told the librarian I'd lost it and paid the $1.75 out of my lawn-mowing money.

The next spring, after graduation, I enlisted and went off to have myself some war. I had some. But that was a very big war, and Sicily and Anzio and Remagen didn't satisfy, somehow. You couldn't see them whole, the way Pancho did. They meant too many things to too many people. Pancho could conceive a battle, plan it, fight it, then give it a name, like Camargo or Zacatecas, and carry it with him afterward to contemplate. I envied him. Besides, by the time of my war they had run out of horses and romance and big sombreros.

When it was over I came back to go to college on the government. After summer school in 1948 a friend of mine, Chap Smith, and I wanted to take off for somewhere different. We were restless. We had six weeks and around two hundred dollars apiece and Chap had an old car. I finally got the idea of driving down to Texas, starting way down at the tip, at Brownsville, and making all the Mexican border towns, all the way across Texas and New Mexico and Arizona to Tijuana, in lower California, or as many as our money would let us. Chap went for it; we packed that night. While I was throwing clothes into a suitcase, for some reason I threw in the cavalry colonel's book.

We took a week reaching Brownsville, for it was very hot, and we had *mucho* higher education to sweat out of our systems. But we did Matamoros up right, then Reynosa, Nuevo Laredo, and Piedras Negras before cutting north and west to El Paso and Juárez. Mexican beer is very good and cheap, and the best brands are Carta Blanca and Bohemia. The next stop was supposed to be Nogales, in Arizona, but we stayed a night in a motel outside El Paso to recover from Juárez. While Chap was asleep I found something in the cavalry colonel's book I had forgotten. In February of 1916, a month before the raid on Columbus, there was trouble all along the border. Gangs of Mexican outlaws were slipping across at night, looting and burning and killing. Our cavalry was stretched thin. A Mr. Charles H. Broadbent, an Associated Press man, was sent to Columbus to cover the situation. He spoke Spanish, and while there became well known and trusted by both Mexicans and Americans. One night emissaries direct from Villa reached him with one of the damnedest, most fantastic propositions ever made any newspaperman. *El León del Norte* wanted Broadbent to conduct him secretly to Washington and to arrange a conference with President Wilson, acting as the bandit's interpreter and consultant.

That started me thinking about Columbus and searching for it on the map. The next morning I got Chap to cut south once we were in New Mexico so I could have a look at the place where the craftiest, guttsiest, guerilla fighter in or out of books had attacked the United States.

It was just a sun-baked little town out in the middle of nowhere with a few whitewashed stores and gas stations and a lot of mesquite desert. There was no sign of Pancho now—no burning buildings, no people yelling, no lead singing in the dry air, no 13th Cavalry bugles shouting boots and saddles. That had been 1916 and the middle of the night. This was the middle of the afternoon thirty-two years later and about 120 degrees in the shade. But Pancho'd put his mark on the town the way he had so many people and it was still there after all these years. Chap and I looked down a street littered with brush. We stared at a store long boarded up, at the 'dobe walls of a house still pocked by bullets. I went on, working a hunch. We walked down the main street and I stopped to ask an old character sitting on a bench if a man named Charles Broadbent happened to live there. He spat and said Charley was probably down at Candelario's, down thataway. I said thanks and started walking fast. History was down thataway.

Candelario's was dark and small and very Mexican, more a cantina than a bar. I couldn't even wait to order, but asked the barkeep, who nodded toward a man sitting at a corner table. I took a dozen steps, hesitated, and introduced myself and Chap to Charles H. Broadbent.

History let me down. A spindly, long-faced elderly gentleman past seventy, wearing a faded denim shirt and a ten-gallon with a hole pinched through the crown, Mr. Broadbent had beer eyes and a beer nose and an empty glass in front of him. He looked as though he'd never raise the price of another.

I sort of swallowed out the question, sure I had the right town but the wrong man. Was he the Charles Broadbent, the AP man who had been contacted by Villa in 1916?

He said he was, although he had not been, might he add, a "working member of the press" for many years.

And then, with a stateliness that surprised me, he invited us to sit down. We did. Thank heavens I had the presence of mind to ask him to have a beer with us.

After he had inquired as to my knowledge of him and my interest in the affair, and after I'd ordered another one for him, he told us the whole story. It was something. I give the gist of it, as much in his own words as I can recall.

"It was a very ticklish thing, Son, with a lot of telegraphing back and forth between here and Washington. All arrangements had to be made through the secretary of state, Mr. Lansing, and the secretary of war, Mr. Newton D. Baker. Villa wouldn't set foot across the border until they swore him safe-conduct, and the secretary of state wouldn't let him unless it was all kept secret. He had to protect the president. Villa was thought of in this country as no better than a bandit—all the papers said he was—and it wouldn't do for word to get out that the president was parleying with a bandit in the White House. It was an election year, you remember. And remember, Villa was gambling, too, as much as the president. We could have stood him up against a wall anywhere, and no one would have been the wiser. Oh, it was a dangerous business all round. But finally everything was settled. A private car was hooked onto a train at El Paso on a Monday night. I was in the car. At midnight a man mentioned in the telegrams only as 'Lion' was escorted aboard by four army officers, who then left. The car doors were sealed from the outside, the window shades nailed down, and I was alone with 'Lion' for nearly three days."

This was Charles Broadbent, all right, come to life out of a book. He might be down and out now at seventy, thirty-two years later, but he still had some of the grandeur that rubs off from the great. His mustache was as thick as Pancho's must have been, even if it was white.

I ordered him another beer and asked him what *El León del Norte* looked like in person.

"Why, he was a big man, with powerful shoulders and hands. He had penetrating eyes, and the whites were very white. His hair was thick and unruly, what you could see of it, for he never took off his sombrero except to sleep. And then he'd tilt it down over his face as though he were sleeping out on campaign. He wore a khaki shirt and trousers and a cartridge belt around his belly. But the thing that first struck me was his pistol. I don't know what caliber it was, but Son, that was the biggest pistol I ever saw. It grew on his hip. He never took it off, either, having been hunted so long. After a while I got the notion Villa and the pistol were the same, and that when he fired it, the bullet came out of him, not out of the barrel. If that pistol were taken away from him, he wouldn't exist."

By now Chap had forgotten he was in a cantina called Candelario's down in Columbus, New Mexico, listening to an old gentleman spin a yarn when we were a hundred miles out of our way and overdue in Nogales. So had I. It was like listening to the lone Ree scout who supposedly escaped the slaughter on the Little Big Horn, or long afterward hearing the hot scoop about Hector from Aeneas.

Mr. Broadbent said the railroad car was well stocked with food and liquor, and they made out very comfortably except that Villa was uneasy about the sealed doors. Once, when he wanted to see out, he took a big knife from a sheath under his shirt and simply slashed one of the window shades to ribbons. He wasn't the kind of man to be trapped. They ate and drank and slept and talked. Villa called him "Pal" and showed him how to make a rose design out of a coiled lariat. He asked him all about the president so that he'd know what manner of man he'd be up against and how to handle him.

"We reached Washington Thursday in the afternoon and stood on a siding until after dark. The door was unsealed, and some Secret Service men came aboard. When they saw Villa's pistol they said he had to leave it in the car. Visitors to the White House weren't allowed to wear guns. Villa refused. He said he had never taken off his gun for any man, and he wouldn't now. If he was trusting the president this far, the president would have to trust him. So they left. I expect they called the White House and the president himself said it was all right. If Villa wasn't afraid, he wasn't. So they came back, and we were put into a big limousine with the shades drawn. We reached the west portico, the side entrance, of the White House around eleven o'clock. It was pitch-dark and a fog had rolled up from the Potomac."

An old jukebox started playing "*La Vida Alegre*—The Happy Life," but I could still hear my heart beating hard.

"We were taken right to the president's study. The Secret Service men left and closed the door behind them. Now try to get the picture, son. There were just four of us in the room—the president standing behind his desk; the secretary of state, Mr. Lansing, beside him; and the two of us opposite. Villa was very natural. He didn't even take off his sombrero when I made the introductions. I said, 'Mr. President, this is General Francisco Villa.' They shook hands. Then things were awkward for a minute. Villa was easy, but I wasn't. I was just a newspaper man mixed up in the middle of the biggest story of his life. The drapes of the big window behind the president were closed and I was thinking, outside those drapes the whole USA is asleep, but would they be asleep if they knew the president and Pancho Villa were standing face to face in the White House? There was only one light on in the study, a little lamp with a green glass shade, on the desk. I can see it yet. It made Villa's pistol gleam, and the bullets around his middle, and the lenses of the president's glasses. Mr. Wilson looked very tired. There was a war on in Europe, you know, and he was having trouble keeping us out of it. But he stood there as easy as Villa, and they sort of measured each other."

I didn't turn my head to buy him another beer, just signaled with my hand.

"Finally the president wanted to know what the trouble was along the border, and what could be done about it. I translated, and Villa started telling him. You see, Son, the revolution they'd begun six years before by getting rid of Diaz had gone sour. Revolutions sometimes do. For instance, the French one got into bad hands. Ours didn't. We were lucky but the Mexicans weren't. Their man Madero was shot by Huerta, and Huerta was very bad. Then Carranza took over, thanks to Zapata and Villa, and they had high hopes for him, but he turned out worse. This had gone on for six years now, and all these men had used Villa for a gun, which he was, and one after the other they'd turned him against his own country as soon as they had power. Now the

Carranzistas had made an outlaw of him and we'd recognized their government. Villa wanted us to withdraw recognition. That would finish Carranza, and if it didn't, he would what was left. Villa said it would be the finest thing we could do for Mexico. I translated as much of this as I could, for Villa was talking fast now, and loud.

"But the president didn't savvy. He didn't care much for revolutions. To him they were bloody things, better to read about than to touch. He'd been a college president, you know, and it's a long way from Princeton, New Jersey, to the Sierra Madre. So he told Villa he wouldn't withdraw recognition of Carranza. It was time the revolution was over and the people of Mexico had a stable government and peace to raise their crops. And it was also time the border quieted down.

"Villa said it did his people no good to raise crops if the government took most of them.

"The president said it did them no good if their fields were stripped over and over by armed bands.

"Villa shouted the border would never be quiet while the people of Mexico were still trying to make their revolution come out right.

"The president said it was his duty to protect the lives and property and sovereignty of the United States, which he would do no matter what.

"You'd never guess what happened next."

"What?" blurted Chap.

Mr. Broadbent sat as straight in his chair as a young man, straighter than we. There may have been foam on his mustache but there was none in his eyes.

"Villa took two steps to the desk and pulled his gun and held it not two inches from the president's chest."

The barkeep brought his beer.

"Villa wasn't roaring now, but still, with kill written all over him. His whole instinct told him to use his gun when he was crossed, even if it was against the whole United States, because, as I said, that's what his time had made of him—a gun. No man had ever said no to his face and lived. I thought for sure I'd see the president killed then and there and all hell and war with Mexico break out even before my eyes. I couldn't move. Neither could the secretary of state, Mr. Lansing.

But after his first surprise that an hombre in the world would dare to draw on him, and one twitch of his hands, Mr. Wilson didn't budge. He wasn't going to say yes to the Kaiser or Clemenceau or Senator Lodge in a few years, or to Pancho Villa now. He was the studying kind and he was where he belonged, in his study, and he matched Villa look for look, as though he was a college boy got too big for his britches. And the fact was, Villa couldn't read or write a word beyond his own name. Oh, they were both fighters, I tell you. Neither one knew what fear was. I was proud of the pair of them."

He was looking far away, right through Chap and me. He was still seeing Pancho and the Professor across from each other, a big pistol between them, neither one afraid of anybody or anything. All of a sudden I realized he had two heroes, not one.

"What happened?" I got out.

"Well, I'll tell you. Villa knew he'd met a man equal to him. So did the president. I reckon they got to respect each other right then, each for what the other was. Finally, after about an hour, or so it seemed, Villa holstered the gun and said, '*Vamanos, amigo,*' and we went out—back to the train and to El Paso. A month later he did take on the whole U.S.A. He shot up this town one night, and the president sent General Pershing and the cavalry after him. Never could catch him, though."

We sat there. After a few minutes I remembered myself enough to light a cigarette.

"Some story," Chap said at last. And then, "Why didn't you use it, Sir? In the newspaper business it would have made you, for life. And no mistake about it."

Charles H. Broadbent took off his ten-gallon and laid it on the table with a gesture that was almost knightly. It was probably the way Don Quixote used to take off his helmet when he swore one of his solemn oaths.

"I'll tell you why, son. Because both the president and Villa asked me as a favor to them to keep it out of the papers. And I have."

We nodded gravely. Thirty-two years is a long time to keep your word, especially in a world full of Sancho Panzas.

Well, we thanked him and said goodbye and went out of Candelario's. I looked back once, and with the story retold, relived, now ended, the man at the table had become once more an old gent intent on an empty glass. It seemed strange to come out of a foggy night in 1916, out of the White House, into the blinding afternoon and main street of Columbus, New Mexico, into the year of 1948. We started down the street, then I stopped, went back, called the barkeep outside, gave him some money, and told him what to do with it.

We kept our thoughts to ourselves for about twenty miles north out of Columbus. Then Chap spoke.

"How much did you give him?"

"Twenty-five bucks. Or as I told the barkeep, enough for 250 beers."

Chap was silent another five miles. I knew what was rubbing him. We were already low on funds; with twenty-five gone we might make Nogales, but not Tijuana. Finally he said:

"Well, I guess it was worth it."

I was glad he'd come to that. Now I could tell him and he might understand. But as I was searching for an approach, he wanted to know why Broadbent or any man who'd been in the big time even for one night in his life would let himself go to pot in a zero-minus-zero town like Columbus for the next thirty-two years.

That gave me the approach. I'd been thinking about it. *El León del Norte* had already given me a lot since I was a kid, and now he was making a low-pressure philosopher out of me.

"Maybe he's been waiting for Pancho," I threw out tentatively. "Everybody waits," I said. "Usually the big thing never happens. But if part of the time you can believe it has, you're lucky. And the rest of the time, while you're still waiting, isn't wasted. In fact, everybody has to have a Pancho."

It wasn't working. Chap was a mechanical engineer and not much for the abstract.

"All right," he said. "What's the twist?"

I took a long breath. "Just that most of the story wasn't true."

He pulled off the road and stopped.

"It just didn't happen, that's all," I went on. "I was telling you this morning about the cavalry colonel's book. That's where I got his name and the hunch to go to Columbus. He was contacted by Villa, yes, and made all the arrangements with Washington. It must have been the biggest thing of his life, being a newspaperman, or just being human. But Villa never showed."

Chap was doing a slow burn. "The old skinflint. I'd like to go back and—"

"No," I said. "You said yourself the story was worth it. And he's told it so often he probably half believes it himself. The rest of the time he waits. I told you, everybody waits."

Chap headed north again. He'd taken it well. After a while he lit up and settled back and let the car drive itself.

"Twenty-five bucks," he said philosophically.

"I earned that *dinero* a long time ago," I said. "I'll never miss it."

"How come?"

"That" I said, "was the last of my lawn-mowing money."

I knew he wouldn't get that. But he had the rest, which was all that mattered.

◆ ◆ ◆

A Horse for Mrs. Custer

Every man lives round the corner from history. Some pass it every day and never make the turning. Others, on their way, are detained by chance and cannot bear it witness. One recalls the Roman who, granting himself the luxury of a stay at Baiae, a resort on the Tyrrhenian coast, did not attend the Senate on the day Gaius Julius Caesar was struck down. One thinks nineteen centuries later of the gunner, fallen ill at the last moment, who was replaced in the ball-turret of the B-29 that flew over Hiroshima. Yet the stories of men who have missed one of the larger human events are frequently as interesting as those who have participated. One of the strangest of these has lately come to light. It is remarkable in that history repeated itself, and the person absent on the first occasion was afforded the unique opportunity of being present at the second.

The tale is told in a small volume entitled Dakota Days, *one of several privately printed in 1928 and written by Brigadier General Alexander Peddie, U.S.A., during the years of his retirement. General Peddie's career was long and distinguished, and since his prose is that of a soldier, honest and direct, it is unfortunate that his reminiscences have not had wider circulation.* Dakota Days *recounts his duty with the Seventh Cavalry Regiment beginning in the autumn of 1876, four months after its*

Originally published in *New World Writing*, volume 5, 1954. Also appeared in *Louis L'Amour Western Magazine*, March 1995, and *The Western Hall of Fame Anthology*, edited by Dale Walker (New York: Berkley Books, 1997).

bloody stand, under George Armstrong Custer, on the Little Big Horn. It contains not only vivid description of the Great Plains but the little-known episode mentioned above, the authenticity of which there can be no doubt. Permission has been granted by his granddaughter, Alice Peddy Wycomb, his only heir, to excerpt such passages as may serve the end of unity.

Historians record that tidings of the Little Big Horn battle came as a dreadful shock to the nation. On 25 June 1876 the Seventh Cavalry was split in three formations by its commander in the face of twelve thousand Sioux, Oglala, and Cheyenne under Sitting Bull. Troops C, E, F, I, and L, those under Custer, were lost to the last man and horse, while other units, with Major Marcus Reno, were severely mauled. But the nation's grief changed soon to indignation as attempts were made in Congress and the press to fix the blame for the disaster. President Grant was personally assailed, but public attention was eventually concentrated on Custer himself. The country, as one pamphlet put it, "chose up sides." To the man in the street or the horse-car, or the saloon, General Custer became either hero or fool, martyr or murderer. Unfortunately, little heed was given to the effects such angry division would have upon the broken remnants of the now-famous Seventh.

It was at this juncture young Alexander Peddie, newly commissioned a second lieutenant of cavalry from West Point, was ordered to Fort Abraham Lincoln in the Dakota Territory.

. . .

It was a long three days by train from St. Paul to Fargo and Bismarck at that time. I was anxious to get my first glimpse of the real West and eager to join the Seventh, whose name had become a household one the length and breadth of the land. I thought myself the luckiest young man alive, and even started a mustachio. Reaching Bismarck, where the railroad ended, I crossed the Missouri by ferry and reported for duty at Fort Abe the first week in November to Major Reno, commanding. I was assigned to I Troop, one of those which had been wiped out by the Sioux in the spring. It was commanded by Captain John C. Thomas, who was sent for to meet me and show me to my quarters. He came presently and we walked along the parade ground together. Captain Thomas was a man of medium height, powerfully built and clean-shaven. His hair was iron-gray, a striking thing in a man no more than forty. He had little to say, showing in every respect the reserve which I was later to understand fully. But for that, I might have made the mistake of questioning him about the Little Big Horn.

Captain Thomas took me into the Custer house, saying I would be quartered here with seven other new lieutenants. Mrs. Custer had gone back East and the house was bare of furniture. As I expressed curiosity, we strolled through the empty rooms in which had echoed only months before the clink of the general's saber and the sound of his voice calling "Livvy! Livvy!" to his wife. In the small study he had written those articles for *Galaxy Magazine* which had stirred the country's blood, while his beloved "Livvy" waited patiently outside, for he could not compose unless she sat near.

Then we went into the long drawing room. On the walls still hung trophies of the General's passion for hunting—the heads of grizzlies, black-tail deer, and antelope. On the mantel were a yellow fox, an owl, and a sandhill crane. But on the floor was a strange arrangement. At one end were four bedrolls, and at the other end three. I stood a moment, then asked what it meant.

"That's the way it is," said the Captain. He was looking out a window. "I expect three of them have one set of ideas about Custer, all favorable, and four have another. You must decide for yourself."

I did not hesitate. "I've always been for a fair fight," I said, and put my bedroll down beside the three. Captain Thomas did not turn round to notice my decision.

That night at mess I met the other seven officers, all of my rank, with whom I was to share quarters. My opposite number in I Troop turned out to be a Lieutenant Alvin Thadius. He was short and chunked, with round red cheeks like apples, and he hailed from Ohio. I took a liking to him at once, but I did not realize how deep the currents ran until we returned to the Custer drawing room to bed down. When Thadius saw where I had put my roll he said he hoped that did not mean I had been taken in by Autie Custer the way half the country had. I replied I disliked passing judgment on a dead man.

"There are five troops dead," said Thadius. "And they have passed judgment, wherever they are, on the man who brought them to it!" In an instant he was as ruffled up as a prairie chicken at mating. "He disobeyed orders, he would not listen to his scouts—Bloody Knife told him they would never see the set of the sun that day! But he took six hundred men with him to the slaughter!

The others were watching me as I sat with one boot already drawn off. I was not on firm ground, for Thadius had arrived two weeks before me and doubtless had more of the facts. But he was not a year older than I, and I resolved to be as stubborn as he was quick-tempered.

"Reno failed to support him," I said. "He heard firing over the hill but he dug in. An officer may think first of the safety of his own command, but not a gentleman."

I regretted this as soon as the words were out of my mouth. Thadius came to his feet with his round cheeks redder than ever.

"A butcher is no gentleman!" he cried.

This stung me to the raw. I hauled off my other boot and stood.

"It takes a gentleman to recognize one," I said.

He started for me with a lunge and we would have had a bobbery then and there had not Lieutenant Nokes, who was a rather sentimental lad, come between us. The eight of us went to bed in silence, four across from four. As I lay accustoming my bones to the plank floor and my mind to this inauspicious beginning, the glass eyes of the grizzlies gleamed down at me, reflecting the light of the dying fire. I tossed and turned for several hours, and I could hear Alvin Thadius doing likewise.

By the first blizzard I found what I had joined. It was not the Seventh Cavalry, nor a fighting force of any kind, but an unruly mass of men divided into two camps. Five hundred recruits and thirty green officers had come from the East too late in the season to train properly, and with them they had brought along the bitterness felt back home about the Little Big Horn. Every troop was split, I Troop included. There were five hundred remounts in the stables, too, and it was hard to tell which was the more cantankerous, animals or men. Only those who had been with Custer, officers like Captains Benteen and Thomas, Lieutenants Varnum and DeRudio, held their peace. All the long, howling winter matters worsened. Discipline became nearly impossible to maintain. The recruits would slip guard at night and cross the Missouri ice to Bismarck to drink and brawl among themselves. A patrol located a little lake near the fort in which warm springs melted the ice along the shore, and here the big pike lay so thick the men could heave them out in piles with pitchforks. But quarrels over dividing them soon stopped the "fishing."

Even Major Reno's attempt to divert the men only increased tension. It had been General Custer's policy to permit "theatricals" now and then, in which the men dressed up and performed skits and dances and so on. But the theatricals that winter ended with the first. One of the pieces announced was a recitation by Tommy Gudge, our Troop I bugler, a boy of eighteen, and when Tommy stood onstage to recite, the Custer-haters had put him up to doing one of Mr. Henry Wadsworth Longfellow's latest poems, called "The Revenge of Rain-in-the-Face." This was based on the yarn that when the general lay fallen, his heart had been cut out of him by the savages. Toward the end of the poem Tommy had worked up such a head of steam that his voice fairly cracked on these lines:

> "Revenge!" cried Rain-in-the-Face,
> "Revenge upon all the race
> Of the White Chief with yellow hair!"

At this point a sergeant in the rear rose up and shouted "Revenge!" himself, and in a flash the fists were flying. A riot was averted only by calling in the guard and banging a few heads with carbine butts.

Fort Lincoln that winter of '76 to '77 was a haunted post. It seemed that all the dead were with us still, making up an unseen regiment, the old Seventh, the immortal Seventh, mocking the new one with the memory of its gallantry. It preyed on the mind. I well recall poor Nokes, for instance. We eight lieutenants still lay separated on the floor of the Custer drawing room those endless nights with the wind helling down out of Canada across the plains and wailing at the eaves. One night we were awakened by Nokes, who jumped out of his roll and commenced to yell at us.

"Hear that singing? Hear it? That's the wives and Mrs. Custer singing as they did the day the news came, crying and singing in this room! I can't stand it! Tell them to stop! Tell them to stop!"

And he began to sing at the top of his voice, "E'en though a cross it be, nearer, my God, to Thee!" It was a terrifying thing, of course, at such an hour, and Allenberry and I seized Nokes and tried to calm him, telling him it was only the wind.

"No, no, it's the wives of the dead! It's the widows singing!" Nokes howled. "I can't stand it!"

We finally got the unfortunate lad back in his roll, but we had to hold him down all night, and in the morning took him to the surgeons because he still shook and did not seem to have control of his limbs. Nokes stayed with them and in the spring was shipped back East to a hospital. I have not heard of him since.

One night in March I learned what lay behind Captain Thomas's reserve. I was officer of the guard, and while inspecting the various sentry boxes saw a light in the stables. Knowing the farriers were all asleep or carousing over in Bismarck, I went to investigate. To my surprise I found the captain currying a small bay horse by the light of a lantern. He told me it was General Custer's horse, "Dandy."

"How can that be, Captain?" I asked. "I understood that neither man nor horse escaped."

"He had two, 'Vic' and this one," said the captain. "On the morning of the battle he took his choice of the two to ride that day. Vic was younger, and he took him. That's how this one comes to be here."

I went round to the head of the stall and looked more closely at the bay. I must admit my flesh crawled, because though he should have been a ghost horse he was very much alive, with lots of spunk in his eyes and the way he carried his head. Though small for cavalry, he belonged at the head of a column. Captain Thomas went on currying and telling me about him. Dandy had been the general's favorite, and had been bought by the government in Kansas for $140. He could run down a deer, and no horse was better alongside the rump of a buffalo bull. When I asked why the captain felt he had to care for him, he replied that feelings were so high, even among the farriers, that most of them would not lay hands on a pet of Custer's.

I commented that that was pretty low, but he said such sympathies were not confined to the farriers. Last fall, before I came, there had been a subscription started among the officers to buy the horse from the government and ship him to Mrs. Custer as a memorial. All the old officers had paid in, but when most of the new arrivals refused, Major Reno returned the money. He would not send Dandy away unless all commissioned names were listed, for he did not want the general's lady to suspect what a state the regiment was in.

It occurred to me that this might be a good time to ask Captain John Thomas about the Little Big Horn and his part in it. I knew nothing about the man except that he had been brevetted colonel during the war, having command of a regiment in Virginia after the cavalry fight at Brandy Station. He was one of those officers growing old in the service, with little to look forward to except gray hairs, which he already had, and retirement at major's rank.

"Captain," I said, "do you mind my asking you about the battle?"

"Ask if you like, Peddie," he said, working away with a comb. "But I have nothing to tell. I was not present. I should have been, since I had I Troop then as now. But before we took the field an officer was needed to conduct some Cheyenne prisoners to Oklahoma and resettle them there. Custer happened to pick me, I do not know why. Captain Keogh took I Troop in my place, and was killed. I could not return to Fort Abe till July, and then it was all over. I met the wounded when they came down by steamer."

"Oh," I said. Then I asked what no man should ask of another under such circumstances. However, I was but twenty-three years of age. "How do you feel about it, Captain?"

For a moment he was silent. Then he turned to me and his face betrayed a terrible look. It was as though his skin had been flayed to ribbons and I could see clear through to his vitals.

"How would you feel?" he asked.

I could not answer. I had no idea how I would feel. But I could see, as if by lightning, how the man must have been tormented. On the one hand, he must have hated Custer for sending him away and denying him the chance a soldier seldom has, the chance to die a hero. That part of him must have blamed the general for the disaster, despised him as much as did young Alvin Thadius and many of the recruits. On the other hand, the instinct to survive which is strong in every man must have made him grateful to his commander for having spared his life. And that gratitude must have made him stand at times on the side of those who worshipped Custer for his daring and leadership. The awful struggle for allegiance in the regiment, which they could fight out among them, had been dueling for a year in John Thomas, and he bore it alone.

When he saw my confusion, the captain looked away and laid a gentle hand on Dandy's neck.

"I am just like this horse, Peddie," he said. "Another went in his place and he did not see that day either. If he can stand it, then I can. And I can care for him if others will not."

I had to leave the stables and be by myself in the cold clear night. Sudden insight into the soul of a fellow human being often matures one in a minute as much as does a full year's campaign.

Spring came. The ice went out of the Missouri, and Major Reno took the Seventh into the gumbo mud daily to train the spleen out of it. The Sioux had left the agencies now. Sitting Bull and Crazy Horse were north behind the mountains and sent word down they intended to scalp every white man in North Dakota. So the Seventh trained, at least learned how to get on and off a horse and which was the business end of a Colt and Springfield. We knew we would take the field, but no man could say when he would return, or if. Not many of the old Seventh had, and this one was scarce its equal.

On 14 May 1877 we marched through the west gate of Fort Abe. I can still hear the leather slapping and gear clinking and fifes squealing a tune, not "Garryowen," which was the regimental song when Autie Custer led it, but "The Girl I Left Behind Me." The last verses of that song I will never forget, for they took on that day a meaning far beyond their words:

> Full many a name our banners bore
> Of former deeds of daring,
> But they were of the days of yore,
> In which we had no sharing;
> But now our laurels freshly won
> With the old ones shall entwined be,
> Still worthy of his sire each son,
> Sweet girl I left behind me.

Few men have seen the plains and prairies, the mountains and rivers and spaces of the Dakota country as it was then as God made it, and I thank Him for the privilege of admiring his handiwork.

We went up to Fort Buford, crossed the Missouri, and then went up the Yellowstone, taking four weeks at it. The ground had not yet started to bloom, and the nights were cold. One day we encountered a hailstorm on Froze-to-Death Creek, with hailstones as big as hickory nuts, and the horses, hit on the hocks by them, thought they were being beaten and became frantic. Another day we went over a rise and before us were buffalo all the way to the horizon. We estimated the herd at thirteen thousand. After the first rains the prairie was covered with grass plover running in pairs. The sickle-billed curlew whistled all day, hovering overhead so still you could drop them with a shot. Little green and purple anemones were the first flowers to come out.

We camped a few days at Sunday Creek in an abandoned cantonment of logs with dirt roofs before heading north to seek Sitting Bull in the mountains. But here Major Reno sent for Captain Thomas, and when the latter returned he said I Troop was detached for special duty. We were to take our four wagons with mules and drivers and mount up at once. F. F. Gerard, the scout, would accompany us. He did not say what the duty would be, and neither Thadius nor I inquired. We left that afternoon and marched up the Yellowstone for a week.

The country here was wilder than could be imagined. We saw elk in bands as large as five hundred. We camped among cottonwoods six feet around the trunk. The men killed some beaver and Gerard showed them how to cook the tails. They were delicious, resembling cold roast pork in flavor. Since we saw no hostiles, the men enjoyed themselves as much as the rate of the march and their own cussedness allowed. It was discovered that the wagons were being hauled empty except for a collection of hammers, saws, planes, and nails.

We crossed the Yellowstone near the mouth of the Big Horn, and here an unpleasant incident showed that I Troop was still composed of boys, not men. The river being high, we slowed the horses behind a skiff, and the lariat of Thadius's came loose. The current wound it around the animal's legs and downstream he went. I dived in under him to cut him free with my knife, but became tangled myself, and both of us would have drowned had not Thadius come in and finished the job, so that the horse brought us ashore clinging to his headstall. But when, having swallowed my pride along with several gallons of snow-water, I tried to thank him for the rescue, he said he had been interested only in rescuing the citizens from the cost of a remount.

"Why, damn you!" I burst out.

"Why, damn you both!" Captain Thomas had come up, mad enough to eat snake. "I will have officers with me, not jabbering squaws! Whether you realize it or not, Sitting Bull has scouts down here, I know he has, and he will have our heads up on a lodge if we don't soldier!"

He saw some of the troopers grinning like apes.

"And that applies to you men!" he said. "Now get those mules and wagons over—if Crazy Horse doesn't make a troop out of this one, I will!"

There was considerable settling down after that. Not that those for Custer were friendlier toward those against, but each was more considerate of his own skin. We were three hundred miles from Fort Abe by then and half that from the regiment. The earth might have swallowed all of I Troop up and not a living soul the wiser.

The next day, to prove the captain right, we saw our first hostiles, a party of three at a distance. F. F. Gerard asked to use the captain's glasses. He was a small, wizened man who wore buckskin and possessed a sense of humor despite the fact that his teeth caused him much pain, doubtless due to his diet over many years on the plains. After a long look he said they were Oglala, and if he was not mistaken one was old Red Moon, a chief not overly fond of cavalry.

We marched another three days, sighting savages on each of them. Captain Thomas gave orders there would be no bugling or shooting or fires at night. We marched up a creek called the Rosebud and found wickiups with skins still tied on them. We also found warnings in Cheyenne scratched in sandstone on the bluffs along the creek. That night we learned from Sergeant Biersdorf where we were going. He had been that way the year before. We were going back to the Little Big Horn.

Midmorning of 25 June, a year to the very day after the battle, I Troop came up a hill in column of twos, wagons to the rear, and Captain Thomas threw up his hand.

"There it is," he said simply.

I heard nothing in his voice, but I could not help conjecture what was in his mind.

Thadius and I looked down a valley. To the west it widened out in swells toward the Big Horns, high and blue. On three of the knolls, C, E, F, and I Troops had stood a year ago that day and given up their lives. Southward were the high bluffs and deep ravines where Reno fought—cut off. Below, a stream sparkled in the sun. It was the Little Big Horn.

"We have come to meet Colonel Mike Sheridan, General Phil's brother, with Captain Nowland and a party of Ree scouts," the Captain went on. "The dead could not be buried properly last year because there was no time. We are to rebury the men in one place and mark their graves. The officers are to be placed in caskets we must build. We will then take them in the wagons back to Fort Union, where the infantry will escort them on to Fort Abe and the railroad. In the East their families are awaiting them. We will then rejoin the regiment."

Thus I Troop learned why it had returned to the Little Big Horn. Camp was pitched near the stream. In the afternoon Colonel Sheridan and Captain Nowland arrived from Fort Miles, guided by two Rees, Horns-in-Front and Two Strikes, who had been with the Seventh the year before. They had sighted many Sioux in parties of various size, and asked Gerard's opinion. The scout replied that he doubted they would trouble us while scattered, but if banded up they might get notions.

The duty was commenced at once, and sad duty it was. The troopers had been laid to rest where they fell, scattered over a lot of ground and buried shallow under heaps of stones. The wolves had been their usual busy selves. And where the valley had been thick with dust from drought and hoofs a year before, now the grass was stirrup-high and flowers were everywhere. The officers were easier to find. By each one a length of lodge pole had been driven in the earth, with a Roman numeral on it, and Captain Nowland had a chart showing the numbers and decorations. Autie Custer's grave was covered with a basket from a Sioux travois, pinned down with stakes. The general's heart may have broken when he saw his regiment was lost, but I can state positively it was not cut out of him.

It was a quiet camp that night, no fires, no calls, and guards out all round.

In the morning my detail began digging graves near the Little Big Horn and bringing the departed comrades to them, while that under Thadius made roughboard coffins out of green willow for the officers. Human nature being what it is, the men got shorter with each other as the day dragged on. Relics found in the grass stuck under their hides like arrows—canteens, a ring, cartridges, knives, boots, gutta-percha buttons from the sleeves of blouses. Once two troopers squared off with fists high until I stopped them. Like as not there would have been a general ruckus had it not been for the Sioux. There were fifty or more of them in evidence now, sitting their ponies out on the knolls a mile off like wooden Indians, not live ones. But they were live, all right.

In the afternoon Captain Thomas sent Gerard and the Rees out to circle. When they returned a parley was held. Gerard reported another hundred Sioux hiding in the hollows, and some Cheyenne.

They're banding, Cap'n," he said. "When Red Moon gets enough parties in, he'll come for us. He was here last year and he knows how."

The scout talked some Ree and sign to Two Strikes, then pulled a blade of grass. "He claims this valley is medicine ground to the Sioux after what they did to Longhair. They ain't going to let anybody dig him up and take him away. Any buck who dies on this ground goes up there on a real fast pony." He pointed to the sky. "Can you follow that, Cap'n?"

"I can," Thomas said. "When will they be ready, Frank?"

"By tomorrow."

Meantime Colonel Sheridan had been pacing. He was a tall man with a spade beard and had been personally sent from Washington by President Grant on this mission. Now he stared off at the Sioux.

"History repeating itself," he said, almost to himself. "Next year my brother can order a command to come for us as we have come for the others." He faced Captain Thomas. "I am no Indian-fighter, Captain, I admit it frankly. But I do recognize odds if Custer did not, and it seems clear there may be another slaughter here tomorrow. If we abandon the wagons and leave during the night we can have a start on them by morning. What do you propose?"

John Thomas turned his face toward the Sioux and we could not see it. I believed I was the only man who understood his terrible position. In this very place a year before the commander to whom he owed both gratitude and enmity, George Armstrong Custer, had made his decision. Now, under almost the same circumstances, John Thomas had to make his. Finally, he answered.

"I will do that if you order it, Colonel. But we came out here to take some brave men home. I would hate to lose this troop, but I would hate to leave the general and the others here again. If we tuck our tails between our legs, the Sioux will think their medicine is stronger in this territory than ours. I think we should leave here in good order with our duty done, or not at all."

No one had anything to say. But even Two Strikes and Horns-in-Front got the drift from Gerard's face.

Colonel Sheridan pulled off his gauntlets. " I have heard about you in St. Paul, Captain. Has the fact that you were not present here last year influenced your tactics now?"

I held my breath, but the captain met his eyes squarely.

"Sir, it has not," he said.

Colonel Sheridan nodded. "I have also heard rumors about the condition and morale of the Seventh, but I know nothing about this troop. Will they fight?"

"I don't know, Colonel," said Captain Thomas. "But they must find out sometime, as we all must."

Colonel Sheridan slapped his gauntlets together. "Very well. When can we be finished here?"

"By noon tomorrow."

The colonel turned his back as though to indicate the responsibility rested now on other shoulders, and the parley ended. Captain Thomas ordered the four wagons driven into a half circle so that we could make a stand behind them with our backs to the Little Big Horn. Seeing this, I Troop knew it was to stay.

That night Captain Thomas ordered as many fires built as the men wished, as if to show the Sioux we were not perturbed about them. The troopers gathered round each blaze to talk in low tones and calculate our chances on the morrow. We were five officers, three scouts, four skinners, and forty-eight men, a total of sixty against no one knew how many hostiles, but the odds were reckoned at more than six to one. The consensus was that Red Moon had kept the bulk of his band concealed to trap us, as Sitting Bull had done successfully. We might stand them off for several hours, but the outcome was assured. The Custer-haters said we were to fight the Second Battle of the Little Big Horn, and that Longhair had led us to it in death as surely as he led the others in life. Many troopers, convinced they would not see another night, turned messages and valuables over to their comrades in the hope that some would survive.

I took no part in this grim vigil, but said my prayers as usual and turned in beside Thadius, who shared a tent with me. I may have expected he would make some peaceful overture, but he did not. The situation seemed unreal to me—being on this hallowed battlefield a year later, the presence of the enemy in overwhelming numbers, the preparations for a stand that must end in tragedy. I fell asleep thinking only that I would never have the chance to display my mustachio in Baltimore.

The day dawned clear. After a cooked breakfast, tents were struck, canteens filled, men posted on guard between the wagons, and the skinners turned into horse-holders at the rear. Captain Thomas ordered that the remainder complete the work we had been sent to do. At this there was muttering that he had gone mad, but my detail proceeded to bring in the last of the heroes and prepare graves while Thadius's finished the carpentry. Except for the scrape of shovel against stone and the bang of hammers, all was silence. There was no sign of the Sioux. They would come when they were ready.

They came near noon, all at once, pouring out of the hollows by the hundreds, spreading out like a swarm. Still a mile away but riding toward us were the brightly painted Cheyenne, who were better horsemen, riding in wide circles and sliding under the necks of their ponies to show what we would have to shoot at. I estimate Red Moon had at least four hundred. And there were many waving carbines, weapons they had taken from our fallen.

We had just filled in the last place of honor, outside the perimeter of wagons, and started running back to form up. I remember troopers' faces staring, figures in blue standing as though rooted. Then Alvin Thadius came on the run to meet me, holding something in his hand and crying like a child. He held up a dirt-stained triangle of cloth, which I recognized as a guidon he must have found with one of the officers.

"You see this, Peddie!" he yelled. "This is what he did to them and what he'll do to us! And before I die, dear God, I'll have it out with you!"

And as I came up short, thunderstruck that this could happen now, Thadius was on me using fists like clubs. My corporal came to pull him off and was pitched upon by someone else at once, and in seconds most of I Troop was battling it out beyond the wagons, standing and swinging or rolling in the grass among the markers, at each others' throats, the line of defense gone and the Sioux not half a mile away. I do not recall an incident like it in the annals of the United States Cavalry. Had something even more unlooked-for not occurred we would have been massacred, every living one.

Thadius and I were at grips near the right front wagon, and suddenly I heard the high-pitched yelp of Frank Gerard.

"Look, Cap'n! Look yonder! They know that horse—blow the charge! Blow the charge!"

And all at once the bell of Tommy Gudge's bugle blew the charge, and the most stirring of all calls was carried above the desperate men and out over the valley. It was so unexpected that men stopped blows in midair or rose from the ground to see. The obstinate lad from Ohio crawled off me, and we stood ourselves.

Over the knolls came a little bay horse upon the lope. When the notes of the bugle reached his ears, he pricked them up, then went into a gallop toward us, right across the front of the swarm of Sioux. And the whole four hundred of the savages stopped their ponies and their yelling. Gerard was right. They did know that horse. They could not believe their eyes any more than we. To them it was a spirit horse with a spirit rider on his back—more powerful medicine than mortal men, red or white, could ever make.

Right between the Sioux and us he galloped, with no sound but the drumming of his hoofs, and he came between the wagons to a halt, blowing and nickering. The Sioux forgotten, we gathered round him. He was all dirt and foam, his eyes sunken and his ribs nearly through his hide. In some way he had broken loose at Fort Abe, and trailing lariat and picket-pin had come two hundred miles over mountains and rivers and prairies, had found his way back to the Little Big Horn where he was the year before and where his master now lay in a box of willow.

Captain Thomas leaped down from his wagon and stood beside him for a time. Then he took off his hat.

"Let there be no more fighting among us," he said at length. "I know what has been in your minds. Some men were picked a year ago to make history here. They made it and they will not be forgotten. But what you bear is a grudge against your luck. You came to the regiment too late and could not share their glory."

He put his hand upon the mane of the little bay. I realized that what he had to say was for his own sake as well as ours.

"This horse was left behind the way you were. But he came two hundred miles to prove he bears no grudge. He missed one fight and he intends to see he does not miss another. If he can do as much, why, so can we. We will now harness these wagons and mount up and march out of here in good order."

For a minute all stood, not a dry eye among us. Then a cheer rang out and troopers shook hands, as did Alvin Thadius and I. If the souls of the departed were present that day, looking down from the blue sky on that scene in the green valley, it must have lifted their hearts.

Mules were harnessed, Tommy Gudge blew boots and saddles, and I Troop came into column. While the Sioux still sat a quarter of a mile away, believing we had joined forces with the Great Beyond, which in a way we had, Captain Thomas threw his hand forward and we marched past them out of the valley as though on parade, our guidon fluttering and our heads high. At the head of the column stepped the little bay.

So there was a kind of Second Battle of the Little Big Horn after all, which was won without a shot being fired. Dandy was returned to Fort Abe with his master and the other heroes. When I Troop rejoined the regiment in the north and related the foregoing, the subscription for him was raised at once. One hundred forty dollars was paid the government, and the general's horse was shipped East to "The Girl He'd Left Behind Him." From her home in Monroe, Michigan, Mrs. Custer sent a moving letter of thanks. It may interest the reader to know that Dandy became the horse of Autie Custer's old father, who was over seventy then, and together they headed up temperance processions and Fourth of July parades for many years.

As for the breach in the ranks of the Seventh Regiment, it was wholly healed, as evidenced by ensuing victories at Wounded Knee and against the Nez Perce at the Bear Paw.

. . .

Alexander Peddie was unable, in Dakota Days, *to describe the action at Bear Paw to which he alludes, since prior to it he was transferred to Fort Huachuca in Arizona. Nor does he mention Captain John Thomas again in his volume. Records of the Adjutant-General disclose, however, that the captain, conducting himself gallantly at the head of I Troop, was killed in action against the Nez Perce. Subsequently a recommendation for the posthumous award of the Congressional Medal of Honor was made in his case, but the citation was never approved. Letters of the day reveal, ironically, that sentiment in both Congress and the War Department was against it and several others on the grounds that too-generous award of the Medal had been made after the Battle of the Little Big Horn.*

◆◆◆

The Attack on the Mountain

This is about a general and a petticoat and three squaws and a rat roast and a sergeant and some other soldiers and a mutt dog and an old maid and a message.

The general was Nelson A. Miles. He followed George Crook in charge of the military department of Arizona, in which vast command the Apaches, still feisty in the eighties, were accustomed to breaking out of the agencies, stealing horses and cattle, burning ranches, deceasing the settlers, and being beat-all scampish. Tender in the beam, Miles was disinclined to spend much time in the saddle, as Crook had done, preferring to reign over military reviews and fancy do's in towns with the locals and let the terrain and the latest in tactics conduct his campaign for him.

To this end he scattered his cavalry in troops across that area most pested by the Indians, ready to strike at any raiding band close-range, and also set up the most intricate, cosmographical system of observation and communication ever seen in the West. The finest telescopes and heliographs were obtained from the chief signal officer in Washington. The heliograph consisted of a

Originally published in *The Saturday Evening Post*, July 4, 1959. Also appeared in *A Century of Great Western Stories*, edited by John Jakes (New York: Forge, 2000) and *Tales of the American West: The Best of Spur Award-Winning Authors*, edited by Richard S. Wheeler (New York: New American Library, 2000).

mirror set on a tripod and covered with a shutter; by means of a lever which alternately removed and interposed the shutter, long or short flashes of light coded out words, the distance depending on the sun's brilliance and the clearness of the atmosphere. Infantrymen were trained at Signal Corps school at Fort Myer, in Virginia, then shipped west and stuck up on peaks so as to form a network. There were thirty-three stations, not only in Arizona but also in New Mexico, and even more were eventually added, reaching down into Sonora, Mexico. The entire system covered a zigzag course of over four hundred miles, a part of it being pieced out by telegraph. It was a monument to science and to General Miles's administrative genius, and it was not worth a tinker's damn.

The Apaches took to moving by night. By day they observed the observers, using their own means of communication—fire, smoke, sunlight on a glittering conch shell. They yanked down the telegraph lines, cut them, and spliced them with wet rawhide, which dried to look like wire, the cuts then being almost impossible for linemen to detect, thus degutting the system.

But whatsoever General Field Order No. 7 established on April 20, 1886, at Fort Bowie must endure. The station could at least transmit messages like the following:

RELAY C O FORT HUACHUCA PREPARE POST
INSPECTION AND REVIEW GENL MILES

So much for the general.

On Bill Williams Mountain, five thousand feet up, set on a ledge, there were five men of the 24th Infantry and two mules and a mutt dog. This was the way they passed their time. Sgt. Ammon Swing was in command. He copied the messages sent and received, made sure there was always an eye to the telescope, and allowed himself only the luxury of an occasional think about Miss Martha Cox. Corporal Bobyne had charge of the heliograph. After two weeks training in the code, he worked the shutter with a flourish, youngster-like. Private Takins cooked. He never bathed, and over the months built up such a singular oniony odor that they said of him he could walk past the pot and season the stew. The guards were Corporal Heintz and Private Mullin.

Reckoning to grow potatoes, Heintz, a stubborn Dutchman from Illinois, hoed and hilled at a great rate while the studious Mullin took up botany, cataloguing specimens of yucca, nopal, and hediondilla. In their brush corral the two mules tucked back their ears and pondered whom to kick next. Their names were Annie and Grover, the latter after Mr. Cleveland, who was then serving his first term in 1886. The mutt dog chased quail and was in turn hunted by sand fleas, who had better luck.

There was no call for the men to be lonely or the mules mean or the dog to mope. Only six miles away, down in the valley, was Cox's Tanks, a ranch from which water was packed up twice weekly on muleback; only twelve miles off, along the range at a pass, was the Rucker Canyon Station; and only thirty-four miles to the south was Fort Buford, whence supplies were hauled once a month. The five men had high, healthy air to breathe, the goings-on over a hundred square miles of nothing to watch, a branding sun by day, and low, fierce stars by night.

In addition, they could gossip via heliograph with Rucker:

YOU SEEN ANY PACHES? NOPE HEINTZ
GROWED ANY TATER YET? NOPE

But after May and June on Bill Williams Mountain they began to be lorn. In July they commenced talking to themselves more than to each other. One day in August the dog turned his eyes heavenward and ran at full speed toward the top of the mountain and death. Dogs had been known to commit suicide in that way hereabouts.

OUR DOG RUN AWAY
SO DID OURN

So much for the mutt.

When they rousted out one September morning there was smoke columning a few hundred yards down the ledge. Taking Mullin with him, Sergeant Swing went out to reconnoiter, snaking along through the greasewood until they reached a rock formation. What they spied was a mite insulting. They had Apaches on their hands, all right, but squaws instead of braves—three of them, and a covey of kids running about. The ladies had come during the night, built a bungalow of brush and old skins, and set up housekeeping. The smoke issued from a stone-lined pit in which they were baking mescal, a species of century plant and a staple of the Apache diet. Ollas and conical baskets were scattered about. The squaws wore calico dresses, which meant they had at one time been on an agency, and one of them was missing the tip of her nose. The whites had not as yet succeeded in arguing the Apache warriors out of their age-old right to snick off a little when they suspected their womenfolk of being unfaithful. But the final indignity was dealt the sergeant when he and Mullin crawled out of the rocks. Two youngsters, who had watched their every move, skittered laughingly back to their mamas.

Apaches or not, they were the station's first real company in six months and the men were glad of them. Sergeant Swing was not. He could not decide if he should start an official message to department headquarters, and if he did, how to word it so that he would not sound ridiculous.

While he hesitated young Bobyne shuttered the news to Rucker Canyon anyway:

THREE SQUAWS COME SARGE
DUNNO WHAT TO DO

The reply was immediate:

HAVE DANCE INVITE US

When this was decoded, since no one but Bobyne could read Morse, there was general laughter.

"Folderol," the sergeant said.

"You tink dem squaws vill 'tack us?" Heintz asked, winking at the others. "Zhould ve zhoot dem kids?"

Swing ruminated. "You fellers listen. If you expect them desert belles come up to cook and sew for us, your expecter is busted. Where there's squaws there's billy-bound to be bucks sooner or later." He said further that he was posting a running guard at once. He wanted someone on the telescope from sunup to dark. "And here's the gist of it," he concluded. "We will stay shy of them Indians. Nobody to go down there calling, and if they come up here you treat them as kindly as 'rantulas, which they are."

"Dats too ztiff," Heintz protested.

"Sarge, you mean we ain't even to be decent to the kiddies?" complained Mullin.

"Not as you love your mother," is the answer, "and calculate to see her again."

They grudged off to their posts, and the sergeant went to sit by a Joshua tree and study his predicament. He was more alarmed than he had let on. The news along the system had for two weeks been all bad. The most varminty among the Warm Springs chiefs had left the agency with bands and were raiding to the south—Naiche and Mangas together, Kaytennay by himself. With their example before him, it would be beneath Geronimo's dignity down in Mexico to behave much longer. General Miles had cavalry rumping out in all directions, but there had as yet been neither catch nor kill. He had heard that the first thing sought by the Apaches on break outs was weapons. What more logical than to camp a few squaws and kids near a heliograph station, cozy up to the personnel, then smite them suddenly with braves, wipe out the sentimental fools, and help yourself to rifles and cartridges? Apaches had been known to wait days, even weeks, for their chance. And how was a mere sergeant to control men who had not mingled with humankind for six months?

Had he been an oathing man, Ammon Swing would have. He had in him a sense of duty like a rod of iron. A small, compact individual, he wore a buggy-whip mustache which youthened his face and made less New England his expression. Pushing back his hat, he let his gaze lay out, first at the far mountains on the sides of which the air was white as milk, then lower, at the specks of Cox's Tanks upon the valley floor. This brought to mind Miss Martha Cox, with whom he might be in love and might not. The sister of Jacob Cox, she was a tanned, leathery customer as old as the sergeant, which put her nigh on forty-four, too old and sensible for male and female farandoles. She ran the ranch with her brother, plowed with a pistol round her waist, spat and scratched herself like a man, and her reputation with a rifle, after twenty years of raids, caused even the Apaches to give the Cox spread leeway. Swing had seen her five times in six months during his turns to go down with Annie and Grover to pack water. Only once, the last trip, had anything passed between them.

"Ain't you considerable mountain-sore, Mister Swing?"

"Suppose I am," says he.

"Seems to me settling down would be suitable to you."

"Ma'am?"

"Sure," says she. "Marry up and raise a fam'ly and whittle your own stick."

"Too old, Miss Cox."

"Too old?"

"Old as you are," says he.

He knew his blunder when he saw the turkey-red under her tan. She squinted at the mules, then gave him a granite eye.

"Mister Swing, if ever you alter your mind, I know the very one would have you."

"Who, Ma'am?"

"Annie," says she.

For the next few days Ammon Swing was much put on. The little Indians soon swarmed over the station, playing games, ingratiating themselves with the soldiers, eventually sitting on their knees to beg for trinkets. Shoo as hard as he might, the sergeant could not put a stop to it. Down the ledge the three squaws went on baking mescal and inevitably there commenced to be visiting back and forth. Takins was the first caught skulking off.

"Takins," says the sergeant, "I told you to stay shy of them."

"I be only humin, Sarge," grumbles the cook, which was doubtful, considering his fragrance.

"You keep off, that's an order!" says Swing, losing his temper. "Or I'll send you back to Buford to the guardhouse!"

"You will, Sarge?" Takins grins. "Nothin' I'd like better'n to git off this cussed mountin!"

Thus it was that the sergeant's authority went to pot and his command to pieces. Men on guard straggled down the ledge to observe the baking and weaving of baskets and converse sociably in sign. The ladies in turn, led by Mrs. Noseless, a powerful brute of a woman, paid daily calls on the station to watch the operation of the heliostat and giggle at the unnatural ways of the whites.

Three days passed. Then a new factor changed the situation on Bill Williams Mountain from absurd to desperate. The supply party from Fort Buford did not arrive. Takins ran entirely out of salt beef and hardtack. Ammon Swing was reduced to swapping with the squaws for mescal, which tasted like molasses candy and brought on the bloat; but the commodity for which the Apaches were most greedy turned out to be castor oil, of which he had only two bottles in his medicine chest. He considered butchering Annie or Grover, but that would mean one less mule to send down to Cox's Tanks for water.

Water! He could not wait on that. But to obtain it, and food as well, would short him by two men. If an attack were ever to come, it would come when the station had only three defenders. Worse yet, it was his turn to go down the mountain day after next, his and Takins', and he wanted very much to go to Cox's again. Why he wanted to so much he would not admit even to himself.

The next morning he traded the last drop of castor oil to the squaws for mescal. In the afternoon the water casks went dry.

At day-die Ammon Swing called Heintz to him and said he was sending him down for water and food with Takins. It was his own turn, but he should stay in case of attack.

The Dutchy puffed his cheeks with pleasure. "Goot. You be zorry."

"Why?"

"I ask dis voman to vedding. I ask before, bud zhe zay no. Dis time zhe zay yez, I tink."

One end of the iron rod of duty in the sergeant stuck in his crop. "Why?" he inquires again.

"I goot farmer. Zhe needs farmer to raunch. Alzo zhe iz nod much young. Nod many chanzes more vill zhe get. You change your mind, Zarge?"

"No," says Ammon Swing.

As soon as Heintz and Takins and Annie and Grover had started down in the morning Sergeant Swing would have bet a month's pay this was the day. Something in the pearl air told him. He ordered Mullin and Bobyne to stand guard near the heliostat and have hands on their weapons at all times. They would change off on the telescope. No man was to leave the sight of the other two.

The morning inched.

They had not had food for twenty-four hours nor water for eighteen. Nor would they until Heintz and Takins returned. The squaws did not come to visit nor the kids to play.

One message winked from Rucker Canyon and was shuttered on:

RELAY GENL MILES REQUESTS
PLEASURE COL AND MRS COTTON OFFICERS
BALL HEADQUARTERS FT BOWIE 22 AUGUST

By noon they were so thirsty they spit dust and so hungry their bellies sang songs. It had never been so lonesome on Bill Williams Mountain.

Then they had visitors. The three squaws came waddling along the ledge, offspring after them, and surrounded a pile of brush not twenty yards off. In one hand they held long forked sticks and in the other small clubs. Mrs. Noseless started a fire. The soldiers had no notion what the Indians could be up to. When all was ready, the fire burned down to hot coals, the squaws and kids began to squeal and shout and poke into the brush pile. Curious, the soldiers came near.

What they soon saw was that the Apaches had discovered a large convention of field rats. Under the brush the animals had cast up a mound of earth by burrowing numerous tunnels. When a stick was thrust into one end of the tunnel, the animal, seeking an escape route, would dart to the opening of another and hesitate for an instant, half in and half out, to scan for his enemy. In that split second another Indian would pin the rat down with forked stick, pull it toward him, bash it over the head with his club, and with a shout of triumph eviscerate it with a stroke of the knife and pitch it into the fire. In a trice the hair was burned off, the carcass roasted to a turn, impaled on the stick and the juicy tidbit lifted to a hungry mouth. Starved and horrified, the soldiers were drawn to the banquet despite themselves. There seemed no end to the victuals or the fun.

A little girl ran laughing to Bobyne with a rat. The young man sniffed, tasted, and with a grin of surprise put down his rifle and commenced to feast. Mullin was next served. Then a squaw bore a plump offering to the sergeant. It was done exactly to his liking, medium rare. He could no longer resist. The taste was that of rodent, sort of like the woodchuck he had shot and cooked as a sprout. He had, however, to keep his eyes closed.

What opened them was the terrible silence immediately smashed by a scream.

For an instant as the food fell from his hands he was stricken with shock and fright. The kids vanished. A dying Mullin staggered toward him, screaming. An arrow transfixed his body, driven with such force into his back that it pierced him completely, feathers on one side, head and shaft on the other.

One squaw ran full-speed toward the tents to plunder, holding high her grimy calico skirt.

Like deer, three Apache bucks leaped from their hiding place in the greasewood and sped toward him, letting arrows go from bows held at waist level.

Another squaw made for the heliograph and, giving the tripod a kick, toppled the instrument onto rock, shattering the mirror.

An arrow skewered through the fleshy part of Swing's left leg. He cried out with pain and went down on one knee, reaching for his rifle.

Young Bobyne retrieved his and began to blaze away at the oncoming bucks when Mrs. Noseless seized him from behind in powerful arms and hurled him backward into the fire of hot coals as she might have barbecued a rat, kneeling on him and setting his hair afire and bashing in his skull with her club.

Shooting from one knee, Ammon Swing brought down one of the bucks at twenty yards and another point-blank. But it was too late to fire at the third, who swept a long knife upward from a hide boot.

He had time only to glimpse the contorted brown face and yellow eyeballs and hear the death yell as a bullet slammed life and wind out of the Apache and the buck fell heavily upon him. He lay wondering if he were dead, stupefied by the fact that the bullet had not been his own.

Then the buck was dragged off him by Miss Martha Cox. She took the

Indian's knife, knelt, and slitting the sergeant's trouser leg, began to cut through the arrow shaft on either side of his thigh.

"Soldiers and wimmen," she snorts.

"You shoot him?" he groans.

"Sure."

He asked about Heintz and Takins. Dead, the both of them, she told him—ambushed on the way down. When they had not shown at the ranch, she rode up to find out why.

She had the arrow cut off close to the meat now and bound his leg with shirt cloth. As he sat up she said he would bleed a little; what was dangerous was the chance of infection, since the Apaches had as much fondness for dirty arrows as they did for dirty everything else. He was to ride her horse down as fast as he could manage. Her brother would have the tools to pull the shaft piece, and water for the wound.

Ammon Swing saw that she wore the best she owned, a long dress of gray taffeta and high-button shoes. When furbished, she was near to handsome.

"Heintz was intending to ask you to marry."

"I figured it would be you coming down today," says she. "So I got out my fancies. Ain't had them on in ten year."

"Oh?" says he. "Well, help me."

With her arm round his waist he was hobbling toward her horse when he caught the flash from the Mogollon Station, to the south.

"Message." He stopped. "I ain't trained to read it, but it better be put down."

"It better not," says she, bossy.

But he made her fetch pencil and paper from a tent and wait while he transcribed the signals according to length, long and short. When the flashes ceased, he cast a glum look at his own shattered heliograph nearby.

"Ought to relay this," says he. "It's maybe important."

"Mister Swing," says she, "infection won't wait. You army around up here much longer and you might have to make do without a leg."

He did not even hear. He sat down on a boulder and tried to think how the Sam Hill to send the message on to Rucker Canyon. The piece of shaft twinged as though it were alive, the pain poisoning all the way to his toes.

There was no other mirror. There was neither pot nor pan bright enough to reflect sun. Miss Martha Cox kept after him about infection, but the more he knew she was right the more dutiful and mule-headed he became. He would not leave with chores undone. Such a stunt would do injustice to his dead. Suddenly he gave a finger snap.

"Making apology, Ma'am, but what do you have on beyunder that dress?"

"Well I never!" says she, coloring up real ripe for a woman who had just put down a rifle after a killing.

"Would you please remove same?"

"Oh!" she cries.

The Sergeant gave a tug at his buggy whip. "Govermint business, Ma'am."

With a female stamp of her foot she obeyed, hoisting the taffeta over her head. Above she wore a white corset cover laced with pink ribbon and below, a muslin petticoat so overstarched it was as stiff and glittering as galvanized tin, touching evidence that it had been a long time since she had made starch.

"We are in luck, Ma'am," says he. "We have a clear day and the whitest unspeakabout this side of heaven, and I calculate they will see us."

Being most gentlemanly, he escorted her near the lip of the ledge facing Rucker Canyon, took her dress, and, reading from the paper, began to transmit the message by using her dress as a shutter, shading her with it, then sweeping it away for long and short periods corresponding to the code letters he had transcribed. And all the while poor Miss Martha Cox was forced to stand five thousand feet high in plain sight of half the military department of Arizona, being alternately covered and revealed, a living heliograph, flashing in the sun like an angel descended from above and blushing like a woman fallen forever into sin. When her ordeal and her glory were ended, and Rucker blinked on and off rapidly to signify receipt, she snatched her dress to herself. To his confusion, a tear splashed down one of her leathery cheeks while at the same time she drew up breathing brimstone.

"Ammon Swing," cries she, "no man has ever in all my days set eyes on me in such a state! Either I put my brother on your evil trail or you harden your mind to marrying me this minute!"

"Already have," says he.

Thoughtfully she pulled on the gray taffeta. "We better kiss on it," says she.

"Folderol," says he. But they did.

Then she helped him on her horse and together they went down Bill Williams Mountain.

So much for the petticoat, the three squaws, the rat roast, the sergeant, the other soldiers and the old maid.

The signals reaching Rucker Canyon Station twelve miles off were less distinct than usual, but by means of the telescope and much cussing they could be deciphered and sent on:

RELAY COL AND MRS. COTTON ACCEPT
WITH PLEASURE OFFICERS BALL
BOWIE 22 AUGUST

So much for the message.

◆ ◆ ◆

Ixion

Not moving, Johnson sat behind the vines as the little girls led a party of tourists along the walk which coiled through the bamboo and listened as they offered to sing an interesting song for a peso and were paid and began to sing in piping voices.

En éste mundo traidor	[In this treacherous world,
Nada es verdad ni mentira;	Nothing is truth or lie;
todo es según el color	All things depend on the tint
Del cristal con ques se mira.	Of the glass before the eye.]

The tourists said it was a very interesting song, but what about the artists?

"Oh, them, well. *Oigame*," the older, seven, started. "The people who live here are all artists except my mother. Mr. Kahn and Mr. Radimersky live in that house. They're painters but they don't paint much. Dorothy Camilla Sugret lives in that one. She's a poetess and drinks tequila *con-sangre*, with blood. That's where we live. Mr. Johnson just moved into that one. He's from Cleveland and going to write a book. So you see they're all artists and all *muy loco* and we usually get a peso for showing people around."

"We could tell you lots more," said the younger, six, "for another peso."

They were paid and lowered their voices. What they said caused the sharp suck of a woman's breath and a man to clear his throat self-consciously.

Johnson sat very still until the little girls led the tourists out of hearing. At their age he had sold lemonade. Of course there had been no poetess on his street.

Johnson had driven down to Mexico by himself. The name of the town was Ajijic, pronouncing the j's like h's. It was on the shore of the biggest lake in Mexico. There were mountains all around the lake, and the bell of the church rang purely during the day and through the night. He came to Ajijic because, being an artist's colony according to the travel folders, it would have atmosphere. One of the best things about the town was that it was four thousand miles from Cleveland and further than that from the advertising business. Johnson wrote copy on a spark plug account. There were only a certain number of things one could say about spark plugs, and when he had said them he gave himself the gift of a year to learn what else there might be in the world. Many other Americans had come to Ajijic, although he did not have much to do with them. There were teachers of English on leave from colleges who said they were never going back, and a man who produced television shows in Los Angeles who said he was never going back either; but on this subject Johnson did not commit himself to himself or to them. He had a fine place to live. He took one of the cottages of the Casa Paraíso, the only hotel. In the small lobby a blossoming tree twisted up through a square in the roof into the air, and outside, spaced around a big patio, hidden from each other by banana palms and thickets of bamboo, were eight cottages girt with vines in which nested birds, red and blue, he had never before seen, while from the porch he could watch, through an eye in the vines, the heat of the sun and the high altitude evaporating the surface of the lake constantly into mist. It was easy to imagine monsters lifting hooded heads out of the mist, or the gods of the lake ancient Indians prayed to for many fish. Then, after a few days, having heard that every man has a book in him, Johnson thought he would try to find his. He would never have a better time or place to be creative. It seemed to him that given such an atmosphere and going to the task as routinely as he went to the office, anyone might write a book. So wearing huaraches and shorts he began to sit at a table on his porch for four hours each morning. His novel, about a young man who left advertising to go to Mexico to write a novel, went well at first. In the afternoons he had a siesta on the beach, letting the sun work on him while he slept, then swam, dressed, walked to the *casa de correos* for his mail, and returned for drinks with Mrs. Temple. She had the cottage next to his. She was six years older than he and she was from New York. After dinner they drank and talked and then retired, either at her place or his, but usually hers because she slept late in the morning while he had his book to write.

Johnson, he told himself, this is so good it is hard to believe. Everything they are supposed to throw in on a deal like this and never do they have thrown in on this one. But this is what can happen if you sell hard and save your money and stay single until you are twenty-nine and then take off. It is right out of the books, Johnson boy, he would say, but here it is.

With the red and blue birds, with his book going well and the mist rising and Mrs. Temple, who was, sensually, all that a woman might be, he would have been completely content if she had not happened to bring her little girls with her. Nearly two years before, living in New York, she had told her husband she was taking the girls to the dentist in the morning. Instead she had packed, gone to the bank, written a large check, and taken them to Mexico. Her husband had divorced her. He had been granted custody of the children but since they lived now in a foreign country, action by him in the courts was useless. Johnson could not understand why she refused to let them return where they might go to school and lead a normal life, unless it was the money their father sent each month which, from her remarks, was supposed to pay for their attendance at the American school in Guadalajara. They did not go and he did not question her about it. He only wished she would send them home.

The morning after the first night at her house he found them sitting on the steps, waiting patiently for their mother to wake up so that they could show her the dolls they had made of sticks tied with string and dressed in palm fronds. If he was embarrassed, they were not. They showed him the dolls. Later, working on his porch, he saw the children watching him through the opening in the vines, waiting for him as though it was now their right when nothing he had done had given them the right. He went on working, hard as it was while being watched, until his four hours were up before acknowledging their presence. Then they showed him the execution of the dolls. They had hung each one by the neck in a noose of vines until it was dead. When he helped them with the burial they said he was very *simpático.* After that he would wake from his siesta on the beach to see them sitting near. As he opened his eyes and stretched they would smile, glad that he was awake, and run to him. He taught them how to swim. He washed them with his soap, for they were usually dirty, and dried them with his towel. Twice he washed their blonde, uncut hair. He drew letters in the sand to try to teach them to read and write. He told them the stories of his childhood. He took them for walks. These things did not give Johnson pleasure. The little girls struck chords in him and took so much of the time and thought and emotion he had to save for his book. He could not let them become important. That was not part of the deal.

One day he found he could not write and went with them down the beach a mile to look for dinosaur bones in a bog where a sluggish stream crawled into the lake. Silently the three oozed their bare feet up and down in the hot black muck.

"If you touch something it's prob'ly a real bone, all right," said the smaller girl. She pumped her legs hopefully. "So feel as hard as you can!"

"I am," Johnson said. He noticed that her hair needed washing again. Either that or the mass of the mountains which overhung them darkened it.

"Have you ever found one?" he asked.

"Some boys in town have," said the girl of seven. One of her front teeth was missing. "And when you do you take it to Mr. Fernandez who runs the cantina and he gives you a peso. I bet he sells them for a lot more, though. The *turistas* will pay anything for stuff if it's old. But what I simply have to know is, how did the dinosaurs ever get in here anyway?"

Johnson understood that parts of several prehistoric skeletons had been found in the bog. He explained how the great beasts must have come here to drink at the mouth of the stream thousands of years before the mountains were made, and stepping into the muck, had been unable with their short legs and heavy tails to lift themselves out and were at last drawn under, thrashing and roaring. The children's eyes were round. Finally the younger made a face.

"Oh, how gooey!" she cried.

"I guess that's what the dinosaurs thought," Johnson grinned.

They bathed their feet in the lake and walked back along the beach past the fishermen drying their nets and the burros grazing the few tufts of grass. In Johnson's, the children's hands were sweaty.

"We like you a lot better than Mr. Spurway," the older girl said.

"*Gracias,*" he said. "Who is Mr. Spurway?"

"The one before you," she said. "He'd never take us to look for a bunch of old bones."

"He wouldn't?"

"And lots more than Paco," said the younger, hopping on a rock.

"Who is Paco?"

"Why, the Mexican, the one before Mr. Spurway." She hopped down again. "He was really gooey!"

They giggled and swung his arms.

That night Johnson sat with Irene Temple on her porch. Usually they talked and usually he read her a few pages from his book while she drank. She had a good critical sense. She drank not just during the evening but steadily through the day, beginning with two or three in the morning and then three or four in the afternoon and then four or five during the evening. Johnson never had more than one or two during the evening, but tonight he was keeping up with her and he had not read from his book. They sat in canvas chairs facing the lake. The night was warm and a wind had come over the mountains as it did at this time. The waves on the beach were monotonous. The pure ringing of the church bell was blown high by the wind. The children were asleep.

"Why so busy with the bottle?" Irene Temple asked.

"I feel like it."

"Good," she said. "Good."

Johnson clicked ice against the side of his glass.

"Why did you happen to come down here?" he asked. "Tell me again."

"If you want to hear it. I wasn't doing anything with my life. I sat down and tried to think of the things I really enjoyed most. I was honest with myself, which most people never are." Her voice was steady and satisfied. "So I decided to do the things I enjoyed most. It was as simple as that. I'm sure there's nothing more syndromic or complex about my coming down than yours."

"*Gracias,*" he said.

"*Por nada.* Why ask again?"

"It's just a little hard to understand."

"Because you're from Cleveland," she said. "And I'm native New York. Cleveland and New York, there's the difference."

Johnson finished his drink.

"One other question." He was being cautious because he did not want to spoil anything. "Why do you keep the girls?"

"I love them," she said. "I love them."

She had a habit of repeating herself in speech.

"I see," he said.

"Do they disturb you?"

"I like them and I think they like me. They say I am *simpático.* What does that mean, exactly?"

"Nice," she said. "Nice."

"Oh," he said.

She was silent, and he knew she would ask one of the big questions. When she does, he thought, watch it.

"Why didn't you marry when you were twenty-two or -three?" she asked.

"Probably I hoped, in the back of my mind," he said, choosing very carefully, "that someday, if I didn't, there would be something like this."

It was right.

"About the children," she said. "You needn't play the father. They have a father." She yawned. "Besides, you'll never do a decent book if you let things disturb you. You'll never be creative. An artist must be *intenso. Intenso* is the opposite of *simpático.*"

"Not exactly," he said.

"They have a father," she said.

Irene Temple yawned again and stood. She was a tall woman with a handsome face and a gray streak in her black hair and the body of a girl of twenty. She wore shorts and a halter and she was barefooted.

"Late," she said, holding out her hand.

Johnson felt the slow deep fill of desire but he made up his mind to think about the children. He did not look at her legs in the light from the door for he knew they were long and straight and smooth as a girl's. He kept his eyes on the lake.

When he did not get up she slapped the flesh of one bare thigh with her fingertips. Sometimes she did things like that.

"Late," she said again.

"Damn," he said. *Intenso* was not the opposite, and they did not have a father.

Then after a minute, "All right."

In the morning Johnson found he could not write again and after two hours' trying drove across the beach into the lake up to the hubs to wash his car. The little girls waded after him. Sun and water were warm. The children ran and splashed, scrubbed the wheels for him, played with a wooden boat, and then the three had a water fight.

"*Hola,*" said the older, stopping the fight.

Johnson turned. Their mother stood on the gray sand at the water's edge. He waded near her.

"Our tourist cards expire in three days, the girls' and mine," she said. "They have to be renewed every six months, you know. I always forget until the last minute. You simply step across the border, step back, pay three dollars, and the cards are good for another six months."

A few yards from them a Mexican woman knelt on a spit of sand, doing her family washing on a large flat stone. The strike of wet clothing against stone sounded in the dry air like slaps. Irene Temple watched the woman for a moment.

"I need to ask a favor of you," she said finally. "Will you drive us to Brownsville? It's only two days each way and we needn't stay in Texas. I don't care to, in fact. We can cross and come right back. I hate dreadfully to ask. Dreadfully."

"Sure, I guess so," Johnson said.

"It's grand of you," she said. "Can we leave in the morning?"

"I don't see why not."

Irene Temple walked up the beach. Johnson waded out to the car and drove it ashore to chamois. He had not sold hard and stayed single and saved his money and taken off to return after a month. More than a matter of crossing a border, even momentarily, between two countries, it was crossing a line between what you had been and what you might be, with the chance that the one who stepped over would not be the one who stepped back. He was already having difficulty writing his book. He made up his mind to think the thing through and decide by tonight. If he decided not to make the trip he would tell her tonight.

That afternoon the girls waited near Johnson until he waked from his siesta, then ran to him.

"Can we go to a movie in Texas with cartoons?" the younger cried, jumping up and down.

"*¿Como no?*" Johnson said.

"And I'd like to get some real ice cream," said the older girl. "The ice cream in Guadalajara is just useless. That's one of the best things about the States, the ice cream. Mr. Spurway bought us some in Brownsville. He took us the last time."

"Who took you the time before that?" Johnson asked.

"Paco, naturally."

After their swim the girls wanted to see the slaughtering. It was just a block from the beach, they begged, and every day they slaughtered a cow for the meat market, which was the store with the red flag hanging in front and all the flies. Johnson asked if their mother wanted them to see it and they said she didn't care, they used to go every day before he came. But in the court behind the *carnicería* the killing was done and two men were dressing out the carcass. The hide hung dripping from a lime tree. The children were disappointed. Sickened, Johnson said they must go back to the *Casa Paraíso* because it would soon be their dinnertime and they would be leaving for the border in the morning. They walked toward the hotel as the sun slanted behind the mountains. On a corner Johnson stopped.

"How would you like to see your father?" he asked.

The little girls regarded him gravely.

"That's a funny question," said the older, scuffing the dust with her sandal.

"You should want to," he said.

"They don't have very much meat in India, I heard," said the girl of six, changing the subject. "They won't kill their cows."

Johnson looked away. "They won't?" he asked.

"Nope," said her sister. "Sometimes they have to eat off one hamburger for a whole week in India."

They went on, picking their way among the sleeping pigs and chickens and brown Mexican babies.

I could drive over to Chapala, to the telegraph, Johnson thought, and get a wire out tonight. It is two days to the border, which would allow time if we start in the morning, but there must be something to hold us over in Brownsville another day, across the line, something she cannot suspect. Being in the States even for minutes will make her very alert. It is very possible. Planning it must mean you are going to try it. Girls do not have lemonade stands in New York. But boys from Cleveland do not have a year and the biggest lake in Mexico and Irene Temple.

. . .

The offices of the dentist in Brownsville, Texas, were on the third floor over a drugstore. Telling the children to stay in the hall and he would have a surprise for them, Johnson went into the reception room. A man in his midforties who wore shell-rimmed glasses and a flannel suit and a camel's-hair coat and had tried to keep something of college about him waited.

"Am I glad to see you!" Johnson grinned, reaching for his hand. "I've been lucky all the way, getting the wire out of Chapala and then setting this up last night over the phone. I had to sneak out at 2 a.m. to call you because she's very suspicious over the border. That's what it does to people who are down there too long, makes them strangers in the States." His palms were wet. Now that it was accomplished he could not seem to stop talking. "They may seem unusual at first until they're adjusted to you or you to them but they'll be normal in no time though they really do need a lot of work done on their teeth. There's your irony. I got her to stay over a day in Texas so I could take them to the dentist."

"I don't want you to misunderstand," Temple said.

"Right here in the hall," Johnson said. Grinning, he opened the door.

Temple hesitated, then went into the hall.

The girls looked at him.

"Well, girls, well, girls," he said, and would have kissed them except that they backed away as though he were a tourist. The younger looked at her sister.

"Should we kiss him?" she asked.

"Maybe *mañana,*" said her sister. "Let's see how it goes."

Johnson suggested they all go down to the drugstore for some of the ice cream he had promised. The little girls clapped hands and led the way. Johnson stopped to look out a window. From that height he could see the tile roofs of Matamoros and then the plains pulsing with heat and the white road splitting south. He would head for El Paso this afternoon and take the central highway down through Chihuahua and keep going through Guadal over to a banana port on the coast called Manzanillo the tourists had not yet found. He had everything with him, even his book, and he had eleven months left of his year. He took another look at Mexico and a fine deep breath and followed them downstairs.

The children climbed on stools at the counter and Johnson ordered double chocolate marshmallow sundaes for them. Then the two men had coffee in a nearby booth.

"I hope I can get through to you on this," Temple said. "Your motives have been the right ones, certainly, and you rate a medal of some kind. I was given custody, although that was pretty much a formality after her conduct, and what it's been since then I can guess. But circumstances alter, you know, and it has been two years. The fact is I have married again, a much younger woman—very young, in fact—and married with the understanding that we will have our own family. The nut of it is, these two just were not and are not part of the package. I am responsible for their support and I accept that responsibility, but that is all."

He was being very businesslike and forty-five to Johnson's twenty-nine, which did not match his button-down shirt and young-man-about-campus tie.

"But my God," Johnson said.

"You wired me, I did not wire you," Temple said firmly. "I flew out only because it was too late to wire back, and last night on the phone you gave me no opportunity to explain."

Johnson heard the girls telling the waitress behind the counter about Ajijic and Dorothy Camilla Sugret and the slaughtering.

"But the life they lead," he burst out. "I can't tell you. My God."

Temple removed his shell-rims and rubbed the bridge of his nose. "I suppose I'm not making any contact at all," he said tiredly. "It may be that you have to experience the situation yourself."

He went on talking and Johnson sat not listening. He was trying to comprehend what he was doing in Brownsville, Texas, really, when a month before he had never heard of Brownsville, Texas. If he says anything about it not being my business in the first place, he thought, I will beat hell out of him.

"I won't take them back to her," he interrupted.

"I don't expect you to," Temple said. "On the flight out I gave the thing a good brain-through. She has a sister living in Waco, north of here. I've put her name and address on this card." He pushed the card toward Johnson. "Mrs. Foster Cole. They were very close, and I'm sure if the circumstances are explained to her she'll be glad to take the girls. I would run them up myself, but I have no car, of course, and my plane leaves in an hour." He checked his watch. "Less than an hour."

Johnson stared at the coffee he had not touched. He stirred the steam from it and the steam made him remember the bog where, thousands of years before, the dinosaurs had been at last sucked under, thrashing and roaring.

"Matter of fact," Temple was saying, "probably the most unemotional thing would be for me to leave now. I doubt if they'll even notice. There's the card."

He leaned out of the booth, glanced at the girls, and standing, cliented his voice. "As I say, you are due a merit badge. Will you tell her sister that as of the first of next month the checks will come to her?" He put a hand on Johnson's shoulder. "What is the Texas jargon? *Adios, amigo?*"

After Temple had gone and Johnson had not hit him, he sat in the booth. He felt so weak that he could scarcely put the card in his pocket and get to the girls and stand between them as they finished their sundaes, scraping with their spoons, and put an arm around each of them. What traveled from their bodies up through his arms was so alive and innocent that, looking round to see that no one was watching, he put his head down.

"You kiss me," he muttered. "Both of you."

"*¿Qué pasa?*" asked the older.

"Right now," he said fiercely.

"He bought us a sundae." said the younger.

So they kissed him and then, taking their hands as though they were walking on the beach together, he walked with them to his car. They did not ask about their father. In the car they helped him find Waco on the map. It was north of Brownsville, four hundred thirty-nine miles north.

Johnson planned as he drove. He would make Waco by midnight. The children could sleep in the backseat. Take an hour or two in Waco, then find a motel and be on his way to El Paso early in the morning. It would cost him only two days. Texas would be a fine place for them to live. When they were eighteen they would be beautiful in a blonde, leggy way and go to T.C.U. or Rice or S.M.U. and wave pom-poms and lead cheers at football games and bear no scars. He remembered Ohio State playing Southern Methodist his sophomore year and beating them. The little girls were very good. Johnson drove tirelessly. He sang "Carmen, Ohio" and "We Don't Give a Damn for the Whole State of Michigan" for them. He wondered what Irene Temple was thinking in the hotel room in Brownsville. He planned what he would tell Mrs. Foster Cole and what he would not. Out of the air-base country and the cotton country by now, he got them into the farming counties with names like Refugio and Lavaca where the cottonwoods were greening under a blue sky and the air, up from the Gulf, was spongy as the flesh of a woman. It was four in the afternoon and three hundred miles before the older girl asked where they were going.

"To Waco," Johnson said. "You're going to live with your mother's sister, Mrs. Foster Cole."

"Aunt Cole?" she said. "That's silly."

"Seems very smart to me."

"It's silly because she won't have us," said the younger.

Johnson was driving seventy and it took him half a mile to brake down and pull off the road.

"What do you mean she won't have you?"

"She just won't," said the older. "She and mother just hate each other.

Once last year Mother asked her for some money and she wrote back and said Mother had made her own bed. Aunt Cole gives us nothing, *más ó menos.*"

The stunning in Johnson's chest was like being hung up on the steering wheel in an accident.

"She's got to take you," he said.

He swung back on the road and put the car up to seventy as soon as possible.

"But she won't," said the younger girl. "Besides, we don't even know if she lives in Waco anymore. She's divorced. She might be getting married again and living in California or Utah or some place, that's what she said."

This time Johnson burnt rubber braking off the road. The car snaked dangerously in the soft dirt of spring. Lied to, he knew then that the woman did not live in Waco, that if he did find her eventually she, too, would lie, and he could go on driving them forever, around and around.

He sat for a minute, then started, but within a mile pulled off the road again. The nose of the car dropped and leaped as the suspensions took the shock.

What he remembered was the federal law against transporting girls across state lines, which probably applied to international borders and to girls regardless of age.

He sat for a minute, started again, reached fifty, and again had to stop.

They could have him for kidnapping. He had taken them from their mother even though she no longer had legal custody and no one would believe their father had asked him to transfer them to an aunt who had remarried and might be living in California or Utah or some place.

He switched off the engine and they sat amid the ticking sounds of the car cooling. The little girls studied him. He looked for police cars in the glass of the rear-view mirror which was tinted against glare and saw that he had chocolate on one cheek and marshmallow on the other where they had kissed him.

"Have you got a problem, *compadre?*" asked the older girl.

Johnson put his forehead down on the horn ring and closed his eyes.

"Do you want us to sing you an int'resting song?"

"I'm hungry," said the younger." And I'm never going to have any children, either."

Johnson addressed himself. I met these little girls in Mexico and did not like the life they were leading so I returned them to their own father who would not have them so I decided to give them a red-white-and-blue childhood in Texas where they could go to college and lead cheers, and I did all this because I am the last *simpático* person left in a world of *intensos.* It is a matter, his secret voice higher and higher, of mores and monsters and a disintegrating society. The only Indians you really care about are the ones who play in the American League and pray for many hits not fish. If you ever get out of this you will get married and settle down and be creative about spark plugs and be an innocent guy the rest of your life, Johnson boy, the only innocent in a treacherous world, but you are not going to get out because there is no out. I don't know what to do! he shouted silently. I can't go on and I can't go back. The truth is, he yelled inside himself, that society is shot to pieces and no single *simpático* person can save it and I am out here in the middle of Texas in the middle of a shot society with my mores and two mixed-up little girls not mine who have not even learned to read and write and I do not know what to do unless I take them home to Cleveland to my mother and ask her what to do!

One of the children put her hand on his cheek near the chocolate.

I will cry if she does that again. The chords in Johnson burst in dissonance. They do not know what to do about me either. I am twenty-nine years old but I will sure as hell cry because this is what you get for goodness.

The little girl touched his cheek again and he began to cry.

◆◆◆

Going to See George

We're all hairs in a hairy world.

Hold that thought.

For example, what a weird night. When did they drop the routine about how the future belongs to you, graduates, so get out there and fight-fight-fight? Our prize was a pep talk on culture. The United States is having a cultural renaissance—reading more books and buying more paintings and listening to more classical music—so while you're grabbing the future and exploding the population, class, also read and appreciate art and keep that stereo hot. We didn't even care who he was, the speaker, because he wore *white sox*. Speakers who wear white socks with dark suits can have *no* message. Besides, at that point, culture. It wasn't even pertinent. Anyway, we the senior class got our diplomas and a wet grip, then marched out in procession to "Pomp and Circumstance," then stood around under the palm trees with our parents, drinking icky punch and letting the folks work up a good proud glow. Finally they dispersed and we were on our own.

It's traditional on commencement night to stay in your caps and gowns and up all night, then assemble at school at six in the morning for breakfast and turn in your apparel. We were triple-dating, Jody and I and Liss, with

Previously published in *Esquire*, July, 1965.

Steve, Harold, and Bate, four in Steve's father's car, Harold and I in his new graduation MG, only it was used. We drove up on a mountain and caucused and drank Airconditioners and the boys smoked Crooks.

Airconditioners you make with vodka and Cointreau and any low-cal cola. You don't need ice and they're really cool.

Crooks are little cigars soaked in rum.

Nobody made out or sexed around because it wasn't actually a date. It was like the last council of six friends who'd been running the show for four years, and now the show was over. We just drank and smoked and discussed what colleges we were going to and how to avoid the draft and what kids were getting married rapidly to make it under the baby wire. And of course took in the view, which was *grandioso*. From up there, three thousand feet up, with California behind us, the whole city of Phoenix and our suburb, Scottsdale, blazing away below, and Mexico beyond them, we could see east for fifty miles, practically to New York. One thing about living in Arizona, you're remote from the masses. I mean, you're *out of sync*. From things like riots and segregation and traffic and poverty pockets you can be aloof. It used to be, back in the granny times, that the blood-and-thunder was out here, in the Old West. Now the settlers back East have all the action. Like now, we felt no pressure. It was only eleven o'clock and we had the whole rest of the night.

Then, on the next street down the mountain, which had some plush homes, right below us a swimming pool suddenly lit up with underwater lights and a man and a woman came out of the house with towels on, took off the towels, and went nude swimming.

Scottsdale's a very money suburb. I'll give examples. One, practically everybody has a pool and belongs to a country club and goes for Goldy Barewater. Two, little kids you mention food to think you mean leftover canapés. Also, some of their parents have been divorced and intermarried so often they have to wear dog tags to be sure of their current name. Three, every year the tennis pro at our club trying to sell sessions puts up a sign on his pro shop: "Give Mother a New Backhand for Christmas."

Only now the man and woman weren't swimming, they were playing intimate water polo. They didn't dream they had an audience. They stood in the shallow end with their arms around each other, producing waves. I don't know who they were or even if they were married and it *was* a hot night and their privilege and I don't want to rank them but it was pretty *mammal.* Because they were old, at least forty or fifty. We weren't exactly embarrassed but it made us nervous. At *their* age.

We switched agenda to what to do. Various ideas were cruising Phoenix offering to drag or floating down the irrigation canals in inner tubes, but they were no big things. On commencement night you should organize some big thing.

"How about the carts?" Bate said.

This was sneaking out to one of the country clubs into the shed where all the electric golf carts stood in a row with their tails to the wall, plugged in, getting their little batteries charged, unplugging some, and having a rally round the course. It was fun but risky. If there's anything that arouses the citizens of Scottsdale more than Communism it's harming our golf greens.

"I'm not in favor," I said. "Not tonight."

"Hey, got it," Harold said. "Let's go see George."

We girls hadn't the faintest what that was. The boys knew, but they were very *mysterioso.* They said going to see George was the thing to do in this era. They all had before and they guaranteed it was different.

So we hit the trail, Harold and I leading. Down the mountain and through Scottsdale and onto the main highway heading into Phoenix. It's an interstate with lights overhead in town and at this hour, around midnight, mostly trucks. Then Harold cornered off the highway onto the road to the Phoenix Zoo. Who goes to a zoo but little kids? Instead of following the road, though, he blacked out and swung into a two-track trail around the back of the zoo. It was real desert here. You had to go slow, between cactus and through dry washes. Finally he stopped and Steve and the others stopped behind us. We got out and the boys went up to a chain-link fence.

"Different, all right," Liss said.

"Thrill-thrill," Jody said sarcastically.

"Just wait a sec," Steve said.

We waited and suddenly heard a roar and something absolutely enormous came at the fence, at us, like a truck. If we hadn't had a limited buzz, we girls would have been scared out of our minds.

"George!" Bate cried.

. . .

Let me interpolate right here that the six of us weren't hoody drop-out types. We were nice, normal, responsible, middle-class kids from nice, normal, responsible, middle-class families. Upper-middle, actually. We'd been treated like adults by our parents. For example, they'd never locked up the liquor on us. And we weren't sloshed now, except maybe Harold. We'd just graduated and all of us were going to college. Every high school has to have a *cadre.* We'd been the leaders of the in-group. Two of us were on the Student Council and Bate was class president and Liss was a power in the pom-pom line and three of us were National Honor Society. Harold was an athlete, true, football and basketball, but he was no *monster.* For four years we'd sort of set the standards. In clothes and lingo and what role to play, et cetera. None of us had ever really been in trouble. As to goals and ideals and things, we were potential Peace Corps material.

What I am trying to communicate is, we were going to be the pillars of society, not the peons.

. . .

George hit the fence so hard it swayed, then backed off and whirled around and trotted away and whirled around again, facing us, snorting and stamping.

If you've never seen a bull buffalo coming at you, you haven't lived, especially at night. I mean, they're *splendido.* They weigh over a ton and are all shoulders and head and woolly and have small vicious eyes and big hooked horns and delicate rears and a beard. Also a short tail and when they lower their head and huff, the dust shoots up from the ground under their nostrils. And they're fast. They can really burn rubber. On the rampage, they put the fear of God in you or an awe of nature or something.

But when you've seen one you've seen 'em all, and we were ready to go.

Not Harold. He kept using the stick and getting George to charge. He took off his gown and shook it. "*Toro! Toro!*" And George, who was practically having a hernia by now, would aim at the gown and about knock the fence down. Harold would make with the cape and we'd cry "*Olé!*" I worried about the fence. It wasn't very sturdy here at the back of the buffalo yard where nobody was supposed to be.

We said let's go, but Harold had to have a big finish. He put his gown back on and stood erect and folded his arms and acted the grieving warrior. There are more Indians in Arizona than any other state and we're very conscious of them. "I am Cola-Low-Cal, chief of the Cointreau nation," he chanted. "My people are cut down. Our braves are dead, in their hogans the squaws and papooses weep. Our hearts are sick, sick. We will fight no more. The white man has killed all the buffalo but this baby. Now we have nothing to eat and nothing to cover our scrawny frames. So I will free the last buffalo, so that he may roam the plains of Disneyland. Okay, George."

He picked up the stick, scraped the fence, and got George revved up again. And this time he made it. He came on head down, stronger than ever, and hit that line like a fullback. The fence went over and he wallowed down onto his hump, then pawed up. We panicked. The girls screamed. But old George couldn't have cared less about us. Like a thundering herd, making chips and spraying pebbles and going huff, huff, huff, he really cut the scene.

. . .

Well, we came untaped. I mean, add it up. A cultural renaissance and swimming pool sex and now George on the loose in one night. About weird I wasn't jesting.

We stood around babbling about what to do till Bate said we should scout him and see where he went and then anonymously phone the fuzz and report a missing buffalo and if they didn't believe it, check the zoo. So we piled in the cars and backtracked onto the zoo road. We were torn.

"Harold, you stupid ass," I said. "You stupid, stupid ass."

"No sweat, we'll find him," he said, chewing hard on a Crook and wheeling the MG, but he was torn too, I could tell.

But just as both cars pulled onto the highway, all of us tied up in knots. Try to get the picture. Not a car in sight because it was about 1:00 A.M. Here was a huge tractor-trailer diesel truck barreling along under the lights in the far lane toward us with "Apache Line" in big letters. And down a little hill, head down and tail up, and across the highway George barreled and across in front of the truck. The driver really laid out the air brakes. They screamed and I screamed. A cloud of smoke went up from the tires and George disappeared in it and the truck shuddered and swerved off the highway. Harold with Steve following, U-turned across and pulled up behind the truck on the shoulder and parked. Just as we got out the truck driver jumped out of his cab.

"What in hell," he said.

Truck drivers are supposed to be brawny characters with hearts of gold who change our flat tires and know where the food is good, that's the cliché. But this one was a little man in a straw cowboy hat and a greasy undershirt and hair growing out of his armpits.

"Did you hit him?" we cried.

"Who?"

"George."

George *who?*"

"A buffalo."

"Don't tell me no buffalo. You drunk?"

"From the zoo," Jody said. "Over the hill there."

"Don't tell me *no* buffalo. Anything I hit I gotta report. Cows, camels, gorillas, Good Humor guys. What you dressed up as?"

"We just graduated," Liss said. "Tonight, from high school."

Bate took over. Once class president, *always* class president. "Listen, it really was a buffalo. It was our fault he broke down the fence and got out, and we were going after him. Usually we wouldn't say anything but we're pretty shook up ourselves."

The driver stood looking at us and our cars with his exhaust pipe going putt-putt-putt and then his face griped up and he took off his cowboy hat and waved it. "Hell yes I hit it. That's what I thought but I wasn't saying it! A buffalo!" He was bald and now blew his mind. He waved his ten-gallon and really ranked us. Rich kids. Rich, no-good, spoiled-rotten, fat-butt, rich kids. Once there'd been sixty million buffalo in this country and now they were practically extinct and he was partly to blame for clipping off one of the last of them poor damn animals. *We* were the ones should be in the zoo. If this was what money and education got you, he wanted no part. He was thirty-seven years old with a wife and three kids, he'd been driving long-line for fourteen years, keeping his nose clean, earning a living and now he'd murdered a buffalo. It was the worst thing he'd ever done, worse than hitting a person even.

Well, we aren't snobs, we're very democratic in fact, so we took it, the profanity and bad grammar and ranking. With the peons of the world you have to be tolerant. But finally Harold had had enough.

"Okay," he interrupted, "okay. We said we're sorry but you have to be a hard-ass about it. So we're splitting and you can hang it in your ear. Let's go, team."

But the driver was *furioso.* He jumped into the cab, turned off the diesel, and jumped out again with a baseball bat. "I carry this in case! You try to take off I'll beat your brains out!"

"Three against one," Harold said, flexing a set of his muscles. "We'll take you apart."

Bate and Steve moved up beside him and I thought, on top of everything else, we're going to have a brawl. What stopped it was the sound. With the motor off we heard this bellowing, hurting sound out in the desert, in the dark, not far away.

"Uii, uii, uii," whimpered the driver. "That buff's out there dying. I told you I hit 'im! Uii, uii."

"You're singing the sad song," Harold argued. "Go put him out of his misery."

That gave the driver an idea besides a trauma. "No, you. Yeah, you! I'll make you a deal. You take off, I'm gonna report you to the cops, you know that. But you go out there and finish off that animal, I seen nothing tonight."

Now Harold looked at us. "It's a way out."

"With what?" Steve asked.

"I got everything. He's half-dead anyway, you ain't even gonna get dirty. Here." He shoved the bat at Harold, then went behind his cab, opened a box or compartment and came back and passed out tools, Wrenches and parts of a jack, heavy iron things.

"Not the girls," Bate said.

"Yeah, girls too, everydamnbody. An' wait, you gotta have light." He went to the box and brought back what looked like a Roman candle on a pointed rod. "Take this flare." He struck a match and the flare blazed up, red and smoky and so bright it hurt our eyes. He handed it to Bate. "Get goin'."

We spun our wheels but we had no choice. It was either apply the coup de grâce or have that ding-ding of a driver inform the cops and have them hammering on our parents' doors like the Gestapo.

"Let's go, team," the armpit said. "You come out tonight t'have fun. Now you have it."

. . .

So the program was to stagger out into the desert, toting our weapons by the lurid light of the flare, and I mean lurid. In our caps and gowns and National Honor Society gold tassels. Some pomp, some circumstances. The last buffalo hunt by about seventy-five years. Just out of the cave, with clubs. Weird, weird. And did we ever care not to. Our air-conditioning had broken down. In the middle of the night and already we had a hangover. Liss started to cry. The boys were very chivalrous. They said they'd do it, we wouldn't even have to look. Back on the highway some cars went by, not even imagining. If they'd known what our mission was, we could have charged admission.

Well, class, we zeroed in on the prey not by the flare but first by the sound he made and second by smell. It was a cross between a sob and a huff. And if you've never smelled buffalo, you have a new nasal thrill coming. There's something raunchy about it, almost primeval. When we finally located old George he was on his last legs. That is, he was sitting down with his hindquarters, the delicate part of him, which must have been where the truck clipped him and broke his spine or injured him internally, folded under, and his huge front, hump and shoulders and head, sitting up on his hoofs like a one-ton dog. Harold planted the flare in sand so we could see. George looked like some creature out of a lagoon in a horror movie. He sat there crying blood. It bubbled out of his nostrils with every huff, like soap bubbles you blow when you're a child, and they popped and ran down his beard. He had a cute pointed tongue hanging out, again like a big dog. And those glaring eyes. And that odor. *History No.5.* You knew he hurt like mad, he was dying anyway, and all the boys were going to be was humane. So Harold took his stance and said something casual about the moment of truth and swung the bat. We girls meant not to watch but we forgot. He slugged old George with all his might beside the head. It broke one horn right off with a crack and George sort of belched and toppled over into a mesquite bush. Then, to make sure, Harold swung down on him again and Steve and Bate joined the party, wielding their tools. And then—and this was the shocker—Liss and Jody and I were kneeling and hitting him with ours on his shaggy hump and head so hard the dust flew out of him like a rug and blood spattered our gowns. All six of us letting old George have it. My advice is, if you've got frustrations and neuroses and complexes to work off, skip the couch and *try beating on a buffalo.* You can practically get rid of the whole twentieth century. And what was really radical, we weren't horrified or sad or urpy, we liked it, liked it, liked it.

Hold that thought.

◆ ◆ ◆

Death to Everybody over Thirty

My roommate has this white rat we call Bobby. It smells up the whole dorm but he's teaching it to drive a car for a term paper in his psych course. Friday afternoon I had Bobby out of the cage and into the battery-powered toy car, trying to get him to hindfoot the accelerator, when the phone rang and it was my father long-distance with a voice of doom. Curt Talbot was dead. In that morning's newspaper. Dead at nineteen, killed in Vietnam eight days before with the 82nd Airborne. Curt was already home, his body. It didn't really register so I said something stupid: "His body home in eight days?"

"They fly them."

"Oh." Then it registered. "Curt," I said. "No." I sat down on the bed. "What a bunch of grunt."

"What a what?"

"That's what he used to say, Curt, when he didn't appreciate something."

He went on. Memorial services were tomorrow afternoon, Saturday, followed by a military ceremony at the grave, and he wanted me to come home for them. I said *destroy the whole weekend for a funeral?* He said he'd been on the phone with Howie's father and Tom's and they agreed with him. If the army could fly Curt home, they, the fathers of his three best high-school friends, could fly them home to pay last respects. Therefore Howie was coming down from Berkeley and Tom up from Tucson, and I could be there by noon from L.A. It was the least we could do. Just then Bobby accidently hit the accelerator and the car ran him across the floor, knocking down over him my lacrosse stick. He panicked and jumped out of the car and got himself tangled in the gut of its mesh pocket. I explained I'd like to show for the events but this was a big weekend coming up, I was supposed to go with some buddies surfing at Doheny tomorrow and also Sunday I'd saved for accounting problems, that if I didn't raise my accounting grade my own draft board might be interested because now, with Curt checked out, the 82nd Airborne would have a vacancy.

A large silence. "My son, my son, Absalom, my son. Do you realize what you're saying? Where you and your friends would be if it weren't for boys like Curt? That there is *no* surf in Vietnam?"

Then I felt what I was supposed to feel: instant guilt. "Okay," I said. "Zing it in to me, I deserve it. I can be just as sorry for him in California as over there but I'll come. Will it be as bad as I think?"

"Worse. There but for the grace of God and a student deferment. And you'll have to confront his parents eyeball to eyeball."

"Super."

"Character construction."

"*Su*-per."

"Have a haircut. And bring a dark suit."

We hung up and I untangled Bobby and put him back in his smelly cage. He looked at me rodently and I could see his bongo heart right through his ribs. He'd never driven a car before. I'd never participated in a military ceremony before. Howie and Tom I knew wouldn't want to make the trek any more than I did. We hadn't even seen Curt since graduation over a year ago because he'd disappeared into the paratroops while we went away to school. But our fathers, from another war and overreacting, were probably right. It was the least we could do. Then my eyes filled because I suddenly remembered what else old Curt used to say. Something he didn't like he also called "laminated ratwhiz."

"They're flying me home this weekend, Bobby," I said. "Flying me home for a first-class mungering."

The next afternoon I met Tom and Howie at the mortuary and we lurked around by Tom's car, with its bumper sticker reading DEATH TO EVERYBODY OVER THIRTY. We were going to be the last ones inside and as anonymous as possible, although Howie was wearing a Homburg hat and carrying over his arm one of those British-type pencil-rolled umbrellas. An umbrella in Arizona with the sun shining. Besides demonstrators they rear a lot of conventional weirds at Berkeley, and besides, Howie was an English major. First we talked about cars. They both had transportation at school and I didn't.

Then about our weekends being down the tube.

Then about funerals. Tom had taken in one, his grandmother's, and Howie an uncle's, so they were veterans, but I drew a blank. They said the trick was not to fight a funeral, not to overreact. To be Bogart about it.

Finally about Curt. One, suppose it had been our names on the Viet Cong bullet and Curt had been on campus instead—he wouldn't have made it to our wakes either unless his father applied pressure. Two, we elected school and he didn't not out of patriotism but because his parents were divorced and the money wasn't there. Also, bravery wasn't why he picked the paratroops but the extra jump pay, which he could hoard and someday afford an education himself. In other words, a mercenary. Three, he'd been hosed. Four, it was life. Five, at least now he would never have term papers.

"A man can die, but once we owe God a death, travel now and you don't have to pay later Shakespeare," Howie said. "Let's pool our smarts. A pact? First tear buys the beer?" He stuck out his hand. "*No*body cracks."

"Nobody cracks," we said.

We gripped. But our palms were slimy. And our souls. Bogartly we marched into the mortuary.

That damned casket! Open! Following an usher with a long fake face down the aisle toward an opened casket with printed cards in our hands we stopped, bumping, milling. Panic. Turning and tangled in the gut of guilt and falling over our feet trying to flee that flesh up there which was ours and hiding in the back row like small, very vulnerable boys. Recorded organ music from softspeakers. A few people. Flowers around the casket. How in hell could it be open after eight days with Curt maybe mangled? Four middle-aged men in VFW uniforms marching down and lining up and one by one saluting old nineteen-year-old Curt. Saluting his remains. The printed card I'd mangled in my hand said "Private First Class Curtis M. Talbot Jan. 2, 1948 Feb. 7, 1967 'Blessed are they that mourn for they shall be comforted.'" Trying to put the card in my pocket and dropping it. Cut the music and a minister saying the right things such as supreme sacrifice on altar of country, defense of freedom, et cetera. Family in the front row. Mr. and Mrs. Talbot divorced but closing ranks for the occasion. Beside them Curt's little brother Collins who was big now and on the high school football team and in a couple of years a fine fodder candidate himself. Beside him his sister Sherry. Remembering Tom and Howie both dated her when she was sophomore so she had to be a senior now. Blonde and quite a queen. Nobody else our age. Three of us like a card section representing a whole generation. Bow heads. Pray. Amen and it was over and we had it made and now for a fast getaway from that flesh which was ours. But the reverend escorted the bereaved family down the aisle first. We had to wait. Then it happened. In black, Curt's mother recognized us and stopped and looked at us. Not crying or anything but sure as hell not blessing us. Her son's best friends and legitimate mourners but she was bestowing no comfort. The kind of a look someone would have if they were sighting a rifle in on the president of the United States. The look of a female assassin.

Destroyed. How we got out of that mortuary and into Tom's car at the tail end of the cortege I'll never know because we cracked wide open, pact or no pact.

A cortege crawls. In front was the family in a white limousine and behind them Curt in a white hearse. These vehicles are white in Arizona because white repels heat. And the tragedy was, it wasn't over, we still had to go through the military bit, so crawling along at the end of the cortege we put the pieces of ourselves together and started emotionally preparing for that. Bogart always hit back. Small, very vulnerable boys also hit back.

"Let's list the worst things we remember about Curt," Howie said. "Everybody participates."

"Well, he was no all-state in basketball."

"He dragged down about a C average."

"I personally pulled him through trig."

"His college boards were way low."

"No prayer for a scholarship."

“Or *any* good school. Some JC.”

“And his vocabulary. Bunch of grunt.”

“Laminated ratwhiz.”

“‘Iss’ for ice.”

“‘Eddel’ for gas.”

“‘Sucket beats’ for bucket seats.”

“Awful.”

“The type who’d wear a sport jacket to a funeral.”

“The immortal Private First Class.”

“Ranking sound no worse than cheers after earth has plugged the ears. A. E. Houseman.” Howie tapped Tom, driving, on the shoulder. “One more item. You lay it on the line, lad, and I will. We both dated Sherry when we were seniors. For your information, I made it with her. The ultimate. You?”

“All the way.”

Howie nodded. “I thought probably. And we weren’t alone. There you are. Everything else plus a pushover sister.”

“You bastards,” I said.

“Us,” Tom said. “Us *live* bastards.”

The military ceremony wasn’t as grim as I thought. The cortege parked and we waited till eight Air Force pallbearers in dress uniforms and white gloves unloaded old Curt and the mourners gathered around the grave, facing a color guard of four more Air Force guys with a flag and a bugle, then slunk up behind the group in order not to be noticed. We weren’t about to take the visual shaft from his mother again. It was quite beautiful there, with the palm trees and green grass and the mountains trembling, holding up the blue sky like a tent. Not far away a tractor with a scoop was digging another grave, and outside the cemetery the whole ingrate world was on its way to the supermarket. I wanted to step out and stop traffic and shout goddammit we’re burying a paratrooper in there so let’s have a few seconds of silence! I kept having irrelevant thoughts such as with the insurance money from the government that Curt’s folks would get they could have sent him to college. The minister said amen, the pallbearers with their white gloves folded up the flag and presented it to Mrs. Talbot, and the bugler blew Taps very mellowly, with a sort of Tijuana Brass effect. Then the three of us in our dignity and dark suits took off for the car. We'd done our duty and survived. Curt's ghost could now cool it. When all at once behind us it sounded like a scrimmage. We turned just in time to see Curt's little brother who was big now and wearing a sport jacket, Collins the football player, bearing down on us like a linebacker and crying. He tackled Howie. Tackled him! The Homburg flew off and they grappled around on the grass and people including the Air Force and minister and Curt's family were running toward us like Keystone Cops and Howie somehow got loose and started sort of fencing with Collins, holding him off by slashing with the point of his British-type pencil-rolled umbrella. I looked for an open grave to jump into and drape myself with dirt.

Later that afternoon I was vacuuming our swimming pool as a favor to my father. He sat on the patio wall, watching me. Tom and Howie had already flaked out back to school.

"Thank you," he said.

"What for?"

"Coming home, attending the services, cleaning the pool. I've been pondering. I promised you a car next year. Well, I've changed my mind, you can have it now. Anything up to four thousand dollars."

"Why now?"

"What happened to Curt, for one thing. For another, who knows how long they'll continue to defer college students. Gather ye MGB's while ye may."

The phone rang in the house. My mother had gone shopping so I sprinted in while he took over the pool. I came out like a fugitive and sat on the patio wall and watched him vacuum. I told him the call was for me from Sherry Talbot and she had asked me to take her out that night, not a date, just an arrangement to get her away from her house and the sadness. I didn't know what to do, what the hell was the protocol with the sister of a friend who'd been killed in Vietnam because his parents were divorced and the money for school wasn't there. So I said I'd call her back yes or no.

"I wouldn't know myself. What to do," he said. "Probably you have to."

"I'm full up to here of having to. And her voice scared me."

"Scared?"

"Whispering. But as though she's screaming inside."

"I wish I knew for you."

"I probably have to."

"You could talk to her but be thinking about a Mustang."

"About that car," I said. "Thanks but no thanks. Before today I'd have prostrated myself for one, but not now. Not until next year, not a damn day sooner. I will not have a car with blood on its wheels. I will not be mungered any more by anybody."

"A white GTO?"

"White," I said on my way to the phone, shaking my head. "White. My God."

I thought Sherry Talbot would immediately apologize for Collins making a stupid adolescent ding-ding of himself at the cemetery but she didn't. She met me at a corner near her house because her parents would have murdered her if they'd known she was going out with me, she said. Her father could be very violent. We just sat there. She really was quite good-looking and unhigh-school. But I still got danger signals. She didn't care to go to a movie or anywhere in particular so I took her to the Cowboy Go-Go, a drink-and-dance joint with a long Western saloon bar and a big nude oil painting behind it. For humor the nude was on a real sweatshirt reading DRAFT BEER NOT STUDENTS. I thought of going there because it's very dark except for the babes dancing in spotlights up in their cages. I showed my card and ordered a drink for myself and a Coke for her because she was only seventeen. We sat there and finally she asked how I could have an official Arizona ID card when I was only nineteen, and to make conversation I told her the complicated story. I'd bought it for $30 from Tom during Christmas vacation, who bought it from a fraternity brother at the University of Arizona who worked part-time for a mortician. Now and then they'd get a middle-of-the-night highway crackup case, with one of the deceased a young guy in his early twenties and in his wallet would be his ID card. The embalmer would slip it to Tom's fraternity brother for $20, who would then resell it for $30 to students with similar physical characteristics. Tom had one himself and had sold three others for $40 each, but made me a special price, being old buddies. The card never failed if when you showed it you held it by one corner with your finger over the photo because all they were interested in was the birth date. "So thanks to some hotrod I don't even know," I said, "I'm drinking. Thanks to some *corpse*."

I stopped. I heard my words. And even over the loud record I could hear her internal screaming. "Sherry," I said, "I have dropped my smarts. Am I ever stupid."

"Let's get out of here," she said.

I didn't even finish my drink. In the car I asked her where to. "Park me," she said.

"Park? You?"

This was it. But I was so vulnerable I had to do anything she asked. I started the car and drove about as expertly as old Bobby in his battery-powered toy car into a lacrosse stick. I drove us a mile into the desert to the Apache Rocks, a big circle of slab rocks placed upright in a circle by human hands where the Apaches are supposed to have tortured prisoners and gotten high on mescal and danced gruesomely. Sort of an aboriginal go-go but a prime place to make out because you had history plus entertainment. I parked away from the other make-outs and just sat there. Wondering what was coming next, my palms were as slimy as they had been outside the mortuary. Do your duty to your friends, I thought, and get destroyed. To your country and killed. Cast your bread upon the waters and you get back wet bread. She had a fine body and chewy lips and nice perfume but her name was wrong for the sister of a war hero. It should have been Camille or Hortense or something morbid.

"Sherry," I said finally, "what do you want? I came home. I mourned. I even turned down a new car my father offered me today on account of Curt. So will you please, please tell me what else?"

"I want us to," she said.

"To what?"

"Don't be dense. I want us to. Now."

"You're not serious."

But she was. She knew how boys talked about girls, she said, which meant that I knew about her and Tom and Howie year before last. So she wanted us to now, in the exact same place, to make it complete, his three best friends alive because he was dead also seducing his sister. It would double-damn us. We'd be double-damned the rest of our lives.

I gushed sweat. I said it wasn't that I didn't appreciate the offer because I did, I really did, she was very attractive and under any other circumstances I'd be prostrate with pleasure, but if there was anything I could skip at this point it was sex, that instead I wished just one human being would admit it wasn't our fault we were in school and not having Taps blown for us, it was the system. The mungering system dreamed up by everybody too old to have to go.

Sherry listened. Then she got out of the car and closed the door and said, "You won't. I thought you wouldn't. College men are so sensitive. I called Tom and Howie first, before you, to go out with them tonight because I owe them more. But they were already gone. So you're the one. I have a plan. Watch." She reached down with both hands and raised the hem of her skirt and ripped it all the way to the hip. Then she looked at me like an assassin. "Now. This is my plan. I'm going to walk home and tell my parents you attacked me. In their mood they'll call the police, or my father will kill you himself, or my brother. After Curt, you know which one of us the police will believe."

She started walking! To overreact this way I realized she was not only serious but insane, probably with grief.

"Very humorous, ha-ha!" I called after her. "The girl's supposed to walk home because she won't not because *he* won't! Ha-ha!"

She was disappearing. "You want guilt, okay, you've got it!" I called. "Any more guilt and I'll break my mind!"

I sat there cliffhanging from the steering wheel. Finally I pulled out, cursing down the road to find her. She crossed in front of me, walking cross-desert toward town. She was actually going to! Going home to zing me with a lie! I jumped out of the car and started after her in a state of shock, but I couldn't stop her because now I didn't dare lay a hand on her. I stayed about twenty yards behind, guiding on her blonde hair in the moonlight. It was like a night patrol in a war except for my shouting and her internal screaming.

"Pardon me for being vertical!" I shouted at her, becoming smaller and smaller. Reduced to a midget. Diminished to a helpless child. "Pardon me for using oxygen!"

Sherry Talbot stumbling on high heels ahead and me clomping along midgetly in my dark suit through the dark, we hiked, getting closer and closer to town and her parents and the police and her revenge and my statutory rape case. This was no dramatic act. She was going *through* with it. Unfortunately I started to cry. And I'd forgotten how to, not having in years. I sounded like somebody dying of pneumonia and at the same time eating popcorn out of a paper bag.

"What *else* am I supposed to do?" I bawled. "Walk barefoot over hot charcoal? Sack out on a bed of nails?"

We dodged through a grove of date palms.

"Crucify myself on a bed of cactus?"

We sloshed right into an irrigation ditch full of water up to my knees.

"Iss! Eddel! Sucket beets!" I yelled, still crying. "He had a terrible vocabulary!"

◆ ◆ ◆

The Ball Really Carries in the Cactus League because the Air Is Dry

Al hit one out when they played Cleveland in Tucson on Monday. Then they flew to Palm Springs on Tuesday and played California and he hit two out. Then they played Chicago at home on Wednesday and Al was in there the last five innings and felt like eighty years old and this was only March. But the Cubs sent some bean name of Hernandez trying to "pilfer second" as the sportswriters would write it and Al threw him out by two steps and not only that, hit another. Four over the fence in three days. Off good fastballs. Thinking that over in the shower took the lead out of his legs because he knew they'd also be thinking it over upstairs.

While he was dressing the guy from the local Chamber of Commerce that sponsored the spring training came around with the loot you got when you hit a homer at home. He got coupons for a necktie from a clothing store, a lube job from a gas station, a car wash, a haircut, and a steak dinner for two. It was maybe a little bush league but the donors went for it because when anybody on the ballclub homered the names of their businesses were read over the p.s. system, so the promo was probably worth the price.

Al thanked the guy and left the locker room. On the way to his car he

Originally published in *Esquire*, March 1, 1978. Also appeared in *Cosmopolitan*, April 1990.

autographed balls for some kids and a program for an old geezer who said he remembered Al from when he was catching for Detroit ten years ago.

"Detroit? I was never with Detroit."

"Hanh? You wasn't?"

"Nope. I been with this club ten years. Up and down between them and their farms. Burlington, Spokane, Valdosta—you name it, I been there."

"Up and down, hanh?"

"That's right, up and down," Al said. He gave the geezer back his program and knew he'd lost interest and would drop it in the nearest trash barrel.

In the club lot parked next to his Chev was the Italian sportscar owned by the bonus catcher he was supposed to instruct in the fine arts of keeping the pitchers happy and base runners honest and hanging on to all five fingers of his throwing hand. And incidentally the hundred thousand he'd gotten for signing fresh out of high school. To Al the car was unpatriotic. Play the great American game, drive an American car. And sexy. The front end of the Ferrari reminded him of a big boob with two nipples.

As he drove to the apartment the darkness shut down over the Arizona desert like a door. But the last of the sun lay red upon the mountains in the distance. They blushed the way Babe used to blush.

He went up to the apartment and onto the balcony, and just then the lights went on in the palm trees around the swimming pool and putting green and he could see Babe and the other three wives putting. What they did every day was sleep late and swim and lay around the pool and go downtown to shop and have lunch, then nap and swim and lay around the pool, then get dressed and have a drink or drinks and while they were waiting for their husbands, putt. They never went to the games. The new wives went to the games. These were married to two outfielders and the third baseman. They were ten-year wives and would rather putt. For dough. There were nine holes in the green and they'd bet on low score. Babe usually won even though she usually had a load on by now, which he could hear she did by how loud she laughed.

Al thought of making himself a drink, but when she came up she'd want another and him to have one with her and then another and by the time they went out to eat she'd have a snootful. So he stood on the balcony and listened to her laugh and watched the stars come out in a sky like a big black mitt waiting for the ball of the world. They flashed on suddenly, like signs. One star for the fastball, two for the curve. He still didn't think it very smart of him to let her come along in the spring. It cost. He got the apartment from the club, and $18.50 per diem for food, and they could eat on that, but the $50 a week walking-around money never covered her buying clothes and crap and his salary didn't start till opening day. No, she should be at home where she could booze it up just as good as here, maybe better, but cheaper. Al's legs were lead again. Oh, Babe, Babe, he thought, where the hell we going when the party's over?

When she came in from putting he was making them a drink. "Hi," he said. "Steak tonight."

"Whoopee."

"Listen, that's four in three days. They'll think that over upstairs."

"Sure they will. Then they'll send you down anyways and go with their hundred thousand."

"Maybe not."

"Then when their bonus baby starts cutting out paper dolls they'll bring you up again. Up an' down, up an' down, like every year."

"You have a nice day?"

"Only maybe he won't start cutting out paper dolls. Maybe he'll stick. Then where are you?"

"He's not ready."

"Famous last words."

"Upstairs they know he's not."

"He's nineteen an' you're thirty-six."

"They're not going with a catcher can't throw."

"Leave us pray."

"Here." Al gave her her drink and touched his glass to hers. "Here's mud."

"Here's t'his broken leg."

They drank.

"Give us a kiss," Al said.

She laid limp lips on him reluctantly. "He can hit, though."

"So can this chicken. Four in three days."

"Sure you can. In the spring. How many'd you hit last spring?"

"Twelve."

"An' how many on the season?"

"You know how many."

"No I don't."

"You should. A guy plays ball, his wife oughta know his record."

"You get a record, I'll know it. How many last season?"

Al sat down. "Ten."

Babe didn't. "Ten. About what I thought. Ten. My God. Twelve in four weeks in the spring an' ten on the whole damn season, when they count, an' what I wanta know is why."

"I told you."

"Tell me again. In plain English."

"Because the ball carries a lot farther out here because the air's dry. I mean, back home, with the muggy air, you hit one just as good it's a long out. So out here I hit twelve in four weeks and back there ten on the season and about twenty long outs."

"You mean," she said, drinking and thinking. "You mean there was a major league club in Arizona an' you was on it you'd hit thirty a year an' we'd be in the bucks on account of dry air?"

"That's right."

She had a piece of ice in her mouth and spat it back into her glass, thoo. "If that ain't the dumbest, damnedest alibi I ever heard. You expect me t'buy that?"

"Christ," Al said.

She turned her back on him and made herself another drink. "What'd the kid do t'day?"

"Up twice, singled twice."

"Ah-ha."

"And also threw into center field and two runs score. I told you, he can't throw yet. They steal him blind. I keep telling him, you gotta feel like you stretch out your arm and touch the guy on second's glove or the guy on first's and once you feel that you never miss. It's all in your mind, not your arm."

She turned. "Quit tellin' 'im."

“That’s my job.”

“That’s your job t’talk yourself out of a job?”

“Somebody showed me once.”

Babe blew on that one. “Showed you? Showed you what? How t’get a hunderd thousand out of high school? How t’pay off a mortgage? How t’knock up your wife? How t’be an up-an’-down second-string dumb-damn catcher hits two-two-nine for ten years?”

“Two-three-one,” Al said.

“My ass,” Babe said.

“Let’s go eat,” Al said.

“Steak,” Babe said.

“Free,” Al said.

“Free my ass,” Babe said.

He drove them past the ballpark about three miles out of Scottsdale in the desert to the OK Steak Corral and parked and they went in. Babe had to stop first to see the grave of the gunfighter in front, a mound of earth with plastic flowers and a Stetson at the head of the mound and boots protruding from the dirt at the foot. There was also a headboard which said HERE LIES LES MOORE KILLED BY A SLUG FROM A .44 NO LESS NO MORE.

“Al,” Babe said.

“What.”

“There ain’t actually anybody actually dead under there, is there?” She asked him every time.

“No. It’s for the tourists.” It was what he told her every time, but he wasn’t actually sure himself.

Al gave the waitress his freebie dinner ticket and they had another drink and ordered.

“You bastard,” Babe said.

“Who me?”

“Lookin’ at that girl that way.”

“Not me,” Al said. “Not with the best-looking broad in the place with me.”

“You bastard.”

They didn’t talk much while waiting because there was so much to see.

The restaurant was full of winter tourists and the ceilings were hung with thousands of neckties cut off at the knot by the waitresses if you wore a tie to dinner here and the walls were covered with thousands of business cards from all over the country. Everyone said the OK Steak Corral had a lot of color. Al found one card on the wall behind him that cracked him up. "Cooney Plumbing, Dover, N.J.," the card said. "Your Sewers Bring Our Bread and Butter."

The girl brought the meal and they ate like from starvation. The only dinner served was a two-pound cowboy T-bone steak, pinto beans, salad, and bread and butter. They started getting along better right away. There were three things, Al had learned, that sobered Babe up fast when she had a load on. 1. Steak. 2. Compliments. 3. Death.

Then they had coffee and she smoked. "Okay, okay," she said. "So what's gonna happen to us?"

"They'll keep me up," Al said. "Most of the year they will. They'll break the kid in easy. I'll work the tail end of doubleheaders and teach him. We got a knuckleballer over from Milwaukee, for instance, and he wouldn't know a knuckleball from his sister. Anyway, they'll keep me up. We're good for this year. One more."

"One more," Babe said. She sucked smoke like a vacuum cleaner. "Tell me the pension thing again."

"Again?"

"You want your piece tonight?"

Al groaned. "Okay. I start drawing at forty-five. Nine years to go. They figure it out on how many days you been in the bigs. You're up there four years and you draw two hundred a month. For life. That's minimum. They keep books on you, and outa my ten years I been up with the big club nearly five. Or will be by fall."

"So how much is that?"

"As close as I can figure, three-twenty a month."

"Three-twenty," Babe said. "God."

"Let's go, huh," Al said.

"Three-twenty," Babe said. "Jesus."

"Let's go, huh," Al said.

He left a dollar for the girl and they left the OK Steak Corral and walked by the gunfighter's grave and got in the Chev and started back toward town.

"'Your Sewers Bring Our Bread and Butter,'" Al said. "Ain't that something, though?"

"You sure we're set for this year?"

"Sure I'm sure. We're ahead in the late innings and they need defense they'll yank the kid and use me. I got a great arm. There's no better throw to second than mine in the league. They don't get cute on me, ever, they don't even lean the wrong way. I don't scare when they come in from third. I'm a rock."

"Okay, they keep you. After this year what? We got nine to go before the pension."

"Well, Ray's been after me to sell cars for him, you know."

"You selling cars," Babe said bitterly. "The best throw to second in the league selling cars."

"Why not?" Al said. "I'm not in no Hall of Fame. What else do I do?"

"Three-twenty a month. God."

"Not only do I sell cars, we get a cat."

"A cat?"

"I like cats."

"I can just see it—me sewing buttons or some damn thing and you playing with a cat."

"Home sweet home."

"Home sweet shit."

"Not only that, I want us to adopt a kid."

Al drove half a mile before Babe said anything. Then she said, slowly, "Not having a kid of our own can be the man's fault, not the woman's. I read that somewhere."

"I didn't say it was your fault."

"No, but that's what you think."

"No, I don't."

"You and your great arm, ha."

Al drove half a mile before he said anything. Then he said, slowly, "Let's bury the bone, huh. I love you. I'd like us to adopt a kid. Boy or girl, it don't matter to me. Whichever you say. Stay off the sauce you'd make a helluva mother."

Babe was silent, wrestling with the concepts of temperance and motherhood. The night was cold. Finally she snuggled up and put her head on his shoulder.

"You have a nice day?" Al asked.

"So-so. I bought some beads. On sale. Indian."

"That's nice. You win, putting?"

"A buck. I never lose."

"You did with me. Marrying me."

"No I didn't."

"I bet you thought you snagged yourself a three-hundred hitter."

"I didn't know from nothing about things like that. All's I knew I was marrying a ballplayer. Going where it's warm in the spring, your name in the papers, things like that. You know, glamoor."

"Two-three-one's not a bad average, lifetime."

"You're not kidding."

"Four in three days outa there—that's not exactly chopping wood neither."

"I don't believe it, Al. I mean, about the dry air."

"It's a fact."

"Unh-hunh. Get a violin."

"Hey," Al said.

"Hey what?"

"I'll prove it."

"What?"

"I'll prove it. I got an idea."

They were passing the ballpark. Al braked and pulled into the entrance and up behind the stands, and stopped in the club lot.

"We gonna neck?"

"C'mon," he said, opening her door. "C'mon, I'll prove it."

"You freaked out or something?"

"I just got one hell of an idea."

He took her by the arm to a gate in the chainlink fence, opened the gate with a key, and led her along the stands.

"I can't see. Al, what is this?"

"Your eyes'll adjust. Anyway, stand right here and I'll turn on the lights. Then you go on up the stairs and sit behind home plate.

"Al, you outa your mind?"

"Babe I got one hell of an idea. Give it a try, huh? Just stand here."

He felt for another key on his ring, unlocked a door under the stands, and went in. On a wall to the right were the switches. He pulled every switch he could find. They played semi-pro ball in this park in the summer, at night. Then he went into the locker room, turned on another light, grabbed one of his bats from the rack and a bag of fungo balls, and climbed the ramp from the locker room into the dugout and stepped up onto the field.

They had a good system. The park was bright as afternoon except for shadows in the outfield corners. In right center on top of the wall was the beer-ad scoreboard, and above the wall in left center were the fans of palm trees, and beyond the wall, beyond the light, out there scouting in the night, were the mountains. First he checked to see if Babe was behind home plate, which she was, standing and hugging herself against the cold and waiting on him like a mother on her adopted child.

"Write me every week," she said.

"From where?"

"The Funny Farm."

He frowned at her, then checked to make sure nobody else was around. Nobody was. Leaving the bat at the plate he trotted out to the bullpen beyond third, located the cord, and plugged it into the outlet. Then, as the cord unreeled, he pushed the Lambert-St. Louis pitching machine out to the mound. It was a big rig but it rolled easily on rubber wheels. He placed it carefully and trod the spikes into the ground for stability. The club used the machine everyday in the spring as an alternative to a lot of sore arms and usually stationed a rook or the batboy behind the netting to feed it. It would throw strikes or breaking balls, and he set it for strikes. Taking six balls from the bag he fed them into the v-tube, flicked the switch and heard the thing hum, and ran around the protective netting for the plate. He had twenty seconds. It fired at twenty-second intervals.

He grabbed the bat and some dirt and wiped his hands on his sportshirt, but before he could dig in the first ball came through the hole in the netting like a cube of ice spat into a glass. Thoo. Past him to the screen.

He looked back at Babe and dug in and waggled the bat and cocked it. Thoo. It was low and away but he swung and topped it foul down the first-base line.

He dug in deeper. Thoo. Low and away again but he swung from the heels and missed and nearly ruptured a disc.

He stepped away from the plate and walked back to the stands. Babe was sitting now and leaning back and pretending to eat peanuts.

"Oh and two," she said.

Thoo.

"Two and oh," Al said. "It's supposed to throw strikes."

"They look good to me," Babe said.

"They're low and away," Al said.

Thoo.

"Busher," Babe said.

"Goddammit," Al said, turned, dropped the bat at the plate, and headed for the machine.

Thoo.

He let the damn thing go on humming and took his time resetting it, raising the spikes, pushing the machine a hair higher on the mound, and aiming through the hole in the netting to line it up dead center of the strike zone. From here his wife looked very small behind the screen in the empty stands and he thought *oh Babe, Babe, what'll we do when we have to pay to get in a park?* Then he stomped the spikes down, fed another six balls into the v-tube, sprinted for the plate, grabbed the bat, for the fun of it pointed at the left-field wall the way Ruth did that series in Chicago in the old days, and dug in deep. He was sweating. He could see his breath in the cold and hear his heart chant.

Thoo.

Down the pipe. He swung and got good wood on it, and the ball sprang off the bat like something alive and soared on up through the light and over the left-field wall between two palm trees right where he'd pointed.

He didn't even look back at the stands. He cocked his wrists and waited.

Thoo.

Down the pipe and he was loose now and had his timing and hit it over the wall in left center.

Thoo.

Like a white bird winging through the light and close to the left-field foul line but fair, fair, and out of there.

Al quit while he was ahead. Three out of five. She had to be a believer now.

He dragged the Lambert-St. Louis back to the bullpen and put away the bat and fungo balls and cut the parking lights and got Babe, and they got in the car and drove to the apartment and were in the living room with a light on before she opened her mouth. She sat down and looked at him like a long putt.

"You conned me," she said.

"About what?"

"The dry air. That show you put on, three out of five. You just lucked out."

Her putt dropped.

"That's right," Al said.

"You oughtn't do that to me, Al."

"I know it. But I ain't really a rock. I get scared sometimes."

"But why'd you con me?"

He sat down. "Listen. We been married fourteen years. It's about time we find out if it's for real. If we're gonna make it. I told you, Babe, I love you. The way you are. Even when you're in the bag. And I'll do any goddamn thing to make you love me the way I am. Even selling cars."

He waited.

"A kid," she said.

"A kid," he said.

"A cat," she said.

"A cat," he said.

She looked away at the mountains.

Al went in the bedroom, hoping she'd follow him, but she turned on the ten o'clock news. He sat on the bed in the dark and after a while shut the door and turned on the lights and stripped down to the raw. Then out of the closet he got the cowboy hat and cowboy boots he wore in the parade opening day each spring and under the bed found one of her dress boxes and tore it apart and using one of her lipsticks printed a sign on the white bottom. Then he put on the boots, lay down on the bed on his back, put the sign on his chest, and covered his face with the hat.

Babe came in. First she saw him bare-assed and out on the bed like dead and second the sign printed in purple lipstick which said—

HERE LIES AL
YOUR LOVING COOKIE
DYING FOR A LITTLE NOOKIE.

He thought she'd laugh. Instead she cried. Babe cried taking off his boots and hat and sign and her clothes, and cried laying down beside him, and cried she swore to God she loved him the way he was and would be, no matter what, and even with the lights on they played the longest, strongest, most beautiful doubleheader of their entire married life. True love had a lot to do with it. So did the protein, probably.

◆◆◆

Mulligans

Dottie got a call from Madge, inviting her to dinner at their country club because she, Madge, said she planned to ask her, Dottie, a very special favor, and since she wanted it to be good and dark when they finished dinner, would eight o'clock be too late? Dottie said no, of course not too late, and thanks, but when she hung up she thought *oh-oh.*

They met at the club, wearing summer prints, and Madge ordered a double martini and asked Dottie to please have one, too.

"I haven't had a double mart in a dog's age!" Dottie protested, thinking *oh-oh* again. "I'd be blotto!"

"No you wouldn't," Madge said. "Just tiddly, which is just what I want. So we'll be brave."

"Brave?" Dottie looked at her.

Madge looked away, out the windows at the lights of Phoenix opening like eyes in the mascara of dusk. They both had double martinis and then singles and went into the dining room. "Tiddly is right," Dottie said. "I hope one of us knows what we're doing."

"Trust me," Madge said.

Dottie did and didn't, trust her. They were both widow members and said hi at parties, but until they bumped into each other at the bank last month that was as far as it went. Madge didn't know thing one about how to clip municipal bond coupons, and Dottie was an old pro. They took their safe-deposit boxes into the same booth and Dottie showed her how and they became friends using the shears, though there was a small age difference. And there was another difference: financial. Madge's box was twice as big. Dottie's broker's eye told her it held at least half a million in securities, whereas Ray had squirreled away only a quarter-million for Dottie. And there was a third difference. Madge was a new widow. The black button on her box, signifying Harvey's demise, had been removed only recently she said, but Ray had passed on to his reward two years ago. That was why Dottie decided to wait and see about Madge. She'd learned the hard way about new widows. If they made it the first year they were usually okay. She had. Thrived in fact. But new widows could also go off the deep end. Crazy as bedbugs.

They had snow crab and wore bibs and clinked white wine glasses and cracked legs and claws and spattered butter and talked about their grandchildren sleeping around and cars. Madge was still truckdriving Harvey's Fleetwood and hating it. "Get rid of it," Dottie advised.

"Well, I would, but Harvey adored it so."

"Ray left me a Mark V. A week later I traded the damn thing in on a darling Mercedes."

"Harvey would turn over in—"

"Harvey's gone bye-bye, Madge, and the sooner you face it and adjust, the better."

"I'm trying."

"Try *harder.*"

"I'd love to take a cruise," Madge said. "To the South Seas or somewhere. Harvey never would. 'If they had nine holes and a putting green on a ship,' he'd say."

"Ray's words exactly."

"That's where Inez and Chris are now, my best friends. They begged me to go, but I felt it was too soon, that it would look—"

"I went on one last year. The shopping in Hong Kong you wouldn't believe."

"If either of them were here, Inez or Chris, I'd have asked her tonight.

But they aren't, and I was desperate. Dottie will know, I said to myself. She knows how to clip coupons, so she'll know how."

"How to what?"

"Don't make me tell you yet, Dottie, please. I'm nervous enough. If I do, you might not." Madge looked away again, out the windows, but it was dark now. "I think I'll have some cheesecake."

Dottie thought *oh-oh* again. That's another sign, when they start having dessert. The next thing, she'll be talking to Harvey when she's home alone.

But the next thing was even crazier. Madge signed the dinner bill, ordered two more double martinis to go, in plastic glasses, then left the clubhouse, said no to the car parker, and led Dottie to her Cadillac, where she had Dottie hold the martinis, heaved something in a paper bag out of the car, something heavy, and informed Dottie she wanted to steal a golf cart—well, not steal one but borrow one for awhile. Dottie was speechless.

"That's why it had to be dark," Madge said. "You drive the cart to where they start—the first tee. Then I'll tell you."

"Good Lordy," Dottie said.

They stood in silence a moment, then walked doubtfully along the road behind the clubhouse. Once, Dottie said, whispering, when Ray was trying to sell her on golf, she'd ridden around the front nine with him, and driven the cart, but what a bore. Compared to duplicate bridge. They reached the shed and light and there were all the club's E-Z-Go carts plugged into Lester Power Chargers like little three-wheeled pigs with black tails sucking electricity from the Arizona Public Service sow. Dottie unplugged the one nearest the door, they set the double martinis in the drinkholders on the dashboard, stowed Madge's heavy paper bag on the floor, and got into the two seats under the canopy, Dottie behind the wheel.

"I've never driven one of these things, but if they can, I can. Let's see. Accelerator and brake." Dottie placed her feet on the pedals. "Here's the shift—neutral, forward, reverse." She raised her plastic glass. Madge raised hers.

"If you drink, don't drive, ha," Dottie said.

They drank. Dottie took hold of the lever between the seats, pulled it into reverse, backed the cart slowly, noiselessly out of the shed, shifted into forward, and steered them up the road, gaining speed with confidence. She zipped through an opening in an oleander hedge, clipping off a lash of leaves, wheeled over a petunia bed onto a blacktop cartway down the hill past the clubhouse, and braked to a stop by the pro shop. "How 'bout that?" she demanded, taking her glass and toasting herself. "Dottie the Dragster!"

Madge caught her breath. "My stars!"

"That's the pro shop. Over there's the first tee. Madge, you should see it, when they start. They march down here like a brass band and the carts are lined up for them, clubs already loaded. They tee off and they cheat—if they don't get a good first drive, they say 'Mulligans' and take another whack. Then off they go in their carts like big fat pooh-bahs riding on elephants, smoking cigars and some even chewing tobacco. And they take it seriously!"

"How much does a cart cost?"

"Twenty dollars a round. Eighteen holes."

"My, that's high."

"A drop in the bucket. Then add clothes, shoes, clubs, balls, bags, lockers, tips, bets—it's a small fortune every year. Don't worry, my dear, Ray and Harvey didn't die in debt to themselves."

"I never realized how much it—"

"I don't intend to, either. Die in debt to myself. And don't you. I know you're well fixed, I saw that safe-deposit box." Dottie leaned back, then sat up suddenly. "Say, you were going to tell me. If you don't mind, what in the world are we doing here?"

"Oh, Dottie."

"Have a drink, Madge."

They had one.

"Now," Dottie said.

"The paper bag," Madge said.

"The paper bag."

"In the bag is an urn."

"Oh my God."

"Yes. Harvey's ashes. That was his last request. Until I called you I thought I'd never get up the courage. They just sat there on the mantel, staring at me. Two years ago he hit a hole-in-one on Number Sixteen. He said it was the high spot of his life. So he asked me to strew his ashes in the sand trap on the right side of the green on Number Sixteen."

"Oh no."

"That's why it had to be at night, dark. I've never been on a golf course in my life."

"Oh no."

"Please help me. I beg you."

"Have a drink, Madge."

They had one.

"What's it look like?" Dottie asked. "The urn."

"It's bronze, and round, with a lid. It weighs almost ten pounds. Do you want to see it?"

"I do not. It's unspeakable of a man to ask a wife to do something like this. Why couldn't he just be buried? I planted Ray and that was that."

"Well, he loved golf."

"Damn golf." Dottie left the cart, went to the pro shop, took something from a wooden box on the wall, and returned with it. "A scorecard. With a diagram of the course. Number Sixteen must be on the back nine, where I've never been, and so dark you can scarcely see your hand before your face. Damn. Anyway, the tenth tee's over there, must be, because both nines start here. We can follow the diagram." She fastened the scorecard to a clip on the steering wheel. "Tiddly hell. I've got to be stinking to do this." She raised her glass. "Cheers, Madge."

"Oh Dottie."

They found the tenth tee and off they went down the middle of the fairway. The night was fetid, there was no moon, but low stars burned like candles and they could see well enough. Dottie angled to one side of the tenth green. "I remember now—there's a cartway around each green to the next tee. What I'd rather do is gun this thing and drive right across their precious green and tear hell out of it."

"Dottie you don't mean it."

"Oh yes I do." She whizzed along the cartway toward Number Eleven tee. "I've had just enough booze to be truthful, Madge, and the truth is, Ray was an old goat. The last three years, that is. For thirty-three years it was a fantastic marriage, but the last three he really pooped out on me. No consideration. He played this course six days a week while I sat home twiddling my thumbs. Then when he came home he'd have a snootful and watch the television news and carry on all evening, ranting and raving about the state of the world. Really lovely to live with. So when he went, just between us, I wasn't sorry—not this chicken. I've been a golf widow most of my life. Now it's *my* turn to howl."

"Dottie, how can you sit there and—"

"I don't care." Dottie stopped the cart at Number Eleven tee. "Most of his stocks had doubled and tripled, but would he sell? Not Ray. Didn't want to pay capital gains, and besides, what would he do with the money? Take me on a cruise, I'd say, and he'd say 'If they had nine holes on a ship'—you know."

"Harvey's words exactly."

Dottie had a drink. "You've got to lay the ghost, Madge. It took me a year, but finally I realized Ray wasn't coming back to bitch about the world and his prostate ever again. Then I finally laid the ghost, finally I was free."

Madge was silent as they started down the eleventh fairway, but two hundred yards from the green she hissed "Dottie! What's that?"

A flashlight winked near the green.

"The night watchman," Dottie said. "They patrol the course every night. Vandalism. Sssshh. I'll just scoot behind those trees."

She scooted them behind a row of eucalyptus until the watchman carted by, but before she could get underway again Madge burst into tears. "Oh, Dottie," she wailed, "I'm sorry, I can't help it, but I was wretched, too—simply wretched!"

"Let it all hang out, dear." Dottie took them onto the fairway and lent a sorority ear while Madge unburdened herself.

"Harvey was a dear for forty years—an absolute darling. Then the last four—I don't know what happens to older men. He nitpicked my clothes, my makeup, my hairdos, everything, and at parties he contradicted me and repeated himself and carried on about inflation and our grandson's long hair and the Democrats—oh, he was impossible!"

"Par for the course." Dottie stopped the cart at the Number Twelve tee and gave Madge her glass. "Here, let's polish these off, they're getting watery."

They polished them off and Dottie pitched the plastic glasses onto the tee. "There you are, boys—tee up on those tomorrow!" And she sped them down the fairway, crying "Yahoo! Ride 'em, cowboy!"

Madge continued her tale of marital woe, which, as they passed an artificial lake, she entwined with a tragedy of ducks. "We had separate bedrooms—he said I snored. We were playing bridge, my Tuesday group, and someone had the idea—we have this dear little lake on the course, why not have some dear little ducks on it? But *he* was the one who snored. And about once a week while he was reading the paper he'd get this insane idea. We thought it was a sweet idea, so we had the manager buy two dear little ducks and a drake and put them down here by the lake. 'The country's going to hell in a handbasket,' he'd say, 'and we're getting out, Madge. Pack up, Madge, we're selling out and moving to New Zealand.' 'New Zealand!' I'd say. 'Why, Harvey, why?' Or it would be Switzerland or South America or somewhere. 'Pack up, Madge!' he'd shout, and have me in tears half the night. But the most terrible thing, three days later all they found was feathers. 'Pack up, Madge!' Can you imagine, every week? Coyotes. The poor little things! 'Pack up, Madge!'"

"I'm drunk," said Dottie.

"Oh so am *I!*"

"Smashed."

"Coyotes."

"Oh my God, what now?"

The E-Z-Go cart had stopped midway of the thirteen fairway.

"What's the matter with it?" Madge asked.

"Out of gas—I mean power. I know what happened. This one was used right up till six o'clock or so, and then only had two or three hours of charging until we took it. They charge them all night. So the battery was low to begin with. Wouldn't you know."

"Whatever will we do?"

"Walk. What else?"

"In the dark?"

"Shall we call a cab?"

"But the coyotes!"

"If they attack, hit 'em with Harvey. The urn, I mean. Come on, you bring that and I'll bring the scorecard." Dottie got out of the cart and squinted at the diagram. "We're on Thirteen, we'll just follow the fairway. If only I had my reading glasses."

Madge got out, hoisted the paper bag, and they started toward the green. They located it without difficulty, and the Number Fourteen tee.

"My feet are killing me already," Dottie groaned. "I'm taking off my shoes."

"What about snakes?"

"You mean Ray and Harvey?"

"Oh, Dottie." Madge removed her shoes.

Dottie carrying both pairs, Madge the paper bag, they stumbled into a sand trap on Fourteen. "How about here?" Dottie challenged.

"What hole is this?"

"Fourteen."

"No, he distinctly said Sixteen."

"Dammit, Madge, sand is sand. How would he know?"

"He'd know. Harvey'd know."

"Pardon my language, Madge, but screw Harvey."

"Dottie!"

"I'm sorry." Dottie sighed. "Come on, only two holes to go, thank God."

Fifteen was a long par five, with a dogleg to the right, and they were just rounding the dogleg and complaining about their girdles when they were slapped almost to the ground by a whirling propeller of water. They screamed, they staggered onward only to be assaulted by another blade. They seized each other and reeled between several propellers of water to the rough.

"Oh! I'm soaked!" Madge wailed.

"The sprinklers!" Dottie wailed. "They water the damned course at night, of course!"

"The bag!" Madge peeled shredding paper from the urn.

"Damn the bag!" Dottie coughed. "What about my hair? What about my dress?" She waved two pairs of sandals at Madge. "Madge, I will not go one step further! I've done all that a friend can be asked to do! Now I've taken care of my deceased old lech and you can take care of your own deceased old lech—because in case you don't know it he was! They both were!"

"Dottie, how dare you!" Madge cried.

"Madge, don't be an idiot! Why do you think they went to Las Vegas every year for the Western Seniors? To play golf? Golf, my foot! They went for the hookers! And I know because Helene Donnell told me because her husband told her!"

"Oh no."

"Oh *yes!*"

"Oh no."

"Oh yes. I'm not going one step further. You can see the lights of the club from here and I'm cutting cross-lots and you can come with me and try again some other night with Inez or Chris or you can stay here till you push up the daisies yourself, but I've had it. Well?"

"I'm coming," Madge said.

"Then shake a leg."

They picked a path through a stand of saguaro cactus and walked wearily, tearily, blearily down the edge of Number Seventeen fairway, keeping to the rough to avoid the sprinklers.

"His stomach rumbled," Madge said.

"Whose?"

"Harvey's."

"Lordy, it's good to see the lights. My head aches, my corns hurt, I'm shot, shot. Bless the club. I feel like a lost lamb coming in to the fold."

"Harvey, you bastard," Madge said.

Dottie clapped her on the back with a shoe. "Attagirl!"

"I've never used that word before in my life."

"You're going to be all right, Madge. I thought *oh-oh* at first, but you'll make it. I tell you, women have to tough it out. We outlive them by eight years on the average, so we have to plan. Have you thought of marrying again?"

"Heavens, no."

"Why not? Mulligans—if you don't make it the first time, have another whack. I'm looking all the time. But somebody younger."

"Harvey, you bastard," Madge said.

They came up Eighteen and neared the clubhouse, Dottie lugging the shoes, Madge hugging the bronze urn. "Whatever will we do now?" Madge despaired. "We can't go through the club looking like this, and if we go around outside, someone will surely see us."

Dottie stopped. "I know. We'll go through the Men's Grill and their locker room. I've always wanted to see their locker room."

"I wouldn't dare!"

"Haven't you heard of Women's Lib? Come on—who'd be in there at this hour? Then we can go out the side door to the parking lot. Let's go!"

They sneaked into the Men's Grill, which was on the lower level of the clubhouse, and surveyed the bar and tables with checked tablecloths. On the walls were mounted the heads of African animals. Air-conditioning and the musky, male smell of the room gave them gooseflesh. They shivered.

"This is where they play gin rummy and poker afterward and drink," Dottie whispered. "For fantastic stakes. Ray often lost several hundred dollars a week. I wormed it out of him. Did Harvey play?"

"I think so. But he never talked about it."

"Of course not. Bastards."

On soggy stocking feet they padded through the Grill and entered the locker room and squinted down the aisle between the rows of lockers to be sure they were alone.

"Coast's clear." Dottie sniffed. "It even smells nice. I thought it would reek of dirty socks and crotches. Say, while we're here, let's use their biffy. I need to repair the damage."

"Dottie, I'm scared. You know we shouldn't be in here. What if we're caught?"

"Pooh. What is it—sacred?" She led the way down the aisle toward a bright light, peeked through a door, said "Oooooh!," and walked in, Madge following timidly. "Oooh, look at this," Dottie marveled. "The throne room!"

The room was immaculate. Walls, floor, and ceiling were tiled in pastel green. Along a wall were six stall showers and six toilet cubicles and six urinals. Facing these were twelve pastel green washbowels with gold fixtures below a fairway of mirror. Over the washbowls, laid out on snowy linen towels on a shelf, was a beauty-salon assortment of lotions and shave creams and hairsprays and soaps and tonics and footpowders and anti-perspirants and mouthwashes and aspirin and stomach-soothers and bandages and cornplasters and electric razors and hot combs and sunburn preparations and denture glues and lip chaps and hand creams and colognes.

"My God," Dottie said. "The women's locker room is a dump, compared. I told you—they *never* die in debt to themselves." She dropped their shoes in a washbowl. "*Look* at my hair. Fifty-dollar tint down the drain."

Madge was goggling at the display on the shelf. "Heavens to Betsy!"

"Well I'm not losing a kidney, too," Dottie said. "Pardon me, dear."

"I will myself," Madge said.

They entered adjoining cubicles, and when they flushed and came out went to the bowls to wash their hands. Madge dropped something thuddy in a wastebasket and turned on the water.

"What was that?" Dottie asked.

"What?"

"In the wastebasket."

"Oh. Empty urn."

"Oh."

They washed their hands and were using linen towels when Dottie froze. "The empty urn!" She stared at Madge. She turned her head toward the cubicles from which they had just emerged. She stared again at Madge. She stepped backward until she had the tile wall close behind her. "Madge, you *didn't.*"

Madge dropped her towel in a wastebasket. "Yes, I did," she said.

Dottie braced her back against the wall and began to slide slowly, inch by inch, toward the floor. Suddenly she began to laugh. "Oh my God, my God!"

Madge began to laugh. "My own hole-in-one!" She rushed to Dottie and embraced her, and laughing, dying laughing, they collapsed together down the wall.

"Hoo-hoo-hoo!" Madge hooted. "I made up my mind—Harvey, I said, I'm not going out on that awful course of yours again!"

"A straight flush!" Dottie gasped. "Hee-hee-hee!"

They were on the floor now, sprawling, clutching each other, tears rolling down their cheeks, helpless with terror and laughter.

"Mulligans!" Madge squealed.

"Mulligans!" Dottie shrieked.

Movin' on Out

We're movin' on out.
Read the obits:
"World War II Army veteran,"
"World War II Navy veteran,"
"World War II Air Force veteran,"
"World War II Marine veteran."
Every day's paper
a few more of us
take silently off into
the small print.

Wish us well.

Once we were sweet-cheeked
and flat-gutted and twelve
million, counting Kilroy.
We got drafted and went
to war whistling.
It was one hell of a fight.
More of us came home

than didn't, and you
called us
heroes.
Maybe.
But we won, didn't we?
Aren't Americans supposed to?

Stateside again, we reassembled
our lives like M1's and
looked around for
targets of opportunity.
Here's what we did:
married;
fathered;
worked;
voted;
paid taxes;
pledged allegiance;
and watched the country
listen to latrine lawyers
and lose a couple and
kept our GI mouths
shut.

Now we grow gray hairs
in our ears.
Wear funny caps and fire
Springfields over graves.
Try to keep step in
parades and fall over
with cardiacs.

So.
Time to move on out.

In the obits every
day a few more
of us go over the
hill into
history.

Listen:
we're glad we went
and proud we won
because
winning's
a damn sight better than
losing.

The U.S.A. forgot that.
Twice.
But now some new heroes
have kicked it back into
our butts.
Bless them.

And us.
You may never see our like
again except in old footage
on TV.

Wish us well.
Wish us well.

Glendon Swarthout,
3rd Infantry Division

Afterword

Afterword

When my father died on September 23, 1992, it was the biggest blow of my life. His lungs finally gave out that morning after he had barely been able to get out of bed, and in a way, it was almost a blessing. Glendon had depended upon my mother's support as his emphysema grew progressively worse, and for the last six months of his life he had been on oxygen assistance nearly full time. It was heartbreaking to see a world-class storyteller cooped up in a townhouse, unable to summon the energy to communicate with the outside world for more than a couple of hours on his best days, and then only for a little time on the telephone or a brief bout with the old Selectric.

Yet Glendon did it to himself, by beginning to smoke while in his teens. He was unable to win a $500 wager with his father that he could go a whole year without smoking by the time he was twenty-one. I won the same bet from him. World War II reinforced dad's sole bad habit, what with the assistance he received from the tobacco companies, who strung out a whole generation of GIs with their gifts of two free cartons of cigarettes (unfiltered) a month to each of our soldiers overseas.

Thereafter Dad was hooked for good and came to feel he couldn't write without a pack-and-a-half's worth of nicotine assistance daily. He was otherwise healthy, but begged his doctors to allow him to continue smoking so he could complete his final manuscript. And since our family doctor smoked, too, what the hell? Glendon finally did manage to quit smoking the last six years of his life, but by then the damage was done. Emphysema knocked at least five extra years off his seventy-four, his pulmonologist estimated. I once asked him later in his life if he had any major regrets. "Only one," Dad replied. "That I wasn't able to quit smoking much, much sooner."

Great artists live on through their works, and Glendon Swarthout was so gifted that he will be remembered and read longer than most. He was twice nominated by his publishers for the Pulitzer Prize in fiction, for *They Came to Cordura* (Random House, 1958) and *Bless the Beasts & Children* (Doubleday, 1970), both of which were bestsellers and subsequently made into fairly good motion pictures. Yet it was probably the very commerciality of his stories that kept my father from greater acceptance by the more literary of the critics, who often dismiss linear plotting and honest, uncomplicated storytelling, as well as interest from Hollywood, out of hand. *Bless the Beasts* evidently went right down to the wire with James Dickey's *Deliverance* among the Pulitzer committee in its year, but the fact that both books had already sold to the films didn't help. The judges chose not to award a prize for fiction in 1970, finding no entry of suitable quality, and his second miss at a Pulitzer was probably the biggest disappointment of Glendon's career.

Yet awards and recognition came anyway. He won a Gold Medal from the National Society of Arts and Letters in 1972 for the body of his work, and the Owen Wister Award for Lifetime Achievement from the Western Writers of America in 1991 for his superb Western novels. Two of them, *The Shootist* (Doubleday, 1975) and *The Homesman* (Weidenfeld and Nicholson, 1988), won the Spur Award for the Best Western Novel of their respective years from the Western Writers of America, and the latter also won the Wrangler Award from the Western Heritage Association, affiliated with the National Cowboy Hall of Fame in Oklahoma City. *The Homesman* was the only novel to pull off this dual sweep of the major Western genre awards in fourteen years, since the great Elmer Kelton did it in 1974 with his masterpiece, *The Time It Never Rained.*

It was the films of his novels which brought my father fame, fortune, and a much wider audience. His novel-to-film sale ratio was phenomenal—of his sixteen published novels, eight have sold to the movies and others have been optioned, in some cases several times over. *Seventh Cavalry*, based on the fine short story "A Horse For Mrs. Custer," found in this collection, was Glendon's first sale. Released in 1956, it was the first film to deal with the aftermath of Custer's defeat by the Sioux. *Seventh Cavalry* was one of Randolph Scott's two-a-year "B" Westerns for Columbia Pictures, but it turned out to be one of his best smaller Westerns. Backed by a good cast of Hollywood character actors (Barbara Hale, Jay C. Flippen, Jeanette Nolan, and Frank Faylen), Scott portrays a cavalry officer who must prove during the military investigation and months-later reburial of the fallen Seventh Cavalrymen that he personally didn't desert Custer at the Little Big Horn.

Glendon Swarthout was both a superb stylist *and* a master storyteller. His interests and choices of material were all over the map, from comedy to tragedy and all the variations in between—including satire, farce, mystery, melodrama, and picaresque adventure. His favorite British publisher, Tom Rosenthal, formerly of Secker and Warburg, said that Glendon had "the widest range of any American writer he knew of." Glendon never repeated himself or wrote any sequels, although book editors were certainly after him for *Where the Girls Are*, and the producers of *The Shootist* were interested in a follow-up film.

No, Dad often said that with both a Master's and a Doctorate degree in English Literature, he probably knew too much about literary theory and the history of world-class fiction, and he was therefore always experimenting and trying new genres and writing styles, attempting to top either himself or the greats of literature. While representative of his literary genius, such professional eclecticism made it tough for the critics, as well as his readers, to follow the body of his work, let alone anticipate what might be coming from his typewriter next.

Glendon Swarthout's varied literary tastes are just as apparent in this wide-ranging selection of short stories, which he aptly titled *Easterns and Westerns*. Leading off is one of his best, "A Glass of Blessings," which really was a forerunner of his bestseller *Where the Boys Are*. MGM quickly turned that groundbreaking novel into one of the biggest low-budget films of all time, and it became the granddaddy of all the generic "beach pictures" to follow. *Where the Boys Are* became a cultural phenomenon, the legendary launcher of twenty years of MTV-sponsored Spring Break Beach Blasts on Florida's sun-drenched sands. Michigan State University professor Swarthout researched his hit novel by spending a wild spring break observing the mating habits of some of his English Honors students on the beaches of south Florida.

Glendon's passion on his own summer vacations was cruising on many of the great ocean liners, and over the decades our family was booked on almost all of the best-known passenger ships belonging to the world's various cruise lines. "A Glass of Blessings" is based on dad's observations of the antics of some of the student passengers returning from a summer tour of Europe.

Published first in *Esquire* (January 1959), "Blessings" surveys a group of spoiled, inebriated collegians in Tourist Class passage on an ocean liner, returning from their drunken summer's vacation in Europe. In it he uses the same literary device he soon made famous in *Where the Boys Are*—a naive heroine narrating her sexual misadventures with college boys and her fumbling attempts to resolve her momentarily pressing problem—lack of funds to buy her father a nice present as a thank you for paying for her vacation. Savage irony is the weapon Professor Swarthout uses in his gimlet-eyed examination of these self-centered, overgrown adolescents. "A Glass Of Blessings" was later anthologized in the college textbook *Short Stories for Young Americans* (1964) and chosen for inclusion in the *O. Henry Awards Best Short Stories of 1960.*

Employing another female Michigan State undergraduate, Merrit, to narrate his huge hit *Where the Boys Are*, only a year after "A Glass of Blessings" saw print, Glendon infused that novel-length tale of college kids on spring vacation with a lot more comic hijinks and fun, and his youthful readers obviously bought it, big-time.

"Four Older Men" is an unpublished story written in the winter of 1952 after my mother and father had returned from his half-year's writing sojourn in Mexico. Prior to that, Glendon had spent two years as an instructor of English at the University of Maryland. This very slight tale of unfulfilled romance between a beautiful, well-to-do divorcee of twenty-six with two kids and no career and her suitor is so sketchily described that their breakup leaves the reader just that—unfulfilled and wanting more. Yet as an example of his earliest writing in the long, bleak days when he was churning out short stories in an attempt to break into print, it suffices.

"Poteet Caught Up in Lust and History," from the spring of 1955, demonstrates a sizeable leap in his writing ability. This unpublished story about another romantic adventure, this time set in Washington, D.C., is much more fleshed out, told from the points of view of both of its two characters, a would-be bureaucrat in his thirties looking for a job with the federal government and a forty-year-old hooker looking to turn a last trick on a slow night in a cocktail lounge off U.S. 1. That their one-night stand remains unrequited is secondary to the fulfillment they find admiring the view from the steps of the U.S. Capitol at four in the morning. This poignant, mildly amusing story displays Glendon's growing skill at evoking interesting characters and settings, even if his plotting is still a bit thin.

"What Every Man Knows" is the first non-Western Glendon ever published, appearing in *Collier's* in February, 1956. It's the semiautobiographical story of a teenager's coming-of-age in a small Michigan town on a memorable day in the early thirties when all the state banks closed. My grandfather, Fred, was a state bank examiner in Michigan during the Great Depression when those banks did close, and this seminal day in America's banking history was the most traumatic thing that ever happened to him professionally. Describing this cataclysmic event through the eyes of a fifteen-year-old boy fighting his teenaged hormones, as well as facing the unpleasant prospect of his father marrying his high school Latin teacher, Glendon puts this tidbit of American history into a much more interesting perspective. Banking, bah! It's how your father's bank closing affects your next necking session with your worried girlfriend that really counts!

Actually, "What Every Man Knows" is the first version of what became chapters 3 through 5 of his comic romance, *Loveland*, which Doubleday published in 1968. Purported to be the tale of one Perry Dunnigan, aged eighteen, who hitchhikes to the fashionable Lake Michigan resort town of Charlevoix during the "dirty" thirties to find employment as an accordion player in a college band, it's really the story of Glendon Swarthout's summer escapades as a singer/accordionist in Charlevoix and later at a large hotel in Grand Rapids, where he sang over a statewide radio network to his fiancee, Kathryn Vaughn, who would eventually become my mother.

No, Glendon never did have a fling with a rich playboy's coed girlfriend, but a quick perusal of the brief life story the novelist has provided shows that his summer gigs and the characters he met and made music with over the course of his formative years provided the cat's pajamas backdrop for *Loveland's* rumble seat ride, looking for love and fortune in the Depression-era haunts of the decadent rich. It's too damned sad nobody ever got *Loveland* to some choreographic genius like Tommy Tune, for this swingin' story would make a dancin' dandy of a Broadway musical.

Another unpublished story from 1956, "Gersham and the Saber," is also an example of a story, which later evolved into a book for juveniles, *The Ghost and the Magic Saber*, by both my parents. Again, this story of a "citified" teenager spending a summer growing up and learning about female affection on his grandfather's farm is based upon a seminal event of Glendon's youth, when his grandfather, Will Chubb, offered him the choice of his great grandfather's pistol or saber from his service with the 10th Michigan Cavalry during the Civil War. My dad got to choose when he turned twenty-one, and he took the pistol, but he wrote about the saber in this fine little story about a ghostly cavalryman who returns to his home ground to upbraid a boy for his foolishness.

This same ghostly Cavalryman, with his Civil War saber and pistol in hand, turned up again much later, in the climax of Glendon's best-selling novel *A Christmas Gift* (aka *The Melodeon*), published by Doubleday in 1977. This little novella was made into a mediocre, much-altered TV movie in 1978 under a third title, "A Christmas To Remember," starring Jason Robards, Eva Marie Saint, and Joanne Woodward. If you enjoy "Gersham and the Saber," you'll probably really like *A Christmas Gift*, which over the years has become a certified Christmas classic.

In 1962 my mother admonished my father enough about the "Gersham" story lying unnourished in a desk drawer that together they reworked and expanded it into their first book for teenagers, which Random House published in the following year. Its excellent reviews and subsequent sales were encouraging enough that my parents went on to write five more books together for teens—*Whichaway* (Random House, 1966, and Rising Moon/ Northland Press, 1997), *The Button Boat* (Doubleday, 1969), *T. V. Thompson* (Doubleday, 1972), *Whales To See The* (Doubleday, 1975), and *Cadbury's Coffin* (Doubleday, 1982). Yet "Gersham and the Saber" remains the initial seed of the story which evolved into a secondary successful career by both my parents writing stories for young teenagers.

Glendon's unpublished novella "O Captain, My Captain" is a tougher call. It was written between 1948 and 1949, and I understand why it never saw print. In his autobiographical sketch, Glendon discusses his adventures with the army's 3rd Division Battle Patrol during World War Two service in France and Italy, and how lucky he was to move to division headquarters to write service awards and citations for soldiers' meritorious conduct. The 3rd Infantry was Audie Murphy's division, and over the course of the entire war it went on to win more Medals of Honor, more medals for valor in combat than any other American division during the Second World War. Glendon always was a good writer, even under combat conditions!

Interviewing live heroes and hearing their stories, as well as researching the valorous deeds of the dead, made a profound impression upon my father and deeply influenced his later professional writing. Heroism is the central theme of many of his best books, especially as it suddenly appears, given the right circumstances, in the otherwise most flawed of characters. Time and again he returns in his war novels to men performing incredible deeds and winning medals for them. *The Eagle and the Iron Cross* (WW II POWs from the German perspective) and *The Tin Lizzie Troop* (about the army's Pershing campaign in Mexico) both touch in their subplots upon soldiers winning medals for valor. Indeed, Glendon's very first best-selling success, *They Came To Cordura*, concerns a cavalry officer branded for cowardice who is detailed to escort five enlisted men cited for the Medal of Honor to a rear railroad depot to be shipped home to safety. Along their grueling journey, Major Thorn interviews these men in order to write up their citations, and the well-researched military background to this rugged tale obviously came from Glendon's personal experience.

"O Captain, My Captain" was written before *Cordura*, but Glendon chose in it to examine the exploitative side of heroism, how America's "Greatest War Hero" is promoted into a movie star and best-selling author. My father actually met Audie Murphy on a movie set out in Hollywood after the war, and the few hours he spent lunching with America's real "Greatest War Hero" made another big impression upon him. Checking 3rd Division war records against Murphy's ghosted military memoirs, *To Hell and Back*, which had just hit the bestseller lists in 1949, bothered Glendon, and this enlightening novella is the result.

The parallels between Audie Murphy and Billy Dow were so obvious and close that no magazine or publishing house in America would touch this story at that time. Timing is so often *everything* in the arts, and in this case Glendon's was very bad. Sergeant Murphy's hit autobiography had been very well received by readers and reviewers, and Dad's peek behind the brass curtain would have been too controversial to print right then. The feedback his agent received from editors and readers in the publishing business was very good and generally laudatory, but the story itself was just too hot to handle. In 1955 Murphy's war movie of the same title was also released and became a big box office success, and Audie was on his way to becoming a movie star. So "O Captain, My Captain" was dead and buried for the duration of both budding authors' careers. Only now that both old soldiers from the same army division are finally at rest does this lengthy short story deserve its moment in the sun. It's up to you, the reader, to decide the "truth" of this largely fictional tale, and how you wish to remember the famous Sgt. Murphy, whose exciting combat exploits during the last of the world's *great* wars, certainly *were* the stuff of legend, both on the battlefields of Europe and on the big screen of Hollywood.

Westerns were the genre in which Glendon really got his professional start, and "Pancho Villa's One-Man War," which *Cosmopolitan* ran in February 1953, was his first published short story. In the early fifties, *Cosmo* wasn't the magazine for younger women it's become today, or it wouldn't have printed this tale of two young men on a summer's vacation drive to Tijuana, stopping to look up an old alcoholic newspaperman in an obscure border town in New Mexico. The technique, used in this story, of American Western history rewritten or retold from firsthand sources, Glendon went on to use a number of times in his writing, most notably in *The Old Colts*, purported to be the last adventures of an aging Wyatt Earp and Bat Masterson (Donald I. Fine, 1985).

In "Pancho Villa's One-Man War," however, Glendon was experimenting with this technique for the first time, and he hadn't quite mastered it. As a character study of a pathetic failure, "Pancho Villa's One-Man War" is a lot less interesting than the newsman's highly dramatic tale of the midnight meeting between two legendary figures in North American history, which is why it's a letdown when we learn it never happened. This story is also significant because it's the first time Glendon used the plot device of a college kid narrating what happened on his vacation, which he later used to much better effect in the award-winning "A Glass Of Blessings" and his trend-setting novel, *Where The Boys Are.*

Glendon was the first writer to use General Pershing's 1916 Border Campaign as a fictional backdrop, and "Pancho Villa's One-Man War" story was his first use of this lesser-known episode in American military history. Five years later, Pershing's punitive expedition against Villa was the setting for his first best-seller, *They Came To Cordura* (Random House, 1958), and Villa's raid on Columbus, New Mexico, turns up again in his comedy *The Tin Lizzie Troop* (Doubleday, 1972) and once more in his mystery-thriller *Skeletons* (Doubleday, 1979).

"A Horse For Mrs. Custer" was the first of Glendon's writings to bring him any serious professional attention. After its publication he received letters from editors at several different magazines and publishing houses, praising the story and asking what else he might have lying around on his desk or in the works. Published in volume 5 of *New World Writing* (April 1954), a biannual compilation of contemporary poetry and stories in all genres put out in soft cover by New American Library, "A Horse For Mrs. Custer" was read by a Britisher named Peter Packer while he stood at the paperback rack in Schwab's famous drugstore in Hollywood. Packer optioned the tale, took it to Harry Joe Brown's production company, and wangled the assignment to write the screenplay. Packer's adaptation varies somewhat from this short story since the lead role had to be tailored for a middle-aged Randolph Scott instead of a shavetail lieutenant, and being a movie, also had to involve a romance with a beauty like Barbara Hale. Still, Packer did a good job researching the military investigation into the Custer massacre. *Seventh Cavalry* turned out to be one of the very best of Randolph Scott's "B" Westerns.

This time Glendon really mastered his "history rewritten" technique. Purportedly an excerpt from a privately printed memoir of his service as an officer of cavalry by Brigadier General Alexander Peddie (retired), "A Horse for Mrs. Custer" relates what befell the remnants of Custer's Seventh Cavalry when it was assigned to rebury the fallen troops at the Little Big Horn a year after the debacle. So thorough and convincing was Glendon's research into the aftermath of the battle and the severe friction that developed among the troopers either supporting or decrying the fabled, fallen general, that he has several letters among his collected papers from Custer buffs and historians asking Professor Swarthout's help in locating a copy of *Dakota Days*, the "lost" memoir they've tried in vain to locate in any American library's Western history collection!

"A Horse for Mrs. Custer" remains a little masterpiece of the traditional Western genre, and confirming that judgment, it was recently reprinted as the "Classic Western" in the first-anniversary issue of *Louis L'Amour Western Magazine* (March 1995), and then again in the *Western Hall of Fame Anthology* edited by Dale Walker for Berkley Books in 1997. It is a classic story indeed.

"The Attack on the Mountain," a *Saturday Evening Post* story from 1959 (4 July), is another traditional Western, equally as good as "A Horse for Mrs. Custer." Glendon was a military history buff and had read all the issues of the *Cavalry Journal*, the magazine of record of the United States Horse Cavalry. His authentic research augmented "The Attack on the Mountain" and "A Horse for Mrs. Custer," and was used to its fullest effect in his comic novel of cavalry misadventures, *The Tin Lizzie Troop* (Doubleday, 1972).

Two elements make "The Attack on the Mountain" notable—Glendon's descriptions of the army's use of the heliograph, a mirrored system of communication with which it had a brief mechanical fascination, and the author's introduction of a strong female character, the rancher's middle-aged sister, who could hoe and shoot and handle Indian trouble better than any of the soldiers assigned to this miserable Arizona mountain outpost. Miss Martha Cox is so tough and forward, in fact, that it's she who proposes marriage to the gruff sergeant, Ammon Swing. Strong frontierswomen characters were fairly unusual in Westerns written in the fifties, and the inclusion of such a character here sets this story apart.

This story's horse cavalry background and the hit-and-miss love relationship between the diffident sergeant and his aggressive sweetheart prefigure the key character set-up of Glendon's later comedy Western, *The Tin Lizzie Troop* (Doubleday, 1972). Furthermore, in the Apaches' attack on the cavalrymen, Glendon didn't dwell on the violence and bloodshed, but paid more descriptive attention to the sergeant's arrow wound and its medical treatment, a physiological technique he would refine to perfection sixteen years later in his Western masterpiece *The Shootist* (Doubleday, 1975).

"The Attack On The Mountain" has been included in the Western

Writers of America's year 2000 volume of Western short stories by Spur winning authors, *Tales of the American West*, edited by Richard Wheeler for New American Library, as well as in *A Century of Great Western Stories*, edited by John Jakes for Forge Books in 2000.

"Ixion," published in volume 13 of *New World Writing* (June 1958), is Glendon's semiautobiographical story of a young ex-advertising man attempting to write his first novel in the little artist's colony of Ajijic, on the shores of Lake Chapala, the biggest lake in Mexico, near Guadalajara in the state of Jalisco. From the autobiographical sketch included herein, you'll learn that ex-ad man Glendon spent six months in Ajijic in 1951 with my mother and me, writing his second novel. *Doyle Dorado* ended up in the stove, making hot water for Dad's shower, but the real reason my parents left Mexico in a hurry was to seek emergency medical treatment in Brownsville, Texas, for five-year-old me, after I'd contracted para-typhoid fever from swallowing sewage water in Lake Chapala. I lived and went on to a normal, productive life, and hopefully so did this story's naive hero and the two wise-beyond-their-years little girls he tries to rescue from the neglect of their alcoholic mother in old Mexico. The tragic irony in this tale builds to a heartbreaking conclusion as the young writer becomes trapped between his good intentions and his own ineptitude.

My only quibble with this excellently crafted story is that the author didn't work some explanation of the title into the text for those of us who are mythologically uninformed. *Ixion* was the mythical Greek king who sought, and imagined he had obtained, the love of Hera, queen of the Olympic deities and wife of Zeus, the father and king of gods and men. When he boasted of his romantic exploit, Ixion was hurled down into Tartarus, a dark abyss beneath the earth where the rebellious titans were punished, and bound to an eternally revolving wheel. Okay, now you remember, too!

"Going to See George" could be described as Glendon Swarthout's breakout short story. His second story to be published in *Esquire*, this savage tale of teenaged angst was heavily influenced by two things—the overwhelming success of his college kids on Spring Break story, *Where The Boys Are*, and William Golding's famous novel, *Lord of the Flies.*

Some parts of "George" actually happened. I was senior class president of Scottsdale High (Arizona) in 1964, and my parents attended my graduation ceremony. One warm spring weekend that year, several buddies, girlfriends, and I drove up the back roads of Papago Peaks Park to Governor Hunt's tomb to drink beer and enjoy the spectacular night view. One of the guys knew that our necking spot overlooked the large back enclosure of the Phoenix Zoo, and while fooling around near the tall fence below in the dark; we managed to disturb one of the resident buffaloes. Protecting his turf, the bull charged us and put a nice dent in the heavy chain-link fence, managing only to stun himself and give us naughty boys a good scare. The bull buffalo never got loose and wasn't really hurt, but I made the fortunate slip of mentioning this little escapade to my father. The rest, as they say, is literary history.

The drinks, the smokes, the lingo, and the attitudes in this story all ring true to their time. Dad was always very, very interested in the tribal rituals of American youth! Glendon made me drive him in the daylight back to the scene of the crime, to "*cerveza* the situation," as we used to say. He imaginatively enhanced my true story, and this tough tale of teenaged brutality appeared in *Esquire* a year later (July 1965), prompting some critical letters to the magazine's editor. The story's primal theme of awakening the predatory beast lurking in all men and women echoed Golding's "man is a savage animal" premise in his tremendous international success, *Lord of the Flies*, which had appeared in print in 1954 and then in Peter Brooks's filmed adaptation of the famous novel in 1963, two years before "George."

The reaction of some disturbed readers to "Going to See George" got Glendon thinking deeper, however, leading him finally to decide that he didn't agree with Golding's provocative premise. After letting his ideas marinate for a few years, back to the Selectric he went. *Bless the Beasts & Children* was published by Doubleday in 1970 to instant acclaim and became Glendon Swarthout's biggest and most enduring success.

The novel *Bless the Beasts* was based on my four summers of experiences as first a camper and then a counselor at Hidden Valley Ranch for Boys, a private summer camp for teens outside of Prescott, in northern Arizona. The story concerns a cabinful of camp "misfits," six psychologically unbalanced, spoiled boys from wealthy families, sent out West for a summer outdoors to toughen up and become young men. On a camping trip, the boys are taken to see Arizona's annual licensed buffalo hunt, the closest thing to a legal bullfight anyone's ever staged in America. Appalled by the bloody spectacle, the boys sneak out of the camp to ride their trail horses to the rescue. That they succeed in freeing the doomed herd instead of beating America's national symbolic animal to death underscores Glendon's rethought, more optimistic attitude about our youth, as he returned to the central theme of his best books—that even misfit, disturbed kids are capable of bonding together in the right, tense circumstances and accomplishing great deeds. There's a hero, not necessarily an animal, lurking inside of all of us, and given the chance and proper circumstance, that hero will emerge. This uplifting, much more positive theme obviously struck a better chord with readers, as *Bless the Beasts & Children* became an international bestseller, which has been continuously in print since the day it was issued, having sold well over three million copies in paperback in the United States and Canada alone, and millions more in hardcover and overseas editions, as well as through book clubs and a Readers Digest Condensed edition. In this case, one downbeat short story like "Going to See George" actually led to a bigger, more upbeat, worldwide success story.

"Death to Everybody over Thirty" makes me personally uncomfortable. Private Curtis Tarkington was a good friend of mine, freshman year president of our high school class and someone who gave me good advice and support when I ran the senior class at Scottsdale High in 1964. He was a great guy and a good athlete, but not a great scholar, who graduated with us and then started his freshman year at Arizona State University. After breaking up with his girlfriend, though, Curt dropped out of school and enlisted in the army in the mid-sixties, presumably to save some money to return to college later on the GI Bill. I got a student deferment and went to a private college in California, Claremont Men's, while Curt got sent to Vietnam. At the mid-point of his year's tour, Tarkington was killed as he jumped out of his helicopter, landing in a backcountry raid.

My Dad read about it in the local paper and called me at college to see if I wished to fly home for his funeral. It was mid-semester and I was very busy with tests and term papers, so I declined, settling for an emotional letter to his mother instead. Glendon, however, old soldier to the core, did attend Curt's funeral and the military ceremony at the gravesite. It obviously made an impression upon him and this highly fictional story is the result. Curt did have a sister, but I never knew her very well and certainly knew no one who dated her. All that bad business is made up.

This well-written but unpleasant short story searingly deals with the grief over the loss of a friend or loved one, and how poorly young people usually handle it. Such a wrenching, revelatory tale of the loss of a young soldier was not going to appeal to too many readers wrestling with their consciences over our own escalating conflict in southeast Asia at that embittered, divided time in America. This is an old World War Two army sergeant's Vietnam story, and a jaundiced view from a stateside perspective it certainly is. Powerful and depressing, it still brings a lump to my throat and a tear to my eye. Reading this tough, grim tale early in 1967, when it was written, must have been very difficult indeed, and it's understandable why no American magazine would then touch it.

"The Ball Really Carries in the Cactus League Because the Air Is Dry," on the other hand, belongs in the Literary Hall of Fame, because it must be the only American short story ever to appear in both *Esquire* for Men and *Cosmopolitan* for Women! *Esquire* ran this story of a second-string major league catcher struggling to hold onto the game and the girl he loves during an Arizona day in spring training in March, 1978. Twelve years later, in April 1990, *Cosmopolitan* took a fancy to this humorous slice of baseball life and its focus on the sputtering, middle-aged romance between a lovelorn ballplayer and his cynical, semialcoholic wife. By that time major league baseball minimum salaries had skyrocketed for players, dating this couples' financial worries somewhat, but that's a minor factual quibble in reading it from a current perspective. Regardless, this exceptionally fine story certainly contains characters of interest to readers of both sexes and is definitely Big League all the way!

"Mulligans" is my personal favorite of all the short stories in this collection, and for the life of me I cannot figure out why it never was published. Written in the winter of 1973, this howlingly funny tale of two golf widows on an inebriated late-night toot at their old country club was perhaps too blackly comic, too close to golfing home for any but feminist tastes. Yet that's really ridiculous, for the midnight misadventures of these two feisty widows are just laugh-out-loud funny.

Funny larded with a tad of chagrin, too, for as a teenager I got arrested and was put on juvenile probation for the very same stunt described here. My buddies and I never really stole or damaged the golf carts, just "borrowed" and raced 'em around the course before returning them to the paddock, out of juice. My father was not amused by my juvenile hijinks, though, making me work off the damages doing housework and pool cleaning for several high school years. Writing what he knew unfortunately all too well, Glendon made my golf cart borrowing adventures the backdrop of this story, as well as an earlier wild chapter in his novel on the commission cattle business in snooty Scottsdale ("the West's Most Western Town!"), the satirical *The Cadillac Cowboys* (Random House, 1964).

Nevertheless, Dottie and Marge make a great Lucy and Ethel for an aging populace in this much more conservative era. "Mulligans," in fact, would make a terrific pilot episode for a sit-com. I filmed it myself as a comedy "short," for a yearlong class in short fiction filmmaking at UCLA Extension in Los Angeles. My little color, 35-millimeter comedy took us eight long nights to film in the spring of 1997, and I endured the usual run of disasters in its making to which first-time directors are prone—broken cameras, scheduling mishaps, damaged film, injured actresses, fog-outs on the golf course, "lost" equipment, overspending, and embezzlement.. Yet we finally got the twenty-three-minute film in the can and our short comedy turned out pretty well.

Mulligans! stars two veteran actresses, Tippi Hedren (actress Melanie Griffith's mother) and Marcia Rodd, in two of their best comic performances. I must say these two gals were "troopers," hanging in with us for many long and exhausting nights in their thin summer outfits, even barefoot out on a damp golf course for most of the night, surviving attacks by "wild" spaniels and mishaps in water sprinklers, but keeping their spirits up and remembering their lines while nearly freezing to death through a chilly California April. *Mulligans!* has since played in forty film festivals around the world and won us eight prizes so far, and is now airing on both the Women's Entertainment and American Movie Classics cable TV channels for two years. Those are "*big* hit" festival numbers in the independent film world, and I think this short comedy's female-oriented timeliness will translate into a funny TV series as well.

To anyone who ever thought Glendon Swarthout was a little chauvinistic in his taste for old Western subject matter and his predilection for heroic males in tales of rugged action, "Mulligans" should give pause for instant re-evaluation.

I believe this collection of stories will cement in the reader's mind Glendon Swarthout's great skill as a storyteller, his versatility and tremendous range as a stylist, and his lifelong attempt as an artist to elucidate mankind's best, most heroic qualities. Never a joiner of groups or a leader of protests (although he did take a public, activist stance with the Arizona State legislature to alter that state's bloody buffalo hunt, which he had excoriated in *Bless the Beasts & Children*), Dad was generally an optimistic humanitarian, and those fine qualities shine through his best writing. He was also a flat-out literary genius, and I don't use that description readily. I only hope these stories will lead the reader to seek out some of his novels and the films made from them that I've mentioned, for a deeper appreciation of this greatly gifted author's work. Glendon's loss at too early an age is a great one to my mother and me, but his storytelling legacy will certainly live on through late-night television and in libraries around the world.

Wish him well.

MILES HOOD SWARTHOUT
Malibu, California 2001